I0762208

LIVE CAUGHT

Live Caught

R. CATHEY DANIELS

BLACK LAWRENCE PRESS

www.blacklawrence.com
Executive Editor: Diane Goettel

Cover Design: Zoe Norvell
Interior Design: www.ineedabookinterior.com
Cover Art: "Human" by Hussam Eissa

ISBN: 978-1-62557-138-0

Published 2020 by Black Lawrence Press

For Pat,
who embraced vulnerability
as his super power.

TABLE OF CONTENTS

Don't look for me no more, I won't be coming back
Unless I left some things behind that I forgot to pack.

—from "Flying Down the Highway" by Mike Cross

BOOK I

CHAPTER 1

A MAN'S LEGS APPEAR NOT THREE FEET from Lenny's face. Slick, flat fish hang vertically one after the other against one leg, their green bronze scales painted in downward streaks of blood from mouths gaffed by a rusted stringer. The man's knees and elbows fold downward and slowly collapse into a skinny squat beside where Lenny is wedged under the dock. The chained fish splat into the mud. Jingle jingle.

"Son?" Grizzled face.

The man reaches toward him, slowly, then snatches his hands away. Claps them three times. Goes still.

Lenny realizes the man thinks he's wide-eyed dead. He stares at the scrawny mess beside him, old-old, his loose and careless face unshaven, maybe dodging the razor's edge for weeks.

Homeless, Lenny will take a guess. And day-old drunk. Well, who else would be mucking along deserted shorelines and busted boat landings?

Lenny can't pull off dead much longer. For starters, if he waits much longer, there's not going to be any need to pretend.

He's already bone cold, unable to unclench any muscle. All of a night and most of a morning now he's been swamped here on his back, not by the speed boats as he'd predicted, but goddamn swallowed by a storm-enraged Lake Norman, his boat disappearing beneath him just before he was spit to shore to battle the mud sucking at his back and the weight of a collapsed dock post on his chest, sinking him deeper. He's dreamed his rescue twice, perfectly. It actually happened. Then it didn't. So maybe he's dreaming now, who knows? Maybe he's already silt. His missing lower arm, goddamn untrusty ex-friend, still feels like it's there. Just loves faking him out. So maybe it's somehow jinxed the rest of his body to disappear like it had disappeared. His whole body gone missing. Except for his tongue, his gritty and caked tongue. And his eyes. Held wide open by the grit. And of course, his ears still echoing out his pulse.

This old smudge swaying beside him in the lake, about two staggers away from face down, might be the only human to drift his way today.

So, exactly one week after finally escaping the family farm, it appears he's caught again.

Lenny's mind drifts as taste buds announce themselves. Mud and blood, metallic and lime, all confusion in his mouth. He considers swallowing it, decides against it, then regrets the trickling out the sides of his mouth.

A fish that won't hit, might just hit in a storm, Buddo.

His dad's chatter, always rattling around inside Lenny's head.

Aren't those days supposed to be over? Isn't that one of the reasons he ran away? Or, paddled away? To get away from his dad's things-always-turn-out-right talk?

Nothing ever turned out right back at the farm. Nothing. What his dad would never understand is that you can't wish things right.

Still, sliding into Lake Norman on his skiff last night, bone hungry, he'd listened up.

Fish might bite in a storm, son. He'd let those words fool him into pushing back out onto the gray, rumbling water just before the storm blacked everything from shore to shore. All for a fish that might, or might not, hit bait in a storm.

Hunting for his dad's goddamn luck.

Buddo, keep watching, cause luck never really runs out.

Lenny watches the old man squatting in the mud beside him.

Green, green eyes, bright like the shield of dragonfly wings, sobering up, hovering out there in the flinty midday sun. Homing in on Lenny. Among a field of bristles, the old man's lips part. Wet, crazy young lips mingling with the rest of his dried apple face.

More muck leaks out Lenny's mouth. He guesses, if he were honest about it, seriously honest, he had been lucky. Yep, there's really no doubting it. To have landed last night under the collapsed dock with his head above water, instead of under, warm summer water instead of cold like it could've been. That's certainly not unlucky. And, hell, for the storm to kick him in the direction of land at all, sheer dumb-ass luck. Even wedged up under the pilings, chest caught under the anchor post, legs tangled in partially submerged, sickly yellowed fish netting, well, he was still breathing. You gotta hand that to the luck gods.

Lenny stares at the washed-up geezer.

Lucky or unlucky? Well, he has a choice.

Lenny forces his eyes to blink against the grit. Then, when the codger doesn't seem to notice, and even though it's like sandpapering the underside of his lids, he blinks a couple of more times.

The old guy peers in closer, hunching there beside the dock. Then blinks three exaggerated blinks back.

A freaking mimic. Lenny waits.

"Taint-ass sweet mother a god," the grizzled codger whispers, shifting in the muck. Jingle jingle. One of the fish on the stringer gives a wavy-tailed flop, lands itself on the old man's bare foot.

Lenny slowly flaps his eyes twice more. Just for assurance. Just to make sure they both understand.

"Sweet mother a god. Sweet motherfucker. Son?"

The old man again stretches his deeply veined hands toward Lenny, and this time one of them reaches Lenny's shoulder. Lenny tries to remember the last time someone reached to touch him. Had his mom touched him on Sunday, the day he left home for good? Maybe during church? One week, and he can't remember. But it would've been an accident, anyway. If she'd have touched him, it would've scared her, and he would for sure remember that. So, no. And certainly not his dad nor his brothers. Nothing on purpose, anyway. He would remember.

Maybe Glenna. Sure, Glenna. But that had ended so badly you couldn't count it.

The old man's hand is firm, warm. Then gone, just like that. Reaching for where the piling presses its weight along Lenny's chest. The young lips part the ancient bristles.

"You're screwed around the axel worse than a pecker without a pecker hole."

The old man straightens to his knees, draws his elbows and face back up and out of sight above the pilings, leaving Lenny with only the legs and the jingling stringer of fish, and like those fish, some small scrap of hope. Lenny wills the old guy's voice to hold the connection that was lost when the warmth of his veined fingers slipped from his shoulder.

"No worries, no worries-worries," the old man mutters from above. "We are just finding things today. Finding things a the utmost interest. A who-knew-Jesus interest. But we will set all things crooked straight. All things. Among other things. No worries."

The bowed legs and the fish jingle away.

Lenny lifts his head to call out, or at least to position himself to keep the fish in sight, but his lungs go another direction, suck in silt-air and he gags a thick drain down the long side of his throat, backwards through his nose. His neck won't hold the weight of his reamed-out brain, his tongue won't let words pass.

Most of a week he'd rowed. Cold stinging sweat dripping into his eyes, he'd imagined monster river boats, their power motors bearing down on him, headlights bright, though that made no sense. Not in such a narrow waterway. Still, he'd dreamed up police fierce and impatient, waiting along the shore at every bend in the river. All week, visions of his mom, not understanding, irritated, and too distracted trying to keep her irritation under wraps, control, control, she could barely manage that on her best days, would she try to find a way to understand? And his dad, perplexed, worried maybe, possibly, but curiosity king almighty over anything else he might feel.

Concentrate. Row.

But his parents asking their endless questions broke through.

Why? No that wasn't right. Neither one of them ever asked him why.

What? Just what do you think you were doing?

Nope, that wouldn't work either. Too concrete, steering too close to getting a true answer from him. They didn't want true. True would kill them.

How? Let's try that one. His mom first.

How could you do this to me? You can never, never understand, you've cut deep, little one, deep.

Yep. That fits. Nothing he can say to that.

And his dad. *How, Buddo? How did you figure the rapids? Hell, those rapids just before you hit Gorge Bridge? Deadly, son, deadly. How did you figure that—in the dark?*

Well, sure, he'd portaged the goddamn rapids—but totally beside the point.

All night he'd imagined his parents paying their drifty attention, not to him, but to how he messed with them. How he got to circling their heads like summer gnats.

And him finally, finally—a total stoner dream on his part, nope, never going to happen—him explaining so that they could listen. So, they would get it. Finally, he could make them understand. He could tell them something true, and they would nod, and they would say *yes, yes, we see that now, you've been fighting for your life all these years, yes, your brothers, Jude, and even Frank, yes we should have paid more attention to your brothers.*

Those thoughts, all of them, bundle them up and toss them in the river too. Because what if they'd finally understood?

Now *that* scared the shit out of him. Home, it scared the shit out of him. He could not let those hopes come true. He could not go back home.

Concentrate. Row.

He'd been lucky.

Lucky to escape.

Lucky to make it through that first night, to see morning light stalk the misty river bank. Lucky to find safe enough coves, hide the skiff, sleep the days, paddle the nights until he hit Lake Norman. He'd made it halfway to the Atlantic, by god.

Paddling into Lake Norman, Lenny had lifted his oars, let the skiff glide through a deep pool, and scanned the dusk for a place to rest. His stump strap was holding. Both upper arms were quaking, but they were equally quaking. At least there was that. One shoulder, really, just as good as the other.

That was the thought he'd hung onto as he turned the skiff toward shore.

His stump and his arm, one just as good as the other.

A deep silence settles over the pilings, except for the gentle lapping of water.

He goddamn dreamed up the green-eyed geezer. Dreamed up another rescue. Number three of the morning, a morning full of boats spouting wakes that ran up his chest, big boats hemorrhaging water up and over his head. The mud swirling, water flooding up his nose, stopping up his ears, sheer choking terror, submerged panic that the dock pilings would shift, hold him under forever.

You couldn't just find your thought hole and dive into it. You had to stay alert. You had to tell yourself, mental yourself into believing, it's not the ocean, it's not a goddamn *rising* tide. No. He can figure the timing, hold his breath between waves of terror, ignore the mud building up under his head, tell himself he's not wearing out, no he's not wearing out, not choking, not gagging, he can shake caked muck from his nose, his eyes, his mouth. Make a game of it. Estimate how many more wakes it will take for the backwash from the bank to start sliding over his hair, over his forehead. Testing, testing whether the numbness in his legs, his arm, his stump, has completed its work.

Shit, would he know when he's dead?

Lenny pushes hope back down into the muck, like the rest of him, but it just won't go. It's too much like drowning your last friend. Or more like your enemy. Even if you could, even if the possibility sits right there at your fingertips, you just won't do it. Besides, could the old man possibly be a dream? Would Lenny have ever put "taint" and "Jesus" in the same sentence?

But if he's not dreaming, what a whacked out, unlucky way

to die. Even for a kid who's been hung by the neck, who's been rolled off a freaking barn roof resulting in half an arm being sawed off. And just as he was starting his first solo and therefore his best adventure.

A long, splintered plank drops into the muck beside Lenny.

"Anything broke-broke down in here?"

The old man's legs reappear, fishless this time, because wouldn't you hang your slimy catch right back in the water to keep it fresh? To keep it alive?

The ridge-lined face drops low as the old man again squats below dock. Green dazzle eyes run from Lenny's head to his toes then back.

"I say, Mister Dead Dick, anything broke?"

Would Lenny call himself "Mr. Dead Dick?"

Lenny gathers his strength, because *getting it over with* was the one thing that three years without a lower right arm had taught him, you gotta do it early because you just absolutely cannot take people by surprise with a thing like a stump, *getting it over with* is one of his only defenses against ignorant scorn, so he siphons in a deep breath and slowly, slowly wills his raw stump into a reverse suction out of the muck. The twisted seam of leathery healed up sutures hang in the air between him and the old man.

In Lenny's experience, people generally head one of two ways when confronted with such an unsightly remnant: hell-bent in the opposite direction, or, and this is what Lenny's hoping for, head-over-heels determined to help out a one-armed boy.

Seemingly of its own accord, Lenny's stump drops back into the mud with a loud thwuck.

The old guy rocks back and splats on his butt. Sits there, peers at Lenny like he's just found him under the dock pilings all over again. Then a raspy giggle escapes the geezer's throat.

"You," he says. "You little fucker you." Abruptly his hands clap twice, then he sucks in a deep breath. "I can see you got a joke or two left, you little pea head."

Again, the hand clapping. Like his own live punctuation.

"Okay, okay worries be gone, we believe you. We believe you, just fine. But don't be thinking I'm easy fooled, though, just because you got only half a what you should have, don't be a thinking that-a-way."

The old man pulls his sweatshirt off over his head and crawls in closer under the dock to flash the dragonfly eyes at Lenny. Neck hairs sprout sporadically over what appears to be…a clerical collar?

Lenny strains to focus.

Where would an old geezer find a clerical collar? In a Goodwill bin? A church shelter? Jesus, maybe he murdered a priest and stole the clothes right off the holy man's back.

Lenny tries to call his neurons to order. Just let this homeless, murdering priest-man, or whoever he is, find a way to release him from this aching muscle press, from this nothingness from the waist down. Then, hopefully, his legs will have time enough to wake up and run the rest of his aching body out of here. Surely, he can outrun this scrap of rags.

The priest-man, muttering as if there were an audience between his own ears, hauls a semi-flat stone out of the muck.

Lenny braces himself for a quick end.

But instead of slamming the stone into Lenny's head, the geezer carefully folds his sweatshirt around the stone, takes care to tidy up the edges.

Then he sits back on his heels and seems to freeze into some kind of trance, eyes closed but moving rapidly beneath his lids.

Eventually, his young lips whisper, "Amen motherfucker," and he lifts Lenny's head to ease the padded stone under Lenny's neck.

The lake is still and quiet and Lenny wonders what the old man is up to, and if he really is trying to help, how the priest-man will react once the wakes start hitting. But mainly he's glad for the padding, he's glad for the relief a rock can give a boy's head. He's glad for the man's fingers firm in his hair and gripping his scalp. And when it comes down to it, and he doesn't want to get all dramatic about this, but still, he's glad for this one last dream, if that's what this is.

The priest-man runs his hands down toward Lenny's legs, and though Lenny can no longer feel his legs he can glimpse the rapid weaving of the ancient fingers, disappearing low, pulling high, nicking knuckles against the dock pilings just above his grizzly head, cursing, muttering as he untangles Lenny's feet from the soggy netting.

"Two skinny legs, two. Just sticking out from under a dock."

The priest-man's eyes flick up toward Lenny's head, then black out as he focuses on the net.

"They could've been cut off! Disembodied legs praise the Lord Jesus-Jesus. They looked so. They did, they looked so."

Lenny tries to imagine how he would look from the bank above, his legs lying tangled in the mud, how the old man might've felt spotting them. The thought gives him a twinge of guilt about the stump thing.

"Then we saw his face, we did. Baby face-baby face. And breathing. Live caught!"

The priest-man has Lenny's legs free from the netting now and is examining the post across Lenny's chest, dragonfly eyes flickering. He creaks to a stand and picks up the splintered plank he'd dropped into the muck.

"But he *was* dead. We saw that he was dead-dead."

Lenny tries again to move his legs, and an awakening pain

shoots up to his knees, his thighs. Or he thinks it does. *Anything broke-broke down in here?* It was a question he hadn't thought to ask yet. He'd skipped right over the broken bone thing, what with the breathing air thing being such an immediate issue.

The priest-man leans his plank against the dock.

"Goddamn resurrection is what we got all up in here."

Lenny hears the click of the man's belt buckle and the slip of the belt being pulled through pants loops. A shirt brushing over a head.

The old guy drops back down to his knees in the mud, his bare, mottled skin barely holding in his ribs, his belly thin but loose over his pants, sagging now for lack of a cinch. Slowly, painstakingly, he secures his shirt to the end of the plank with his belt. He takes hold of the board, begins to wedge the shirt end between Lenny's chest and the stuck dock post.

The clerical shirt encasing the plank is practically zero defense against the wood digging into Lenny's chest, but Lenny's not going to stop the old guy now.

"Do it."

Lenny's own voice startles him. Chiseled. A failed dry heave.

A puzzled look takes hold of the geezer's face. His eyes wander for a moment like they might be in danger of rolling backwards for a view of the inside of his own brain. But then the dragonfly eyes recover and dart off across the water, only to follow the water right back to Lenny's chest where it's suddenly lapping. The old man cocks his head, hearing the same thing Lenny's hearing: the high-pitched saw of an outboard. Large by the sound of it, signaling a grand wake.

The priest-man starts to hum, his fingers jittering a beat against his plank. Lenny wants to tell the old crackbrain not to worry, that he can take it. But the thought has arrived in his brain that the repercussions of the wake, now licking up onto his chin, closing in on his mouth and nose, might just scare the priest-man into a fit of strength that could finally, finally set him free. So Lenny tries his best to look even more desperate than he is, but that turns out not all that difficult, because when the wave hits, it's a gusher, washing completely over Lenny's head in a rush he was in no way prepared for. He chokes out muck as the water eases back. He gulps in air just before the lake erupts again.

Please God let the priest be real.

The water rises, and the old man wrenches the splintered plank in both arms, shoves it beneath the post that's trapped Lenny in the mud, carves his plank deep into Lenny's chest, and throws his whole body to the downward side of his makeshift lever.

"Let a loose, ye fungal-infested load of oppression," the priest-man yells. "Let a loose."

His plank creaks, bows to what must be the breaking point, the rail-thin geezer pulsating on his end, the *load of oppression* seemingly immobile on the other. But as the water builds speed toward the bank, the piling suddenly rocks along Lenny's chest, settles back, rocks again, harder. The old man gives one last heave and the plank snaps, knocking him face down into the rushing water. The log rolls right back into place, but the shift across the knot in Lenny's chest inspires him to dig into the muck with his good elbow and stump and wrench his body just as the largest contingent of the wake washes back over him. Lenny holds his breath under the silty lake and, working with the wave, twists hard to his side.

The piling pops him in the head as it rolls free.

Lenny pushes up on his good elbow, his back screaming. Lake Norman washes the foamy debris of its wimpy encore back up onto the shore.

The dripping priest-man turns and sits up in the water, panting, struggling for air.

The thing about the priest-man? He does not ask Lenny how he got stuck up under that dock. Nor how long he'd been wedged there, exposed and cold. Nor even whether Lenny is okay.

Instead, once he's breathing easier, once the lake has died down and they are sitting side by side in its calm shallows bordering the big city of Charlotte, North Carolina, the city that had been Lenny's destination for the past week, but was still less than halfway to his quest, the old man turns to him and asks the one question Lenny will absolutely not answer.

"Where the hell you from?"

CHAPTER 2

YOU DON'T GROW UP WITH A shrink for a mom—albeit a crazy shrink—without learning some neuro facts. The hippocampus, for instance. Camping out dead center of the brain. The great god gardener of your brain farm, just to put it like his mom would. All those thoughts up there? All those cucumbers, tomatoes, okra? Well they don't get gathered and pickled into memories without your hippocampus.

Lenny might not have much, but he's got a helluva hippocampus. He can flat out recall every ounce of crap he's survived for most of his fourteen years.

Where the hell you from?

A pontoon boat chugs its way down the lake.

To be honest, he wants to tell everything to the old codger sitting bare-chested beside him in the lake. Everything. Every single sorry, pickled memory. He hasn't talked to another soul in five long days. But he can't tell *anyone*, not *anything*. So instead, he joins the old man to gaze out at the rippling, sun-settled water.

Lenny's eyes bore into the surface as if he could spray a hole right down the middle to find and retrieve his skiff, his rod, his father's tackle box that was really his grandfather's tackle box, his rope, his bungee cord, his dad's two-way radio, his mom's St. Christopher that she wouldn't have given him so he just took it, his shoes, and the money he borrowed from Buford—or just admit it, *stole* from beneath the warped floorboards of Buford's kitchen. Buford the only adult he'd ever trusted. If he could just drill through the water and pull everything he'd lost right up from the bottom of Lake Norman, he would give that cash right back.

Lenny's eyes ache against the shimmering surface of the lake.

What's he hoping to find? His boat surfacing, against all odds? Buford's hard-earned cash, ones and fives and tens, floating along the shoreline?

Don't. Don't think about it.

Hold your mind steady, don't let it row itself back up the river, back to Buford and Buford's neat but crinkled stash of bills, over five hundred dollars of cold cash. A life's savings.

Buford. A man willing to hire a one-armed kid, no questions asked.

Lenny can hardly remember a Saturday since he was 11 that he hadn't worked at Buford's car shop. It was the first good thing that happened after losing his arm. Buford showing up at their back door, asking Lenny's dad if he could spare a boy to help down at the shop.

"Just ever now and then," Buford had said. Grey speckles brushing across his forehead and under his eyes, all lighting up whenever Buford smiled. Reddish grey hair cropped short and sprouting from beneath his grease-stained ball cap.

His dad had immediately offered all three of his sons, Jude, Frank, and Lenny. But Buford had lifted a freckled, grease-smeared forefinger toward Lenny, whose bandages along his stump were still seeping.

"Just the one'll do."

You could sit back on your bike seat, drop both your good hand and your stump to your sides and coast steady, steering with your thighs just like you would a horse, slow and easy down the long slope that leads directly into Buford's three-sided grease shop, which sits directly in front of Buford's squatter's house.

And if you were the lucky boy, at the end of each work day, Buford would trust you to pry up the floorboards and drop his cash to safety.

Lenny turns from the water and eyes this priest-man who'd worked himself into a wheezing fit rescuing him. What does he owe this man? What does this man want from Lenny? Hair sprouting everywhere, wily across his worn-out scalp, down his bony back, poking out his ears, his nostrils, smooth under his chin, along his Adam's apple. His chest bare and sweaty, his pants drifting slick fish entrails just beneath the clear surface of the lake.

"My skiff," Lenny finally says, unsure if his words are intelligible, still throttled as they are by the thick, cracked obstacle in his mouth which he understands but can hardly believe is his tongue. He slides down to lower his face into the scummy water and drinks. Swishes the water around inside his mouth. Spits.

"My skiff," he tries again, but it's too hard to continue. His left arm is still semi-asleep, so he lifts his stump toward the middle of the lake.

The old man's face puzzles up.

"No, that's not right," he says, then stops to cough, to wheeze a clear path through his ancient throat. "Not like that," he says. "Not out a that lake...Last night? Son? That sucker last night? Had to be a hundred-year storm."

The old guy waits. Then turns back to the lake, gives a low whistle. "Holy mercy," he says at the end of another wavering whistle. "I don't guess you going to recall much then. Not after *that* blower."

The man continues to watch the water and Lenny continues to watch the man. He is not unlike the old farmers, plowing fields or baling hay, that Lenny and his dad had often drifted past while fishing along the silver river running south from their farm. *Hungry men, Buddo, but of deceptive great strength,* his dad, ever the romantic, would say.

This guy didn't look like he had a home, much less a farm or a field.

The old man peers sidewise at Lenny.

"Yes, I am, son," he pipes up. "I am truly-truly."

The soft wake of a speed boat long disappeared around the far cove rolls in soft against Lenny's belly.

"What?" Lenny says, finally finding his voice. "You are truly what?"

"A priest, son. I am, truly. A special-made holy-man-a-God."

He says this like maybe it's a wonderment even to himself.

The man rises to his feet, untangles his belt and his clerical shirt from the broken board, his sweatshirt from the flat stone, wrings his clothes out and pulls them back on, all askew, before sloshing deeper into the lake. There he bends, reaches into the water with both hands, searching, searching, his rolled sleeves darkening beneath the lake's flinty surface. Suddenly, he jerks his hands clear and pops a finger into his mouth. Sucking blood, Lenny's pretty sure. Found his stringer, and from the looks of it also a razor gill of one of the fish he'd dropped below surface to keep fresh. The man wipes his fingers on his pants, bends again to draw the dripping stringer out of the lake.

One fish after the other emerge, each tail waving gently as harsh air cuts against their soft gills. Jingle, jingle.

The old man trips as he hits dry land, steadies himself, plucks a beauty of a rod and reel from between the concrete abutments at the base of the bank.

"Get your butt up out a that water, little peckerwood," he croaks over his shoulder. Then a hoarse whisper, "You with me now."

Go or Hold, Buddo, Go or Hold.

His dad's WWII stories. They always, always came back to that one thing, *Go or Hold.* Flying fast just above the thick white haze, the Germans plinking planes down all around them, and him and his combat buddies straining every single muscle to locate that ever shifting and elusive hole in the clouds, that hole that would allow them to drop magically through and skid their plane to safety.

"Air traffic control? Didn't exist. No sir. *Go or Hold*, Lenny, *Go or Hold.* Sometimes that's all you can count on, son. Sometimes the only instructions you got up there above those clouds were goddamned scrawled across some blackboard down on the *ground*! Some grunt *writing*. Lord we'd have to calculate fast. If you did not find that hole and drop through *right then*—well that was our greatest fear."

His dad would settle the oars of their boat and lean toward him.

"What's worse than your nose buried deep into the earth, Lenny, due to your own goddamn mistakes? What's worse? Forget the German eighty-eights, forget the enemy flak. You understand what I'm saying, son? *Go or hold.* It always comes down to that."

Lenny takes one more look at the lake, which now possesses his skiff, his only transport to the Atlantic, and basically everything else he ever needed. He is belly-to-bone hungry, and the most likely means to food—that fishing rod clutched between an old man's bony fingers—is rapidly disappearing up the bank. The codger already proved himself of *deceptive great strength*, absolutely he did. Still, Lenny thinks he can relieve the old man of his fishing gear.

Lenny rises slowly from the shallows of Lake Norman and follows the priest onto dry land.

#

The old man lopes along, his rod held loosely in the crook of his hand like he might cast into the bushes at any moment. Up ahead of Lenny, his angled bare feet gain easy purchase against the rocky brambles of the lake bank.

Lenny's own legs tremble, anchored in sneakers that squish and bubble with each soggy step. Even with the sun already baking the back of his neck, his upper body is still a shiver. Behind him, a speedboat motors around the far side of the lake.

One foot in front of the other, Buddo. If that's all you've got, take it!

Lenny trudges up the embankment and his legs finally solidify as the ground levels off and becomes a field of thick green leaves topped by golden fronds, tall, as tall as his dad. He spots the old man further ahead, aiming for a wooden gate that's propped wide open, its post mired in the sand like a permanent open invitation from the lake to the fields. A path winds from the open gate up into the high, wavering gold.

But the old man veers from the gate, hops a ditch to short cut the angle to the fields. There, he splays barbed wire between his hands, negotiates his rod between the pricks and steps through the fence into the field. Once inside, the geezer pauses, adjusts the stringer hanging from his hip with his free hand. The fish are losing steam, but manage to tail flap against his knees. The jingle, jingle of the stringer drifts along the bank toward Lenny. The old man breaks his rod down at its joints and secures the line, then disappears into the green and golden thicket.

Lenny hesitates at the fence line. If the old man had meant to harm him, he could've bashed his head in an hour ago. Instead, he'd saved his life.

But what for? Where was the old man leading him?

Maybe he should just turn back, right now. But to what? A lake with no boat?

Crappy choices, as usual. Once, just once, he'd like to choose between good and better instead of bad and worse.

Lenny splays the fence and steps through.

The old man is quiet, but amber fronds shutter opposite the breeze about 50 yards ahead, giving him away. Lenny hacks in that direction through the sharp green stalks that claw at his arms and face, and give off a rich, glandular odor, not unlike deer musk from back on the farm. Not corn, not sorghum. But what? The musk drifts against the back of his throat, then dissolves. Lenny is too deep into the thicket to sight the old man's movement, so he pauses to listen.

Nothing but the breeze.

The cold from the lake has turned into sweltering heat in the thicket, and he lifts his stump to wipe the sweat that's dripping into his eyes.

How did he get here? Why is he following a crazy vagrant? Just for his expensive rod and reel? He could turn back now, likely find dozens of rods sitting unprotected in boats along the shoreline.

But just as that thought begins to make headway inside his brain, the old man calls to him.

"You off center, peckerwood."

Lenny turns toward the voice. Like hunting, shoot the deer in your sights.

"Yeah, that's right," the old man says. "We coming now, we finding the row. Stop your dithering."

Sure enough, about three feet to his right is a clear row and the priest man is hunched at the far end. Lenny trots to catch up.

Together they step out of the field and onto a dirt access road where a yellow pick-up truck sits angled in a ditch, a State of North Carolina emblem rubbed thin on the driver's side.

Lenny glances at the priest-man.

"You work for the State?"

"Hell no, done told ye, I'm a man a god."

The geezer chatters his teeth together, rapid fire, like maybe he's trying to re-hinge a loose jaw. A slip of drool edges out the corner of his mouth, and he swipes it away with his rod arm.

"That truck? Son, that's just unwanted inventory."

He squints at Lenny, green eyes sparkling, and hacks out a laugh.

"My specialty, I guess you could say, is unwanted inventory."

He climbs up into the truck bed, more nimble than Lenny would've guessed, lays his rod gently down, unhooks the stringer from his rope belt, detaches a long key chain from the stringer, and layers the fish down inside a small ice chest. He chooses a key from the chain, bends and jiggles it into the padlock of the truck's wooden toolbox.

"But to obtain that shit," he murmurs, "you gotta be positioned just right-just right."

Lenny wonders where the old man would be positioned to obtain a rod and reel of that quality. Then realizes that if he's going to take the gear—and the fish, now that he thinks about it—now is the time.

Lenny edges up onto the truck's running board and peers into the bed. Easy peasey. Grab the rod, shove the old man, not too hard, just enough to jimmy time and space to snake the stringer from the ice chest.

But then what? In which direction would he run? How far in that direction? What would he do once he gets there? And, the bitterest pill, with no boat, how will he get back on track to the Atlantic?

The geezer's bony hand reaches down and grabs the rod. Holds it up just inches from Lenny's nose.

"Two-pound test, you see that, you little pin head? You see that?"

Of course Lenny had noticed the ultra-light test line, spooled around the sleek reel right in front of him, now blurry with the priest holding it so close.

The fishing line of stealth, Buddo, the line of the purist, his dad liked to say. *A man fishing with two-pound test is a man taking risks.*

He and his dad hardly fished with anything else. It was light and feathery, so a big fish would snap it, quick. Unless, of course, you had sure hands, or hand, in Lenny's case. A hand that could feel the big fish, anticipate which way it would run with the bait. Let it run. Pull it back ever so gently. Let it run again, pull back. Until the big fish had nothing left. Then usher it right into the net.

"We seeing you appreciating what's in front of you," the old man says.

Lenny nods. "You don't just fish for food," he says.

"Hah. You know nothing." He lays the rod into the truck box, snaps the padlock shut. Fastens the key chain back to his rope belt. "Speaking a food, get into the truck. We got young mouths waiting."

The priest-man guns the truck out of the ditch, up onto the dirt road, bumps around the circumference of the field and swishes onto black top as they reach a two-lane road, not unlike the farm lane back home.

Lenny reaches across his body with his good hand to unroll his window, let the hot air finish drying the sweat from his neck and the river water from his t-shirt. He rubs his stump across the short bristles of his itchy scalp. His older brothers grew their hair long,

Jude with black curls to his shoulders, Frank blond as a broomstick with shanks skimming his ears. Lenny still allows, or, that is, did allow, their father to buzz the razor in whatever direction came to his creative mind. If you avoid mirrors, which Lenny does anyway, what difference does it make?

The truck rounds a corner into a sparse neighborhood, the few houses square and without porches, the windows dull and without shutters. There's a sidewalk, though, and there's a woman striding fast up ahead of the truck, the back of her long shift ragged with dirt. Two stair-step, sunny blond kids clutch tight to a rope stretched taut between them and the woman's waist.

The priest-man downshifts and the truck shutters to a halt in the road beside the woman.

"Hey, you!" The old man leans over the cab seat to peer at the woman through Lenny's window. She and her kids glance over, simultaneously, like they might be attached to a whacked-out puppeteer in the sky.

"Hey, you," the priest says again. "You on the back row there. Do I know you?"

The littlest kid stares up at the priest, unsmiling. Lenny looks closer.

Those assessing eyes, knowing who you are before you even knew yourself. The same eyes as the girl in the road back home. Pushing her goddamn bicycle. He hadn't left home due to his brothers hanging him by the neck, their crazy sex experiment. And he hadn't left because they'd turned him into a one-armed boy by rolling him off his dad's barn in a go cart. Or sure, yes, all that played a part. Glenna certainly played a part, too. But that girl in the road, looking at him. Her seeing he was just the same as his brothers before he even realized it.

The day they picked her up was the day Lenny left home.

Jude driving, saying they were doing the girl a favor, teaching her not to be out on the roads by herself. *For her own good, boys. For her own good.* His black curls, up in the front seat, catching light, hinting at what they could do with the girl. At what Lenny could do. Making Lenny's eyes sting.

She'd made her move when they got out of the car to argue about it.

She couldn't have been more than eleven, but she goddamned scrambled from the backseat over into the driver's seat and gunned it clear down the farm road. The car jerking, sputtering, picking up speed toward the ditch until she located second gear, her head popping up and peering over the steering wheel as the car swerved into a U-turn faster than Lenny would ever attempt, swinging dangerously close to the opposite shoulder and riding the edge of that ditch until she could wrestle herself back onto the pavement and up to Buford's grease shop to safety.

Lenny had stood straddling the yellow lines in the middle of the farm road that day with his two brothers, all of them stranded, but him thinking, *so that's how you do it.*

And he'd done it.

Lenny realizes the kid is not staring at the old man, or him, but taking in Lenny's stump resting along the window ledge. Lenny slips his stump back inside the truck.

The two kids set their blue eyes on each other. The woman shepherds them closer to the truck, all three still held together by the dangling rope.

"Father Damien," she says.

Father? Seriously?

"Miss May," the geezer croaks. "I been studying on a curious, curious matter."

The woman smiles, and that smile seems to make its way

through the rope to the kids. The taller one possibly a girl. The small one for sure a boy. June and July, Lenny decides.

The old man leans further across the cab to eye the kids below. His breath blows warm and sour.

"Yes, a curious, curious matter. I got three fish back a this here truck, and don't you know? They reeled in just about the same size as those bellies you got trailing behind you."

Lenny thinks Miss May's eyes go watery for a second. She looks down at her kids, back at the priest.

"Well, that's a pretty small catch, then Father," she says.

"Hah! You right about that. Climb on up," he gestures over his shoulder with his thumb. "I gotta clean those suckers afore handing 'em out."

Lenny reaches across for the door handle, intending to offer the woman his seat, ride in the back with the kids. But the priest lays a hand on his good arm.

"Nah," he says. "They won't separate."

Miss May, June and July, climb up into the truck bed and soon the truck is sliding into heavier city traffic, passing run-down shop fronts with lopsided awnings, squealing pre-teens racing spray from a busted yellow fire hydrant, its water arcing a double rainbow in the harsh sunlight, young women shooing small children back from curbs, their strollers full of groceries.

The priest-man, *Father* Damien, pulls the truck to a halt in front of a large, concrete, two-story building. Across the street several couplets of old men play chess along the top of a retaining wall, a few rangy dogs sleeping beneath their feet.

Lenny takes a closer look at the graffiti-dotted wall beneath the swinging legs. Paper flyers, tacked haphazardly, display in big black letters the words **ANTI-MIRACLE**.

That's all. **ANTI-MIRACLE**.

There must be twenty flyers under the men and their chess boards. Probably a hundred more tacked across the concrete building's wall next to where the priest has parked.

ANTI-MIRACLE.

Broken concrete steps lead up the front of the building where wide, ornately carved wooden doors are overhung by strings of waxy fake flowers, purple and yellow, that droop from the weight of a narrow wooden cross.

"The Block!" The old man claps his hands three times in Lenny's direction. "Church. You gonna find out all about."

To hell I am, Lenny thinks.

Nope. The idea is to put as much distance from back home as possible. Which means replenishing stores, stealing somebody's boat, heading back down Lake Norman and directly through the Wateree Dam. He hadn't made his way down the French Broad River, paddled for miles *against* the current of the Swannanoa, stayed afloat next to the goddamn speed hogs of Lake James, then, evidently, survived a hundred-year storm on Lake Norman, all for nothing.

The great Atlantic Ocean was waiting.

He just needs to find the right boat. And keep an eye out for a chance to snag that long key chain swinging from the priest's belt as he hops out the driver's side and scrambles into the truck bed.

"Let's clean us up some bream!" the old man yells, seemingly to the entire street.

Lenny swivels loose of the truck just in time to see the priest lean down to unlock the tool box and pull the stringer of cold fish from the ice, once again attaching them and the key chain to his hip. Next, he pulls out a large cleaver, elbows the lid shut, hops over the truck rail and heads up the concrete steps. When he reaches the concrete building, what he'd called the Block, he pushes one of the massive wooden doors open with his bare foot and disappears inside.

Miss May and little June and July settle themselves on the stone wall that encases the Block's strip of yard, their rope draped across their laps. A knot of soaking wet kids break loose from the arc of fire department spray to chase a ball across the street.

Once again, Lenny finds himself hesitating to follow the priest, especially given that the old man is clutching a cleaver. But when all three of the Sunny Family turn and smile at him, as if masterminded by that invisible puppeteer, he backs away, turns and takes the front steps two at a time. He shoulders his way through the wooden doors and into the dark interior of the priest-man's church.

CHAPTER 3

"YOU SAVED!" THE PRIEST-MAN CALLS OUT. Lenny stops to let his eyes adjust. "That's where you at now, son! The Block. Hallowed special, you'll see."

Uh huh, Lenny thinks. *I just need your keys.*

But he gut-checks himself. He's not going anywhere without a boat. Without money. So yeah, he might find out more than he'd planned about the geezer's so-called church.

Candlelight wavers along metal folding chairs lining the aisle leading up to what appears to be an altar. Lenny takes a few steps forward.

"Don't be coming up in here empty handed! Fetch me that tithing plate."

Lenny glances behind him, retrieves the collection plate from atop an overturned wooden barrel, then advances up the aisle to where the priest is laying his fish out along the altar. A baptismal font sits behind the altar and a stair-stepped set of wooden boxes leads to a small, planked raft that Lenny guesses must serve as the perch from which the old man delivers his sermons.

The priest steadies a fish with one hand, raises the cleaver with the other, and brings it down cleanly to lodge into the altar between the cold gills and the body. The fish head flips in the air and skids along the floor. The old man dislodges the cleaver.

"Catch that head next time, little peckerwood," the old man says, nodding toward the plate in Lenny's hand.

Lenny lowers the tithing plate and chop, chop, catches the next two heads.

"You a one-handed wonder," the priest says, as he guts the fish from gills to tail.

Lenny angles the plate to scoop fish entrails with his stump. The priest rapidly scales his catch with a few more swift strokes of the cleaver, then washes the blade slick with their residue in the baptismal font.

"Dip that plate, too," he says, nodding at the font and heading back down the aisle. "Celebrants clean the rest a this shit up afore morning service."

By the time Lenny reaches the curb, Miss May and the two sunny kids are making their way down the street, the bag of fish swinging from the rope stringing them all together.

Lenny climbs back into the truck beside the priest.

The old man cranks the engine. "Can't see it," he says.

Lenny waits. Then when the priest doesn't continue, "What? Can't see what?"

"Can't see how you catch a fish one-handed. Or cast a line, for that matter."

The priest stares straight out the windshield like he might be waiting on Lenny's answer, then gives up and pulls the truck out into the street.

Lenny turns to watch a policeman clamp down the rainbow spray from the broken fire hydrant. The cool water is already finding its way into the gutters in front of the Block, already turning to steam and rising from the blacktop.

#

Lenny steps down from the truck onto a stone drive that leads up to a stone house, which the folks back home would call a mansion, although every single one of those folks would wonder why in the world you'd build such a big house and then forget to add on the front porch.

Take Buford. There's no road to Buford's house, just to his shop. You have to walk around the shop and up the dirt path to get to his house. But, by god, he's got a front porch. Buford bought his property first, years ago, then built the shop, then slept on a rickety cot in the shop until he made enough money to build the house. You could look east from Buford's porch, over the grease shed and up the slope of pine trees to where the land flattens and the farm road curves toward the gravel drive leading to Lenny's home. Used-to-be home. His parents' home. His brothers' home. Not his. Not any longer.

Never? It was hard to think about never. Never seemed like a long time, although the way his luck twisted and turned, you couldn't be sure. Never, it seemed in his experience, could turn out short. *I'm never going to let you do that again.* Which, he guesses, is why he left home. One wild attempt to extend Never.

"Can you believe this shit?" the priest says.

Large windows splay across the front of the stone house and reflect the trees bordering the marbled drive spooling out behind the two of them.

"Rectory," the priest-man says, heading for the front door. "Catholic Church got no idea. A fucking palace. Living like a king-king, while my congregation…well, you gonna see."

#

Lenny does begin to see.

Over the week since the priest crow-barred him out of the lake, he's made little progress locating a boat. But he's learned plenty about the old man's congregation.

"Celebrants" the priest calls them, though to Lenny they don't look all that celebratory. More like downtrodden, more like the scrawny rag-tag families down the farm lane back home. Whatever he expected to find in the city, it sure wasn't more of the same hungry faces. Skinny folks, like the Sunny Family, except not so sunny, trudging through the Rectory, dusting shelves, mopping floors, canning parsnips and tomatoes harvested from the Rectory's vast farmland. Dragging meal sacks full of potatoes up to the Rectory's back door for more Celebrants to pick over before peddling them down at the market.

And he's watched the priest draw his lips down into a tight stitch and shutter his green eyes to ward off any complaints. Like when a local cop, who the priest-man calls Basilios, attempted to shoo a couple of families off the street near the Block.

"Cop ain't nothing, not down the Block way," he told Lenny. "We fix that shit."

So when Sunday arrives, and the geezer climbs the wooden boxes to stand atop his raft, Lenny finds himself looking forward to hearing what kind of sermon will pop out the old man's bristly mouth.

Dressed in a black robe with belled sleeves and maroon sash cinched at the waist, the priest keeps his head bowed as the downtrodden stream off the neighborhood streets, shuffling along the makeshift aisle of the Block, clanging the folding chairs as they migrate away from, or closer to, one another.

Lenny leans against the wall and makes room for a tall, lanky gentleman with a skullcap. The man reaches to shake Lenny's right hand but takes quick note of Lenny's stump so instead reaches to pat him on the shoulder, then, predictably, adjusts his aim to miss altogether. He ends up jiggling his own arm as if he was just fine-tuning his suit sleeve all along.

Lenny can never stop himself from feeling bad for folks when this happens. Are they afraid the world's going to end if they grab hold of a stump instead of a hand?

He pulls his mind to the altar, which is covered with a tattered but clean white cloth, reminding Lenny of his parents' bed sheets. Stubby candles litter the floor beneath the altar, their flames pulling dangerously close to fire hazard. Nothing like the stout, creamy votives his mom lit throughout their farm house. No, these are low on wax, smoking and not coming close to masking the mildew and old sweat hanging in the air.

The walls of the Block remind him of the bare clapboard shacks his mom visits up and down the river. No wonder the priest calls it the Block. Nothing ornate, nothing soul lifting when you walk in, no pure and holy feeling like the little sanctuary back home, sheltered beneath the peaks of Rosey Face and Chub Ridge. Religion tucked away, his mom called it, when she was in one of her good spells. *No matter where you go, little man, God's got a pocketful of Catholics.*

Lenny's throat tightens. Concentrate. Stay on the Block, don't stray down the river routes toward home. Stay in the middle of a Sunday morning where no one has any idea who you are or where you're from.

Lenny glances around for the Sunny Family, and spots them, side by side on the back row. Miss May, June, and July. Both the little Sunny kids cut their eyes toward Lenny, but their towheads stay the course toward the priest who has begun to sing his Gloria, in Latin no less, which Lenny knows a little from his elementary school days. Catechism classes. Enough to recognize...*et in terra pax hominibus bonae voluntatis...*

The old man extends both skinny arms toward the crowd and his hands emerge from his robe with boney fingers spread wide as if to hold them at bay.

The Celebrants fall silent as the old man leans forward. The boxes waggle beneath him, but he stays aboard.

"Today," he croaks out, then pauses. Lenny is pretty sure the pause is due to an effort to hold in one of his *motherfuckers*, like someone might pause for a hiccup. "Today...we gonna pierce that black lie a blind faith!"

Slowly, the priest's fingers rotate and beckon, *come here, come here*. But his head moves side to side, *don't do it, don't do it*. Before Lenny can think through this garbled body language, the old man calls out, "Blind faith? Belief without thought? I tell ye true! Ye falling for a sucker Siren!"

The priest's fingers and head continue their confusing battle, *yes-yes, no-no, yes-yes, no-no.*

"Ye wanna follow that sucker Siren?" Y*es-yes, no-no.* And suddenly, Lenny gets it. Like a third base coach, the priest is signaling a choice. A runner's choice.

A pilot's choice. *Go or hold, Buddo, go or hold.*

Lenny's throat now tightens into a such an acute clench that he can hardly keep his eyes on the old man, now thundering his way toward his point.

"Then ye gonna be a sucker! God's truth! Gonna be a sucker to follow that sugar-sweet blind faith nonsense into those deep, blackened waters!"

Finally—and it seems to Lenny against the old man's own will—he captures his hands at his waist sash and grows still.

Someone from one of the back rows lets out what sounds like an exasperated sigh, but a woman across the aisle, directly opposite from where Lenny is standing, rises slowly from her metal chair, a woman taller than any he's ever seen. For that matter, taller than most men he's seen. Spiky red hair, maybe fake red, it's hard to tell, growing from her head. Spiky hair from hell.

Artemis. Leaping right off the pages of Ms. Petrie's eighth-grade mythology textbook and into crazy church. Sister of Apollo, just like the pictures, right here, towering over the congregation. Unlike Artemis, her boobs swing beneath a tie-dyed hippie tunic. Magnificent chest, kind of reminding him of Ms. Petrie herself, now that Lenny thinks about it.

She lets out a small burp, but on further thought, Lenny realizes she's emitted a short, high-pitched, "Amen."

The priest nods her back down into her seat, where she folds her arms across her chest to settle her boobs.

No one stirs. The old man seems to have his wiry hands around their necks. He surveys his Celebrants a moment longer, then squeezes his eyes shut so that they become just two more of the many wrinkles rejoicing on his face.

He drops his voice to a whisper, like maybe he's talking to himself.

"We gonna invoke Buddha."

Motherfuckers, Lenny thinks, then worries that the old man is so deep inside his head.

"We gonna turn a loose the false Gods a blind faith."

Motherfuckers.

"Instead, we gonna *make an act* a faith. Shoot that shit directly into all ya'lls flimsy veins."

"English, please!" the gentleman in the skullcap blurts out. "And don't expect me to translate whatever it is you are saying unless you speak up!"

Across the aisle, Artemis shoves on her reading glasses.

"Good God, Elias," she says into the open bible on her lap. "Why buy a hearing aid just to leave it on your bedside table?"

Elias blinks. Several times.

The priest looks from Elias to Artemis, then grins and sends his green dragonfly eyes winging off Lenny.

Lenny shifts his feet to steady himself at the swift connection. He barely manages to keep his own grin from escaping.

The priest nods.

"Well, I'm gonna tell ye what I'm sayin, Mr. Elias. An *act*—it's what we *do*. Got that? It *moves*. Got that? Blind faith gonna let you off that goddamn hook! No fish there. Action? Why that's a testable reliable. And a testable reliable requires a brain cell or two. Does it work? Does it help? I tell you straight, that *act* a faith is near-by *perfection*."

He raises his eyes to call to the rafters.

"That Blind scoundrel will set your faith in stone. Don't be fooled! There's nothing blind about faith. No, no. Faith requires a clear head. And certain action, motherfuckers, certain action."

The priest scans the crowd.

"Do we have Islam in the house?"

Several men near the front rise, nod to the priest, nod to each other, sit back down.

The priest nods back.

"Islam be filled with the creative spirit from God by which God enlivened Adam and inspired angels and prophets."

His eyes rest on Elias.

"Let's add on you Jews out there, may you find the spirit a that holy place, yes! Our most high-high God, creator a the cosmos… Yahhhhhhweh!"

He closes his eyes in reverence, but pops them right back open to ask, matter-of-factly, "Any followers a Bahá'u'lláh?"

No one responds.

"Never mind. If you out there, praise through that oneness a spirit right-here-right-here! Our *global* humanity! Praise our *global* humanity, praise!"

He pauses, as if he's forgotten someone. Then yells, "Oh yes!" and shakes his fists toward heaven, like he might have scored a touchdown. "And don't forget, we gonna let Jesus keep all ye Baptists!"

The priest pulls himself to a full stop, panting, and his wiry fingers join once again at his sash.

The congregation waits.

He lets them wait for so long that Lenny's pretty sure the codger nodded off, eyes open, atop his raft.

No one seems perplexed, though, or concerned. More interesting to Lenny, no one appears bored, like in their church back home with their solemn, monotone priest. This is more like the Southern Baptists at the tent revivals he attended with Glenna. The preachers there might not display a lick of logic, but they sure could show off an enthusiasm that moved sturdy farmers to their knees. And afterward inspired him and Glenna, still flushed with their mixed-up passions, in the backseat of her car.

This priest had that same enthusiasm, plus the benefit of what seemed to Lenny a logic that didn't try to fool your brain into performing useless somersaults.

Eventually the old man's young lips start vibrating, and a low ommm rattles up from his chest, carrying words along its swift and wayward current.

"Ommm...we gonna cherish-cherish every messenger a God, ommm...and in every single everlasting soul...the pure, the burning bush, the sacred fire, the dove, the angel Gabriel, ommm...plus that maid a heaven yes...we thank ye, we thank ye, every last one a-ye-gods up there and everywhere, we thank ye, we thank ye..."

The Celebrants become a hive. Metal chairs scrape. Prayer cloths appear and flutter to the floor, like an exotic picture book come to life. Knees drop to the aisle. Ommms mimicking the priest's push against the bare-boarded ceiling of the Block.

Lenny's thoughts walk out the wide wooden doors at the back of the sanctuary and keep right on walking. It's a lot of hard work to herd them from the path back home. How can you miss a place that drives you away? Lenny nudges his dumb-ass thoughts the other way, toward his dream, toward the Atlantic Ocean. Toward the only place harboring mostly good memories for his family. The one place his dad promised him they'd go together, the two of them in his dad's boat, *fishing the whole way, Buddo, fishing the whole way.*

His thoughts come to a full stop, swing into a half turn, and signal that he might just be stuck here for a while. Steady up, they tell him. Steady up. Stay with folks who stand up in church and burp out their Amens.

But why? Why is he wobbling? Just like a skiff in uncharted rapids, it's hard to find a place to slice in your oar. So you just let the rapids take you and hope for the best? That's exactly what he's doing. This past week, listening to the old man's silence on all the things Lenny needed him to be silent on. Never asking Lenny any questions, not even his name. Letting him tend the garden to the side of the Rectory, one of the few things Lenny is good at. The old man quietly letting him work for his food.

Lenny sighs. To escape, well, finding the right boat takes time. And the priest's keys to the primo rod and reel aren't exactly jumping off the old man's hip.

But mainly, he can't get past the fact of the priest. This feeble old man somehow spotted Lenny's legs poking out from under a busted dock—then managed to locate enough strength to dislodge him from probable death.

Does he owe the crazy coot anything?

"Go forth and make them acts a faith, each one a ye motherfuckers," the old man yells out. "Find hurt within your own square a dirt. Then we gonna vanquish hurt!"

The priest raises his hands to the roof, his back bending so far this time that the raft tilts, almost emptying the priest to the wooden floor.

"The ANTI-MIRACLE cometh!" he calls out, once balance is restored.

"The ANTI-MIRACLE is directly upon ye! I tell ye true! Lift up your hearts and *prepare your minds!* Contemplate the pure, the burning bush, the sacred fire, the dove, the angel Gabriel, the maid a heaven. Whatever god speaks in your ear, listen up!

"Cause we ain't leavin' nobody out!

"Amen-Amen."

CHAPTER 4

LENNY KNEELS IN THE DIRT AND observes what he guesses is the end of the turnip cycle. The priest's pruning shears, dewy and grass flecked, are tucked up under his stump. He inhales the familiar vinegary scent of oregano, the soft licorice of the priest's rapidly bolting basil. But every so often an earthy waft nags at Lenny's brain. Not unlike the puzzling scent from his first venture into the vast fields surrounding the Rectory, the day he followed the priest up from the lake.

Snake musk? Skunk?

He'd smelled it again on the night he stole the boat.

Which hadn't been as difficult as he'd imagined. Once he located the right dock with the right skiff, tied onto some wealthy family's outsized pontoon with a hold full of rods and reels. It was a trick, though, swimming his way to the cove in the dark. He got lost the first night and had to turn back, reset his bearings in the daylight, then return the next night. After that, it was just a matter of climbing aboard the pontoon and, feeling around in the dark, nabbing a bag of jigs, a rod, a spool of two-pound test line, a stringer, a pocket knife, a life jacket, and, at the last minute, a couple of large bumper lures on the off chance big fish were biting. He'd tossed it all into the skiff and quickly eased the boat from its mooring to swim it back up the lake, because, of course, he couldn't row until he built a stump brace. He hauled the skiff up the lake bank and left it upside down in the funky smelling fields, the tackle hidden safely underneath.

Every time he thinks of the gear lying neatly beneath that sturdy hull, his stomach jumps with the ache to be out on the water. It wouldn't be long now. He could be back out on the lake, through the Wateree dam, and skimming his father's river route to the Atlantic in a few weeks, a month at most.

He just needs materials for a stump brace. He could use the life jacket from the pontoon boat for shoulder pads. But he still needs straps or rope, maybe, a clamp for the stump hold, screws and a smooth board for the portage brace.

And for that, he needs to figure out where at the Rectory he can find the equivalent of Buford's floorboard full of ones and fives and tens.

Lenny picks up a turnip with his good hand, rubs his thumb across its smooth skin. His missing thumb aches to join in. What he would give to rotate the bulb in two strong hands and shine its purple slur against its white flesh. The bruise of a healthy bulb, the hefty, gnarly result of a seed planted. Not something his mom had the patience for. His mom would snip the green leaves young, way before anything below surface had a chance to develop. She would sit on her butt in the garden soil, her swirly, rust-orange maxi skirt bunched around her thighs, eating the bright green sprouts. Humming some Jackson Brown song, or maybe James Taylor—Lenny could never keep them straight. Cupping the plants in her bare hands, her grimy fingers full of tender root tendrils. Eating as she plucked them.

Lenny must've been seven or eight back then, because he remembers he still had two hands, a luxury for pulling weeds in his parents' garden. Lenny would pause and watch the sun on his mother's face. It could steady her like your breath can steady a skittered colt.

From where he knelt in the dirt, it seemed that his mom was growing straight out of her own garden.

Lenny sets the turnip on the ground, slides the shears from beneath his stump to his good hand and snips the heavy fall greens from the bulb, layers the greens into a bag, slides the shears back under his stump, recovers the bulb and lobs it into the bucket. Continues down the row.

A shadow too scant to be a cloud moves over Lenny's shoulder. The priest, directly behind him.

"God-a-mighty Jesus. Stop rocket-launching our groceries."

Lenny peers into the bucket.

"I guess you thinking a bruise or two'll add specialty down-and-out flavor."

Lenny drags the bucket closer, pulls, snips, then carefully eases the turnip bulb atop the others.

"That's right. But don't be hacking 'em ever single one like that either. Leave a third for full leaf. You gotta leave about a third *under*ground." He points up the row. "Leave that sunny-sunny third right there, just like I said."

"Just like you said," Lenny mutters.

The shadow sways, sprouts wings for a second, then folds in on itself not unlike an emaciated hawk attempting a half-hearted dive.

Lenny pops another bulb from the ground. Tries for a more brown-nosing approach.

"For seed. Right? For next year?"

"You got ears! We gonna bury those suckers deep in sand down the cellar. Pull 'em out an roast 'em. Roast 'em against the winter cold. Give 'em out down the Block way. Celebrants, now, they love them some roasted turnips when the air goes crispy."

"Sure," Lenny says, though clearly without the enthusiasm the priest was hoping for. Sure enough, the shadow's wings rise and fall.

"I can see I ain't taught your sorry runaway ass nothing. Nothing."

Lenny brushes a wave across the coarse turnip leaves with the shears.

"You ever eat these young?" he says. "I mean, before the turnip develops?" Like my mom does, he wants to say. Lenny clears his throat, not having expected the sudden constriction. "I mean, do you ever eat them green, just...well, green?"

The priest steps into Lenny's view, peers down at him for what seems like a lot longer than it would take to think that through, even for an old man. His dragonfly eyes glimmer under their thin lids.

"I mighta, yeah. You talkin sprouts. I reckon probably so. Tasty-tasty. But I tell ye, not since Celebrants started coming out a the woodwork, I ain't. Nah, we got too many hungry mouths for fancy sprout shit."

Lenny nods. Pulls, snips, drops. Repeats. The feel of the bulb erupting from the earth, the clean cut, the misshapen globes rising in the dirt bucket, well, it's a difficult thing to get stopped.

The old man studies the sky.

Lenny wonders if he's hunting for luck up there. That's where Lenny used to hunt. Any time he caught his mom throttled down in the dirt, he would lift his arm to the sky, tilt his head, and blow through his fingers to the clouds for luck. Slow though, so as not to get noticed. Slow, so as not to disturb the gods' possible cease-fire inside her head, nor any random gods that might be keeping guard over him.

But the gods could not protect him from his brothers. And his dad was too distracted with his mom to protect him. Which is why he's never going back. Never. He's extended Never for one month, now, and he intends to keep on extending.

"Peckerwood want a learner's permit?"

The priest talks to the sky like he talks to the rafters in church.

A learner's permit? What's the priest talking about? Of course he wants a learner's permit. Lenny looks up at the old man who's studying him right back.

"Seems we been knowing each other long enough for a sucker ass to start wanting something?"

Bait, Lenny decides. That's what's dangling. With a barbed hook. A learner's permit would require a name. Not happening. Taking that bait would be trusting the priest, and he's done with trusting. Done with hope. Just one phone call could send him packing back to the western end of the state, back to face crap he doesn't plan to face again. Or maybe they'd ship him off to a group home. Who knows what city folks do with runaways? It's not like he's got loads of experience.

"You forgetting I'm waiting on an answer?"

The priest taps the turnip bucket with his bare foot.

"Nah," Lenny says. "There's nothing I want."

"Don't believe ye," the priest says. "I been seeing your eyes on things. Looking here, looking there. Don't like it."

"I'm not—"

"*I'm not* don't start no sentences around here. A sentence like *I'm not* gonna get cut short. Just like a snooper. You a snooper?"

Lenny tries to recall when the priest might've seen him snooping.

"And don't be staring at me like a slack-jawed doubting Didymus. You think I can't pull that off? A learner's permit for a runaway?"

"It's not that, it's just—"

"You thinking short-skirted girls in this parish not getting the help they need? Hell, you thinking addicts on my Block corner ain't getting clean needles? You thinking our fine city civil servants, high and mighty assholes as they are, not paying for all that shit?"

He pauses to wheeze. "Oh, they paying. One way or another, they paying. Ha. A rube, a babe, ye know nothing. Nothing a this Block, nothing a this parish."

Before Lenny can sort out who is paying for what, the old man plows on.

"Okey-doke then. We needing a legitimate driver. Besides me. Mostly legitimate, that is. Listen up! We gonna return all fourteen-year-old calves back to their mamas. Don't think I won't, you little pecker hole. Them fourteens don't stick. Nor do snoopers. So. You gonna be sixteen. Got that?"

The priest hacks through a complicated throat clearing which for a moment covers up the whoosh of a car speeding along the stone drive to the Rectory.

The old man stiffens and Lenny rises to his knees. They both swivel to watch a police cruiser slide to a halt just inside the stone walled entrance to the Rectory.

A patrolman eases out of the cruiser, hitches his gun belt higher on his hips, squares his shoulders and stares at the grey stone Rectory with its high glass windows reflecting all before it.

Two of the priest's bony fingers, light as horse's breath, light on Lenny's shoulder.

"Holy Mary mother of Jesus," the old man whispers.

Lenny doesn't want to think he's visibly shaking. But probably he is, like when Jude starts his circling, his oldest brother homing in on Lenny for yet another of his weirdo "experiments."

It's just a theory now boys, just a theory.

Jude always started out with just a theory. *You got to prove my theory now, don't you boys? That's how a kid would need to swing, gently, so's you can see for sure that it works. And, of course, so's you don't kill him.*

Lenny could never stop himself from hoping for a smile, or a wink, any sign at all of a joke inside Jude's head when he said something like, *And so's you don't kill him.* But Jude stayed wrapped up in his theory.

So, Lenny would sit there waiting to test Jude's theory. Waiting to swing gently.

Tie his hands, Frank. Tighten the noose, Frank. Roll him off the roof, Frank.

The priest coughs up a wad of phlegm, spits. The patrolman looks around, searching for them through the garden hedge.

The priest murmurs, "Cometh, Basilios. Cometh, cometh."

Then louder, "Over here you rat ass!"

The patrol officer doesn't startle, just pivots their way.

The old man's fingers slide from Lenny's shoulder and point to the earth. Lenny drops back to the soil and moves the bucket further up the row, follows it with the one-hand-two-knee lurch he'd learned as a kid. Pulls a turnip and snips. Pulls and snips.

The priest high-steps across the turnip rows to meet the officer at the hedge. The officer waits there, lighting and taking a long draw on the slender cigarette wavering between his soft, plump lips. Lenny's never seen a man smoking one of the new women's cigarettes, the you've-come-a-long-way-baby kind. The cop's eyes run down the row to Lenny but then directly on past. Like Lenny's just another weed, or worse, a just another turnip.

"Father," the officer says.

"Motherfucker," the priest says.

The officer nods. Takes another draw then drops his arm below the hedge as if the slim cigarette needs hiding.

The priest's chest barely tops hedge height. His pants drape from his rope belt like there's no butt there at all, and his coveted key chain pulls the rope belt low on one side. Today, he's wearing a flannel shirt with the sleeves cut out, so his deeply grooved and gritty elbows protrude back toward Lenny. Maybe he never could see to wash back there. Lenny's seen him pull clothes from the donation boxes down the Block way. Street folks pick through those boxes, take what they need. Others drop in crap they no longer want.

The officer removes his hat, tosses it on top of the hedge. Gives his bald scalp a good scratch, causing ash to drop along his ear. Which he doesn't seem to notice.

"Quite the bed of turnips you got there, Father Damien. I been hearing about 'em. Appears to be just exactly what I been looking for."

The two men observe each other across the hedge like they might be peering into a mirror. Except one looks to be fed on burgers, the other on fresh-caught lake fish and garden greens.

"The Lord provides, Basil," the priest says. "The Lord provides."

The officer takes another drag on his cigarette.

"Yeah I heard that. I sure did. And I can *see* that too, Father. The Lord does provide."

The cop flips the cigarette butt below hedge, watches his own foot grind it out. When he looks up, it's directly into Lenny's eyes.

"Nothing better than fine a patch of turnips," he says. "Fact of the matter, wouldn't surprise me if you didn't have *vagrants* snapping 'em up at sundown. You keeping an eye out for *vagrants*?"

Lenny's pretty sure being called a vagrant is better than being called a turnip, but still, his face flushes deep into his neck at the officer's words.

The priest's hands fiddle along the hedge, snapping off a twig here, another twig there. Searching and snapping.

Lenny pulls another turnip, but as he shears the greens he

misses and slices the bulb. Stark white scars stare up at him from the dirt.

The officer turns away from the hedge and spits. Wipes his mouth with his sleeve.

"In fact, that's what I'm here to discuss, Father Damien. *Vagrants*. Things going missing. You hearing anything about *things going missing*?"

Sweat drips from Lenny's nose onto the blemished turnip.

The priest's fingers continue their fidget.

"You know that Block of yours is a tough beat," the cop says. "Sure is. And it takes time to patrol. Lots of shit going down the Block way, is my way of thinking."

Lenny can't recall the priest silent, ever, for this long a stretch. He edges further down the row. The closer he gets to the end of the row, the closer he is to the path leading around the fields and down to the lake. It's too soon to run. But it occurs to him that he could put the boat in the water and just float away, stump brace or no stump brace. A risky float, but still.

"Taxpayers, now they want their money's worth," the cop continues. "You know that's the truth of it. Sometimes arrests gotta be made." He brushes his hand across the top of the hedge and in one quick motion grabs his cap and flips it onto his head. Pulls it down snug. "And others, like your holiness, well, you folks gotta pay taxes to protect your special assets. *Turnips*, just for argument's sake."

The priest finally settles his fingers, places his hands behind his back.

"Uh-huh, Basilios. Uh-huh. Seems to me what you got up under that official-looking cap a yours is an astounding redundancy of thought pattern."

The gurgle in the back of the old man's throat lands in the hedge between the two of them.

"Uh-huh, just about ever' two weeks, all this agitating about me paying what you like to call taxes. Seems to me, more akin to a habit than to any clear indication of oscillating brain waves."

The officer's plump lips seem wary of the idea of a smile. They test it anyway, then let it go, then test it again. Like minnows nipping at a worm too large to swallow.

Finally the cop recovers himself.

"Not that it matters so much one way or another, Father," he says. "Fact of the matter being, I reckon tax is tax, and it always comes due."

The priest hesitates, like a rabbit twitching against a risky scent on the wind. Slowly, he loops his thumbs into the front of his rope belt, turns and edges down the hedge row toward the Rectory. The officer follows down the other side and sidles through a narrow opening, holding his revolver close to his hip so it doesn't catch. The priest waits for him. Together, they head through the dappled shade of the crepe myrtles bordering the grounds.

But the officer pauses, turns back toward Lenny.

He lifts a hand, directs it down the turnip row like he might be standing in an intersection directing a car into a left-hand turn. Between them lie the dark green okra stalks left to their fall riot, the red-veined chard just emerging, the sweet funky white flowers of chives already dropping seed.

"You gotta leave at least a third of that sunny patch below ground, son," he calls. "But the old man done told you that, right?"

They disappear around the corner of the Rectory, heading toward the shed in back of the Rectory, the priest reaching down for his keys.

Lenny cuts a thick, coarse turnip leaf, holds it out flat in his good hand, like a book. He presses it up against his closed eyes. Slowly he slides it down past his nose to fill his mouth, his tongue drawing up tight and the back of his throat filling with its harshness.

The shed. The keys. Buford's floorboards?

CHAPTER 5

RAYMOND PULLS A HANDKERCHIEF FROM HIS back pocket, waves it toward Lenny. Voila! Quickly polishes then pats the metal folding chair beside him.

From behind the altar, the priest pauses his homily, boney hands hovering over a flickering altar votive, his eyes on Raymond. Then continues.

"*Are ye consumed in transient desire*?"

Lenny slides into the short row beside Raymond.

"Transient?" Raymond stage-whispers, doing his usual Priest baiting. "First off, just show me one single un-transient *anything*, man. I'll take that, please and thank you."

Raymond could find forty-nine ways from the highway to disagree with just a single strand of the priest's thought web.

Especially when the priest got cranked up about the upcoming ANTI-MIRACLE.

"Man, why attach an *anti* to a miracle? What's the fun in that? And how would you perform such a thing?"

Lenny's been sitting with Raymond in services for a few weeks now. Ever since his first Raymond sighting, alongside the Rectory hedge. Raymond cutting the engine of his convertible sports coupe, unfolding slender legs to stand on the driver's seat, and peering over the hedge into the garden where Lenny was raking leaves. One-handed, of course. Lenny pausing, waiting for *the look*. The stump magnet. Will the sports coupe guy make fun? Ignore his stump all together? Would anyone ever simply be impressed with his one-handed gardening skills? It's not like *they* could pull it off.

Lenny went ahead and raised his stump in greeting. First order of business. Get it over with.

Raymond nodded, like he was agreeing with something, then folded his own arm in half, raised his elbow, and circled it right back at Lenny.

Called out over the hedge, "See you in church, man!"

Dropped back into his convertible and buzzed out the Rectory drive.

"Desire ever so vast, ever so breath-grabbing, that ye seem descended from heaven?"

"Hello-a-licious yes," Raymond whispers. "I could just eat that priest up! Have no idea what he's saying, but keep it coming, baby, keep it coming."

"Be ye wary, lest desire disappear ye destiny!"

The homily ends. Amens echo around the Block, followed by a stir and focus as the old man circulates the collection plate. It's a reverse operation. The plate, clean and shiny, which is surprising given its fishy use on off days, starts out full, then drains to zero by the time it returns to the priest's hands. Artemis the Amazon, Elias, and a few others, drop bills in, but for the most part, Celebrants leave the Block a little more secure than when they arrived.

Each week Raymond drops in two tens, enough to fund Lenny's

escape plan. But Lenny can't bring himself to reach in, not with the Sunny kids waiting their turn.

The problem with Raymond, all flowy angel hair and tight jeans, is that he sends Lenny's mind spinning toward Glenna. Same ache. Same urges all headed in the same direction. Down toward disaster. Relief, yes. But disaster.

Lenny might be unsure what to do about Raymond, but the phone in the priest's study could go a long way toward easing his worries about Glenna. He can't imagine calling her. Just the thought of her voice on the other end of a phone line rattles him. But more than her voice, her likely reaction to his voice is what stays him.

Of course, *not* calling her is impossible, too. He needs to find out the end to that story. If he could just make sure she came through okay, he could get on with...with getting on. It's a risk though. Not only that he might find out she isn't okay. But also, he can't afford to be caught snooping or be overheard. As far anyone knows, he has no connections, no one to call. No past.

And he intends to keep it that way.

Which eliminates phone booths and just about every other phone he can think of, but one. Upstairs in the Rectory, the priest's private study. *We gonna return all fourteen-year-old calves back to their mamas. Snoopers too.*

If he chooses his time carefully, makes sure the priest and his Celebrants are well out of earshot...

The priest presides over communion, letting each Celebrant linger at the cup, refilling often from the wine jugs behind the pulpit, painstakingly wiping the rim with a bar towel. The votives have long since burned out and the sanctuary reeks now of his dad's hangover breath.

The service ends with the usual peace-be-with-you milling about, and the flock files out.

Raymond nudges Lenny's stump with his elbow as they part ways.

#

Lenny stands in the bed of the priest's pickup truck and drops corn onto the sidewalk, watches the Celebrants bag their week's dinner. Wednesday Market Day. Just down from the Block.

The air is warm and gritty for September, the street hairy with wayward silks and shucks. The swirl of hands reach and sort through the corn piled high on the cracked sidewalk. Every now and then a silkworm falls to the curb, its home shredded by eager fingers judging kernel color and texture.

After the corn, the Celebrants move on down the street for okra, peppers, the late tomatoes. Two wheelbarrows, one full of bruised apples and the other tipping day old bakery bread, draw attention.

When Lenny remarked on the picked-over nature of some of the produce, the priest had simply replied, "First, second, third pick, they's still calories, son."

Last week the priest unearthed five cantaloupes wedged under a rain spout behind the A&P Store, probably rolled off a cart. They'd sliced them for Sunday morning services, the body of Christ distributed on a toothpick. Several Celebrants refused communion, resulting in the priest calling out from the altar, "Some folks taking symbolism way too far!"

Lenny waits for a pause in the sorting action, an opening, so he can dump more corn.

Crisp, blue pants shift and shimmer in Lenny's peripheral vision.

"I'm just guessing you know the difference between a hook and a sinker?"

Officer Basilios. Cap under arm, bald head glistening. Long, slim cigarette popping between his lips as he speaks.

A hook and a sinker. Lenny stares down at the officer on the sidewalk, struggles to latch onto the man's thought line.

"Nope," is all he can think to say. Then, "Yep."

Everyone knows the difference between a hook and sinker, right?

Basilios pulls on his cigarette, removes it with thumb and four fingers, examines it before dropping it to the sidewalk and grinding it out. A small eddy ripples along the sides of his mouth, a grin idling there. Or maybe a frown?

"You're either a lot smarter than you look, or…"

The officer clears his throat and raises his voice so suddenly that Lenny momentarily loses his balance.

"Where's Father Damien?" the cop yells. The milling crowd comes to an uncertain attention. "I need to inquire as to a person, or persons, with knowledge of a small fishing vessel, gone missing. And an expensive fishing rod, also gone missing!"

Now it's Lenny's brain that's knocked off balance.

The officer pipes down as quickly as he'd piped up, drops the hat under his arm to his hands, rolls it round and round.

"The good Father tells me you already sixteen," he says.

Lenny scoops another arm full of corn, using his stump as a brace, and lets the ears filter over the tailgate to the pile. He doesn't much like the officer's choice of topics, and he doesn't much like a conversation that jumps. Police tactics?

"Now a boy who's not yet sixteen, does not seem to have a family? That could be a problem. Especially when things go missing. Fact is, that's what we call a problem of magnitude, and we do investigate magnitudinous problems."

"What makes you think he's not?"

Raymond. Sporting a bright red bandana that irons his

Goldilocks hair flat back off his face. Yellow flowered knee patches on high water jeans. High water enough that Lenny suspects he's pulled them from the clothes bin outside the Block. But maybe that's just what rich folks wear, how would he know?

Raymond's fingers string loosely along the metal handles of a stroller, a small baby inside. Tiny. Its nose just a bump with two peep holes. Wrinkled forehead, deep in a frowning sleep. Naked, except for its matching red bandana diaper which is streaked dark with what Lenny guesses is tiny baby pee. Fingers of both hands grip the hot air, then let it go.

Lenny wants to jump down to the sidewalk and touch its pink palm. The urge is strong and jolts his heart like a cattle prod.

Officer Basilios gives an exaggerated sniff toward the baby, and steps away to the sidewalk fountain, runs cold water into his hat and places it on his head.

"Not what?" he says.

"Well, man. Sixteen. Just like you said. Why wouldn't he be sixteen?"

Basilios turns toward the street, looks left, looks right, and steps off the curb. Back on patrol.

Raymond swivels a thumb over his shoulder at the retreating officer.

Mental, he mouths, before lifting both hands to check his bandana. The stroller, now free, twists away in a half circle toward the street.

Raymond keeps an eye on the stroller, but finishes fixing his hair before rescuing it.

"Knocked her mama up," he says.

Lenny waits.

"Man, does it have to be this difficult? I mean, don't get me wrong, I could bat cleanup on town cushy. But I'm feeling safer in the dugout these days. Running those bases? Too hard on the heart, man, too hard on the heart. You dig that, right?"

Yes, Lenny wants to say. Yes.

Raymond wheelies the stroller back and forth on its rear axle.

"Now I got responsibilities."

"She kept it?"

Lenny wants to jerk those words back like you yank a misfired lure headed for a tree branch. Yank it clear of a sure snag, watch it fall safely into deep water. But you can't do that with words.

Raymond looks up at Lenny in the truck bed. "Well, *obviously*. What would *you* know about *that*?"

Lenny shrugs. Glenna isn't a subject he plans to discuss.

Raymond moves closer to the truck.

"Man, I pleaded with her, I did plead. But she was zilch-o. Nada. She wanted that kid. Thought maybe it could turn a *profit*. That's what she said. A *profit*. Lots of possibility thrown into a doomed argument. Woman's moving downtown, now. Taking the kid with her. Downtown where nobody lacks for *opportunity*. She says. Scouting it out as we speak. Claims it's my responsibility to, well, I guess stroll it until she gets back?"

Raymond rolls his eyes. "She said one week, tops. Makes me nervous, man."

"What? What makes you nervous?"

"Her taking the kid, *obviously*. Her plans for the kid. Makes me nervous."

"Who," Lenny says. "I mean, who's the girl?"

Raymond points at the stroller. "I've been telling you, man. She's *my kid*."

"No. I mean, who's *the girl*?"

Raymond braces the stroller against his hip hugger jeans, shakes his hair loose from the bandana, reties it.

"Not a girl. Nothing girl to her. Name is Shawnee. Stout and wild, man. Stout and wild."

"What's she mean by *profit*?"

Raymond stands down there on the hot pavement, thinking. Sharp nose slightly sun burnt. Pale eyes. Pale blue fading toward yellow. Eyes trying their best to match the few escaped strands of hair drifting in the hot breeze.

He frowns. "But you gotta ask, is *that* shit worth *this* shit?" He gives the stroller a nudge for emphasis. "We should think that through, man, you and me. We should discuss that little problem."

He nods, places a hand on his hip. His *I'm pretty satisfied with myself* look.

"I got my eye on you, man. Brain power."

Raymond moves on down the street, zig-zagging the stroller, steering clear of the wake of hungry kids and their parents combing the bins.

Lenny watches Raymond, and Raymond's heart-jolting baby, *a profit?* until they disappear around the corner.

Lenny dumps two more loads of corn into the pile on the hot cracked sidewalk. The truck is still about a third full. The last of it will be harder for him to pick up. Scooping with one-and-a-half arms is much quicker than plucking. Pretty soon he'll have to start scraping it out the end of the truck with his feet.

"You probably understand a thing such as taxes."

Basilios, drifting back in.

Lenny looks up to the corner, hoping Raymond might again appear out of nowhere. The Celebrant tide has ebbed. Or, more to the point, been washed away. It's like Basilios jumped into the lake and splashed everyone to the shallows. When Baslios floats away, they'll flow back in, redistribute along the sidewalk. Restore the natural order.

"I'm just guessing," the officer says.

He picks up a hand full of shucks, flattens them out, layers them neatly between his thick fingers. Silks fall away, drift back toward the street.

Basilios and his taxes.

All Lenny can see is Jude, tossing a rope over a tree limb, tying the other end around Lenny's neck. Hoisting him up. It might not be the same thing, but it sure feels the same. A trap being laid.

Well, he's bone tired of traps.

"Do you need some corn, Officer?" he says.

Basilios steps in close to the truck to look directly up into Lenny's eyes. The shucks are smooth now between his fingers, but still he continues to pave them out. Over and over.

"You want to be sixteen? Then yes. Yes, that's *exactly* what I want. I want corn. But not *this* corn. No, I want that particular kind of corn that's in the old man's shed. Lots of it. Lots more than the good Father Damien is willing to cough up. You hear me? You pay *your* taxes, you pay *your* fair share, you bring me *that* corn, and you'll be sixteen, here and forever more."

He tosses the ironed shucks into the truck bed.

"Shit slingers, especially *one-armed* shit slingers, are easy to track. You understand what I'm saying?"

"Who's holding up that corn line?"

Basilios closes his eyes at the voice of Artemis the Amazon, her red spikes bobbing above her flowing peasant dress, boobs swinging at wide angles as she charges across the street toward them. Behind her, on the opposite curb, Elias lingers at a news stand, his skullcap neatly in place.

Basilios reluctantly turns toward her. "I got a job to do, Marva. I guess you know that."

"Well, if your job is to ferment this corn, I'd say you're stepping right up the ladder of success."

She gestures up the sidewalk where families are milling about, pretending they aren't waiting for the officer to wade out.

Elias seems hesitant to cross the street. There are no cars. But still, he looks both ways. Like he's hoping for traffic.

Artemis, or, Lenny guesses, Marva, reaches inside her bag, pulls out an envelope and hands it up to Lenny. But her eyes never leave Basilios.

"For Father Damien," she says. "For what he just happens to get done on a daily basis."

She takes Basilios by the elbow. "Let's leave the Block folks alone for just one afternoon, Basil. I'm sure you've got important patrols elsewhere."

He flinches at her touch, but lets her steer him away from the corn.

Elias finally crosses over and nods at Lenny as he follows them down the sidewalk.

Lenny sits on the truck's tailgate to open the envelope, hoping there's enough cash to send him on his way. But before he has a chance to look inside, the Sunny Family shows up. Miss May with June and July trailing, the rope dangling from hand to hand.

"You doing good work now," Miss May says. She smiles. The kids smile.

"Yes ma'am. I mean...I guess I'm figuring things out."

"Yes," she says. "I see that. You staying around?"

"No ma'am. I mean...yes, for now."

She winds the rope up under her arm, pulls the kids in close to pluck corn from the pile. It occurs to Lenny that having kids might be a close estimation to what life is like one-handed.

July, the little boy, edges in toward Lenny, his eyes glued to Lenny's stump.

"I see you got a friend," Miss May says, still bagging her corn.

"Ma'am?"

"A friend," she says, nodding down the street. "Marva. That's a fine friend to have. Handy. And tall!"

"Oh, you mean Artem…uh, yes. Marva. I guess so."

July crowds in closer. Pries his eyes off Lenny's bald elbow, trying to gauge Lenny's thoughts on such a serious matter as a stump. Lenny'd seen kids do this plenty of times. But July, he reaches his little index finger upward and without hesitation runs it over Lenny's stump seam. He watches his fingertip trace the edge of the scar, checks again for Lenny's reaction, then offers up his opinion.

"Feels like rope," he says.

Lenny nods, his heart feeling a bit ambushed, but in a good way.

"It's tough, alright," he says.

June tugs at the rope, her eyes on the wheelbarrow of apples. Miss May tugs her children back in line.

"You have any troubles with that Basilios?" she says. "Or any police in town? Just in case you didn't know yet. Cause I've had *my* troubles and you might have yours. Marva. She's a fine friend to have."

"Well," Lenny says. "Well okay, then. Thanks."

Miss May gives a short tug on the rope and strings her family down the sidewalk toward the apples.

Lenny wedges Marva's envelope into his thumb crease, tears it open with his teeth. Lots of ones and fives and tens and even twenties. Just exactly what he's been looking for.

But maybe he needs to be on the right side of Artemis.

He transfers the envelope up under his stump to brace it, slips two fingers in and pulls out two ones. Waves the bills toward a couple of kids who've drifted in to pick through the corn.

"You two empty this truck? These are yours." He lays the ones on tailgate beside him. Time to plan, *to cogitate*, as Buford would suggest.

Job 1: Don't think about Job 1. Too difficult to think about.

Job 2: Drag the boat deeper into the Rectory fields, before someone finds it.

Job 3: Find out what's in the priest's shed. Whatever it is, it's valuable enough for the cop to want it. Which means, Lenny wants it. *I'm just guessing you know the difference between a hook and sinker?* Yes, Lenny thinks he probably does.

Job 4: Secure funding that's not Marva's, and build a stump brace.

Lenny watches the kids in the truck bed, their stringy fingers reaching for the corn, their tough faces watchful but satisfied to be tossing corn to the street, working for their dollars.

Which reminds him of Raymond. What the heck does Raymond do? Where does he get off driving a sports coupe?

Job 5: Figure out Raymond. Or, at least, his ricocheting thoughts about Raymond. And, jeeze, that baby. Lenny's not used to babies. So why all of a sudden the heart jolt?

Which brings him right back around to Job 1.

Work his nerve up to call Glenna.

CHAPTER 6

LENNY SLIPS INSIDE THE PRIEST'S PRIVATE study and slides the door closed behind him.

The priest is down the Block way for afternoon services, as are the committee of Celebrants who clean and cook and fiddle around the Rectory throughout the day. Plenty of time to make one call, just one call. And maybe time left over to check out the shed before shucking and scraping the last of the corn for canning, which was his excuse for staying behind from services.

"Shucking and scraping gonna be a one-handed trick?" the priest, not looking all that surprised anymore at Lenny's skill set, but still curious.

Only for folks who can't use their feet and teeth, Lenny thought, though he only said, "It'll get done."

The study is bigger than he'd imagined, huge floor to ceiling windows looking out over the fields behind the Rectory, a white picket fence squaring off one field big enough for a couple of horses. But there's no horses because it's no pasture. Instead, it's thick with rows of tobacco that the Celebrants cut and sell, under the promise to return a fraction of their earnings back to the Block.

It's a small-time operation, little peckerwood. But each operation counts.

Behind the tobacco there's more land, planted in sorghum, the same amber fronds they'd hacked through that first day when the priest pulled him from under the dock. Sorghum running across the low, wavy hills all the way down to Lake Norman.

The windows lay down misshapen light rectangles and trapezoids across the red oak floor, and Lenny steps in closer to their warmth. Patches of purple, or maybe blue, it's hard to tell from this distance, darken the amber across field after field. Orange and blue, orange and blue.

Maybe that's how sorghum dies. How would he know?

The priest's shed is in full view to his right. Lenny's noticed that the cop's not the only person the priest takes back there.

A shiny black phone sits heavy on the priest's shiny black desk. He's heard it ring from his bunk just off the second-floor screened porch.

Lenny pulls back the rolling chair, sits at the priest's desk, stares at the phone.

He'd laid awake in his bunk last night, allowing the chirping crickets outside the screen porch to remind him of home and to help him make up his mind to call Glenna.

Call Glenna before his brain explodes from the need to hear her voice. Even if it was for the last time. No more thinking it through. He'd been gone six weeks now, and the need to ask her had grown inside his head like a bolted autumn gourd. Glenna was the one person that he could call. She might not care. She might not even talk to him. But she wouldn't tell anyone about him, either. That's the key. She wouldn't ever tell. So, he'll just call. By the time the charge shows up on the priest's phone bill, Lenny will be long gone, back on the river and headed for the ocean.

He swivels the desk chair. Somehow, he can't imagine the priest sitting here, then realizes the old man probably never sits here. Why would he? Lenny pulls open a drawer, watches a spider skitter to the back corner. A dime and a nickel lay flat on the dusty wooden base along with an A&P Store receipt too faded to read. A few mouse droppings. There's no papers here or on the desk, no pens, no paperclips, no tape, no scissors.

Lenny picks up the phone in his good hand, extends his forefinger and quickly dials Glenna's number. It's not like she's going to be home in the middle of the day, anyway. Probably she got a job, working downtown at the creamery, or the women's boutique selling vases and ashtrays and knickknacks.

Glenna picks up on the second ring.

Lenny holds his breath. Hears her say "Hello?" "Hello?"

Long, long pause. Then she lets out a giving-up kind of "Hello."

"Glenna?" Lenny doesn't like the way his voice wavers. And why did he ask her name like a question, like he's unsure. Like he might not recognize her voice, which he absolutely does. He should've just said her name like he meant it.

Glenna.

He should've said it like he'd said back when they were just kids, back when he'd come upon the three of them, his two brothers and Glenna in the tall grass, and she'd needed him to come upon them.

Glenna clutching at her shredded blouse.

He'd ridden his horse up the ridge to their hide out, which Jude swore was built by *the Native Americans, boys, Native Americans*, but to Lenny and Frank it looked more like an abandoned sheep shed. A trail led from the shed through a copse of hemlocks to a sheer cliff face two stories high and covered in mountain laurel. They would climb the cliff face, toss a rope over a sturdy branch, and swing from the cliff clear across the spring to the trail head.

At the base of the cliff was a mountain spring, and if the rains were strong enough in the spring and early summer, the cool, fresh water would rise up through the earth and form a waist-high pool where they could swim.

But Glenna and his brothers weren't swimming that day.

That day, they'd had her down in the weeds, and when he spotted them, he'd clamped down on his breath and ridden his horse directly into his brothers' angry eyes. She swung up behind him and they'd held tight where the trail angles steeply in its descent to the river bend leading to Gorge Bridge. In that flat stretch along the river sits the Rader farm. Glenna's home.

They'd ridden in silence except for that one word he'd said. *Glenna.*

Lenny wills her to speak now, but she's not saying anything.

He takes a deep breath. He wants to speak again, but then she might think he's crying or something. He holds his hand over the mouthpiece so she can't hear him breathing.

She sighs. *Her* hand isn't over *her* mouthpiece.

"Why are you calling?" she says.

He imagines her black hair, long and silky-flat, shifting down around her shoulders. Around his shoulders.

"Lenny?"

"You been riding any?" he says.

Her abrupt warning laugh, usually reserved for his older brothers. Warning you that you aren't funny.

"Riding, Lenny? Really?"

"The horses," he says. "Are you riding the horses?"

What *was* he talking about? Why was he asking her stupid horse questions?

Glenna exhales. Gathers it back in.

"Did you make it to the Atlantic Ocean? Have you found work? A place to stay?"

Steadier ground. "Yes," he says. "I mean, no. Not to the Atlantic. I will though. I'll make it. My boat sunk. I made it to Charlotte."

"Charlotte?"

"Yeah, holed up in Charlotte. With some priest."

"Some priest?"

"Father Damien. The Block. He's got what he calls Celebrants. They sell tobacco like the folks back home..."

Her silence lingers.

"You should hear his sermons—"

"I thought you were serious about this, Lenny. This isn't a joke. Your parents are...if you weren't serious...Lenny if you are not serious you should just come home. We talked about this. Why are you calling?"

"What about my parents?"

The line goes absolutely still. It could be that she's not even breathing. She's not going to give up any information about his parents. Not if he's truly gone for good. She's not going to make it worse on him. Or easy on him. That's Glenna.

He needs to hang up. But he also needs to get to the point. He needs information only she has. He should know, shouldn't he?

Lenny pauses to listen for any sounds outside the study, any signs of church over.

"I just wanted to find out," he says. "You know."

He clears his throat, surprised how much he sounds like the priest coughing up crap. "I wanted to know if you are okay, and everything. With everything."

Was that clear enough? Does she understand what he's trying to ask? Should he say the word? Would she be hurt if he said the word?

How did your abortion go, Glenna? Is that something people said? Or would he say, *our* abortion? *How did our abortion go?*

Another stupid question. There's only one way these things go, right? What's he supposed to ask her? He doesn't even know why he's thinking about it. She's obviously fine, because she's on the other end of the phone talking to him. And it's legal now. She'd said she could go somewhere close to home, clinics opening all over the place. Everything was fine. Is fine. Why is he asking?

The phone sweats where it's wedged between his shoulder and ear. He twists the cord up tight against the receiver, releases it to unspool.

"Glenna?"

Her words come quick, sudden, like a big lake bass striking hard on a thin line. Two-pound test. Lenny would not have the dexterity to manage that today.

"You know what Lenny? You know what? That wasn't what we said. We said, *you* said, it was too dangerous to stay. You were suffocating. That's what *you* said. And you were right. You *had* to leave. God, what you've been through. Your *brothers*. Remember? That's what we agreed on and you by gosh better be serious. And you know what? You are too far away from me to know anything more."

Then she's gone. The ultra-light line snapped. The fish hooked forever in the gut, dragging the bait and the broken line into deep, cold water.

CHAPTER 7

LENNY SNAKES ALONG THE GROUND BENEATH the rusted barbed wire fence and rises in the sorghum field on the other side.

He hesitates, listens for any movement among the thick rows of orange fronds fanned by just a whisper of a breeze. Most Celebrants are down in the lower fields, dragging the last of the tobacco to the barn. But a few loaded into the priest's yellow pickup truck headed for the Sunny Family's neighborhood to clean gutters and haul trash down the row houses.

Just as soon as the priest rounded the bend, Lenny was out the back and headed for the fields.

Job 2: Drag his boat deeper into the fields, out of range of Basilios. Lenny's pretty sure the cop wouldn't heave his way too deep into the hot fields on foot.

Lenny scans the sorghum downslope, then up the next rise. Its sweet scent is dusty in his mouth. A hot autumn day. Does it ever get cool in this flat city land? He guesses folks here wouldn't call it flat. But back home, on their little farm nestled between the double peaks of Rosey Face and Chub Ridge, the mountain air begins to brisk up in September and is downright bracing by October. But here, nothing seems to be shifting. Hot and dry. Hot and dry. Day after day.

Lenny counts five of the weird purple-blue patches stitched in among the amber fronds, and decides those plants are not dying sorghum.

He heads out for the boat, counting along twelve rows before turning in at the thirteenth which leads to where he hid the little skiff and the fishing tackle. He trots along, keeping his good arm and stump high to brush back the green leaves swiping at his face. Amber buds, disturbed by his journey, float on the thick air. Lenny slows, then comes to an abrupt halt when he hits a blue patch.

He must've counted wrong, or, thinking back, maybe he'd counted from the lakeside, because there'd been no blue near where he hid the skiff. He floats his good hand across the spiny, prickly blue spiders. Pretty and ugly all at the same time. He breathes in the funk, heavy enough to taste.

So. Now he knows where that whiff of musk comes from, its scent blowing down from these upper fields to mingle alongside the oregano and sweet basil of the priest's garden.

He pulls on the blue feathery spider legs of the leaves, then he pinches off one of the centers. Holds it close to his nose. Places it on his tongue.

Sweet, then a bitter burn. And just like that, it's familiar. He pinches a few more buds, rubs them between his thumb and first two fingers, and stares at the short threads sprinkling into his palm. He juggles the shreds into a pile. Gives a low whistle.

Skunk weed. In full Fall bloom. The shit Jude and his friends talk about, brag about when they can get it.

And here it is, hidden yet growing crazy among in the priest's quilted fields. Fields you hear about on the news from time to time, patches of weed spotted by overly energetic drug agents in their helicopters. Lenny glances skyward. *Goddamn DEA, Buddo,* his dad would say. *Alerted by your friendly neighbor narcs.* They'd land their helicopters on the spot, dig wide firebreaks around a farmer's field. Burn that family's land to ash.

His dad swore the entire community got high watching their neighbor's food source disappear. *Goddamn distracting. All the while, the Cali cartel's hopping borders easy as you please. Cocaine in their britches. Goddamn.*

And just like that, the priest's shed is not all that mysterious. Lenny lets the weed filter through his fingers and drift to the ground.

He's got to find out for sure, of course. If the priest is dealing in illegal weed, *and,* if the priest knows Lenny knows he's dealing, well then…well then, it seems the scales would be different. The priest can't just rat him out to the authorities, *toss him back into the lake* as he put it. If the priest is a dealer, then Lenny has what Jude would call *leverage.*

A shudder runs up Lenny's chest. Isn't this one of the reasons he left home? To make sure he didn't become Jude? That girl in the road they'd picked up, that girl with her bicycle, he'd seen her see it in his eyes. Her eyes saying he was no better than his brothers.

But already that chest shudder is shaking out thoughts that hatch and surface quick as minnows chased by hungry fish. Skim the crop. Not much, just enough for quick money. Enough to pay off Officer Basilios, keep him out of his hair. Enough to get the hell back on the water. He could sell packets, like those little baggies his brothers bought from pushers down the valley and hid under the porch of their farmhouse.

He could hide it in the fields. Have a business even Jude would admire.

But not like Jude. That's not his final destination. It's just a way to get there.

Lenny gathers more of the soft, moist buds, fills the front pockets of his cutoffs.

He hurries to the far end of the field, counts rows back from the lake until he locates his stolen boat and drags it further into the priest's patchwork fields.

#

A sliver of moonlight finds its way through the roaming clouds and glints off the back of the tool shed, making its hairy cedar boards sparkle for a moment before fading back to dark.

Like on the river, at night. The clouds will open, shine off the water, disappear. Lenny often wonders what that's like for the fish below. Do they swim toward the sudden glimpse of light? Away from it into the cold deep? What do they do with those few seconds of light?

With his good hand, he feels along the boards tacked neatly across the cracked window of the shed. The priest has been too wily about his keys, so after weeks of watching and waiting, Lenny's trying another route.

Slowly, night by night, he's pried one board loose, then another, careful to ease all nails back into their holes for daylight eyes. He'd taken his time, waited for his chances. Waited for the priest to settle in from his big shoe drive or corn grilling or banjo fest down the Block way. Waited for the Celebrants to finish their canning, their mopping, their jabbering. Waited for the priest to finish off his third glass of red wine. You don't grow up fishing for food without learning how to wait.

Tonight, Lenny had dozed off in his bed by the upstairs porch, then startled awake from a dream of the river, him in his sunken skiff, his dad popping a jig from the lips of a largemouth bass the length of Lenny's stump, the bass disappearing. Sweat soaked and a little chilled, he'd listened for the deep snoring of the priest down the hall before making his way down the steps, cringing with each creak of hardwood, and slipped through the kitchen and out the back door.

Lenny eases the three previously loosened boards from their purchase across the window, leans them against the shed. Tonight, the fourth board should break free, giving him plenty of room to enter. He's swiped a small penlight from the priest's kitchen. He just needs to get into the shed and steal enough of the priest's pot to fund his escape.

Lenny gently works at the final board, listening for the groan of old, rotted cedar under stress. He could jerk it loose in about a half a second. But the trick is to pry it without busting it so he can put it all back together again. No suspicions, no evidence.

Slipping through a busted window has its drawbacks.

Lenny runs his stump up under his shirt and across prickles of glass caught along his belly. He lifts the shirt with his stump and picks them with his good hand the best he can while waiting for his eyes to adjust to the cool dark of the shed's interior. He'd had to jerk harder than expected on the window sash and the panes shattered, leaving the window still jammed.

He pulls the penlight from his pocket, beams it around in broad circles, catching hand tools strewn along the floor, a hack saw, a couple of hammers, along with moldy boots, random pieces of scrap wood, nails of all sizes. Saw dust. Cobwebbed brooms, shovels, rakes in one corner and worn out garden gloves in another.

He beams his light wider to the shelves along the wall. Rows and rows of canning jars, mostly quarts, some squat pints, full of beans and tomatoes, pickles, corn, jellies and jams. Useful supplies, even in a boat. He spots a spool of thin wire on a high shelf, mentally marks it for his brace. He runs his light across a tool bench, then beneath, but no evidence of the "taxes" Basilios is so keen to get his hands on.

Lenny places the penlight in his teeth, reaches to pull open a toolbox but the beam jumps too erratically for him to focus. He clamps the light tighter in his teeth to steady the jumping beam. It's only when the beam takes off across the wall that he realizes it's not his penlight. As Lenny swings back around to the broken window, his penlight falls to the shed floor, popping dark on impact, and a flashlight beam from the busted-out panes of the window catches him full in the face.

This light runs him up and down. Twice. Holds again in his eyes, which Lenny shields with his stump. Quickly, Lenny mentally ticks off his excuses to the priest. He needs to re-rig the hoe, the shovel, the rake, with stump braces, make them easier to use? Of course he does. And he couldn't sleep, so he might as well make the best use of his time. He couldn't help it if the priest wouldn't cough up his keys. Lame, lame.

But maybe it's not the priest. Maybe it's the cop?

The flashlight flicks off and a silhouette disappears from the window to be replaced by bumping and a metallic rattle against the shed wall.

Lenny drops to his knees, his good hand feeling across the floor, hair balls webbing his fingers before he finally seizes on the penlight. He flicks it off and on twice, then shakes it until its thin beam emerges. He points the light toward the window just in time to see the front wheels of a baby stroller emerge.

"Grab a wheel, man, would you?"

The stroller jams in the window frame. Several blades of glass hit and shatter across the concrete floor.

"Shit," Lenny whispers. "Just…quiet. Just—"

Lenny slips the penlight into his pocket, braces the front of the stroller between his stump and body, reaches with his good hand for the handle to shimmy the stroller through the window and air lift it to the floor of the shed.

He's not sure how he was hoping otherwise, but the stroller is sure enough full of baby.

Raymond lets out several low groans and a louder *ow!* as he edges through the window.

"Been staking out your slinky butt, man. But finally, finally. Hey, next time you gotta pop out that back porch light. Made you too easy to see from the street. But that priest, he's a sick sleeper. Drowned. Am I right?"

"Staking out?" Lenny whispers, hoping Raymond drops to the same volume. He shines his penlight on the baby tucked into the sack of the stroller. Eyes half shut. Miniature arms doing slow motion wind mills. Bare feet circling.

"Well, yeah, staking out." Raymond at least now stage whispering. "You got access, man. Living with the crazy man. Just a matter of time before you snooped out the old guy. So, is it true? Do we have what I think we have?"

"Just…just be quiet." Lenny leans down and picks a shard of glass from between the baby's diaper and the stroller sack. His fingers come back wet. He lifts them to his nose to make sure it's urine and not blood.

"What if it cries?" he whispers, wiping his hand on his pants.

"This shed, man. You busted it. Notorious. Did you even have a clue?"

Lenny picks a shard from the stroller's foot rest. Pulls out his penlight and shines it across it's little baby head, searching for glass sparkles.

"I thought you were only keeping it one week," he says.

"*Her*. Keeping *her*. Turned into three. Three weeks." Raymond circling, swinging his beam too fast for focusing, but the light sweeps an odd shape along one wall.

"Woman's doing recognizance in Raleigh, man. Shawnee evidently now needs to skip town, lay low. All cool. Says she's coming for the kid. Today, tomorrow, the next day, who knows? I kinda hate giving her up."

Raymond pauses his circling, grabs Lenny's bicep just above his stump seam and gives it a quick shake.

"But a man needs his sleep."

Raymond's touch sends a surprising urgency through Lenny. Surprising and unwanted. He doesn't have time for a goddamn body betrayal, not now. He needs to think.

"Flash your light toward that wall again," he says.

Raymond beams in the direction Lenny indicates. The light catches on a colony of protrusions along the wall, floor to ceiling, and on each side of the window.

Wasp nests? Bats? Lenny edges over to the wall, gingerly investigates with the fingers of his good hand.

Burlap. Coarse, burlap sacks, torn open and quilted together, from what he can tell. Hanging in large swaths, roping down from the slanted tin roof of the shed. Gingerly, Lenny lifts a corner of the sacking, shielding his eyes with his stump in case birds or bats or whatever fly out at him. But nothing flies out, nothing moves. He drapes the burlap over his shoulder and runs his good hand across the wall beneath. Raymond moves in behind him, casting light under the burlap.

Rows and rows of plastic bags, pint bags, quart bags like his dad used to freeze blueberries and squash and okra back home. Tacked to the shed's cedar wall, bulging bags blossoming on top of each other like fungus stacked up the base of a tree trunk. He won't have to tear open any bags to know what's inside, to know his theory was correct, to know why the priest locks the shed door and boards the windows. Or why Basilios shows up every other week jawing about "taxes."

Raymond lets out a giggle.

The baby lets out a whimper.

"We're in business," Raymond's whisper breath brushing Lenny's ear. Lenny closes his eyes, tries to concentrate away the urgency Raymond is creating.

The baby lets out a short squeak, then a longer one, tilting on the edge of a cry.

Raymond snaps one of the baggies off the wall and backs out from under the burlap, leaving Lenny in the semi-dark of his penlight.

Lenny takes his time settling himself. He needs to sweep up the glass and hope the priest blames someone else if he discovers the break. He needs to grab the wire for his brace and a few bags of pot in case he runs into Basilios. And he needs to get the hell out of the shed. But more important, he needs to get Raymond and a potentially screaming baby out of the shed. After a couple of deep breaths, he eases back from the burlap and shines his penlight at Raymond, who is now kneeling beside the stroller, licking his finger, dipping it into the baggie, placing his finger into the baby's mouth.

"Hey," Lenny says.

"Quiet," Raymond whispers. "Working like a charm."

"Hey!"

"Snoozes her," Raymond whispers. "And it's not her first time."

The baby's lips pucker. Lenny shines the light from the baby to Raymond, back to the baby. Same lips. Pucker, pucker. Quiver, quiver. Both of them.

Raymond rocks back, sits on the concrete. His face shadowed in the weak beam.

"Takes just the tiniest thread," he says, like he's made some scientific discovery. Like he's the king of babysitting knowledge. He looks up at Lenny.

"Well, well, Mister Notorious. You understand what we got here, right?"

Lenny thinks he does.

"We?" he says.

Raymond's lips form a fine, silk line. His *I'm trying to concentrate* look.

"Yeah," he says. "If Shawnee takes the brat and leaves, then yeah. We."

Lenny flicks the light to the baby.

"What's her name?"

"Romey. Name's Romey."

"Don't give her any more weed," Lenny says, shifting the light to Raymond's eyes. "Not…not ever."

Raymond grins. "I like where you're going with that, man. Not very practical, but I like it." He tries to shield his face from Lenny's light. "Wait till you see my apartment. It's my dad's, just to be perfectly transparent, but he's never there. Smells like diapers right now, but wait for the candles, man. Let the priest keep working his end of this magic show, let Shawnee disappear. Vamoose goes the baby. Then *we* are in business. You need a home, right? I got one. Hey, where are you from?"

Where's he from?

The goddamned lake, that's where. Washed up from the lake. And he's returning to the lake, heading for the ocean, the Atlantic Ocean. The big dream.

But, *his dad's* big dream, now that he thinks about it.

Is it truly a clean break from home, if he's still following his dad's goddamn word map? Maybe he should head up a different cove. Take a different route. *His own* route.

Maybe that route is lying on the shed floor right in front of him. What would *that* be like? He's worked his way out of Jude's pocket. Now maybe he's staring at a way out of the priest's pocket, plus the cop's. Maybe it's time to cut bait on all lines. Explore what's right there front of him. Check out *those* options.

It's not like the Atlantic Ocean is going to walk off without him.

"Vamoose goes *Romey*," Lenny says.

"Romey? Yeah, man. Vamoose."

Lenny lifts the penlight to his chin, shines it upward across his face. Tilts his eyes downward so the light beams harsh into one eye, then into the other, then back again until blue and red and green lines are all that he can see.

Raymond eases up from the floor.

"Man, you're tripping me out. I like it though, I do like it."

Lenny flicks the light off, slips it back into his pocket. Grabs a stroller handle with his good hand, twists the carriage toward the window.

"Let's get Romey out of here," he says.

Blue John. That's what his mom called it. Blue John.

Milk the cow, set the jug on the stoop, watch the cream rise to the top. Skim the cream off for butter. Or just lather up your apple pie with the rich mess. Drink what's left, the watery Blue John underneath the cream. What city people call skimmed milk.

So. Code name for their new business. Operation Blue John. Lenny skims from the priest's supplies, Raymond sells downtown, or anywhere outside the sphere of the Block, the sphere of the priest. They'd pick the weed themselves, but they couldn't afford that much time in the fields, especially in broad daylight.

Lenny stores the baggies of weed under the stolen boat. Once Raymond finds a buyer, he picks up the stash by approaching from the underside of the fields, near the lake, so he's never associated with the Rectory.

Lenny has to admit, it's pretty genius for a farm boy and a stoner.

CHAPTER 8

THE PRIEST'S SCALY FOREARMS EMERGE FROM the watery depths of the baptismal font, fingers encased in yellow rubber gloves, dripping, dripping. He shakes his hands twice and water flecks away, spatting the single blue flame of a Bunsen burner set on the altar. Cords of kite string dangle in individual strands from the altar like rosary beads, each anchored there by individual votive candles.

Lenny did not mean to get stuck inside the sanctuary of the Block watching the priest performing crazy chemistry shit. He'd been hauling the local grocer's nightly dump of spotty fruit and day-old bread into the sanctuary, storing it in the back closets of the pantry to hand out before services, when he heard the Block doors gently shut and the locks click. The priest trotted past him up the aisle, even more feverish than usual, intent, and it being the night before the mysterious Anti-Miracle, Lenny's curiosity piped up. Even the Celebrants seemed more addled than usual, and many had taken to praying out on the front sidewalk. So Lenny stilled his breath and slid deeper into the darkened alcove to watch the priest set up at the altar.

Lately, the old man hadn't been able to stop talking about his Anti-Miracle.

The holy fire of the tomb? We must de-bunk-de-bunk. Do not be played by tricks of trade. Remember that! Do not fall on your knees in passion-passion. Not when mere science is before ye.

Mere science. His dad, the numbers guy, would love that. Mere science. Raymond had jumped on it one afternoon back at his apartment. The window fan whirring, Lenny lying back on Raymond's couch, Raymond lying on the floor beside him.

"A holy fire at the tomb of Jesus? Man, *that's* the miracle, pure and simple. Am I right? So, what constitutes an Anti-Miracle? And why does the old geezer talk smack on the...what did you call it?"

Romey was slumped in sweaty sleep deep in the bucket of her stroller, which Lenny had angled close to the fan. Raymond had laid her on the floor, squalling, so he'd finally scooped her up, awkwardly, he had to admit, until he figured out how to settle her into the crook of his stump. He dripped cold milk into her mouth with a spoon plucked from Raymond's sink, and after more spoonfuls than he thought possible for a baby to consume, she fell asleep, surprising him with the slackness of her round mouth and the warmth of her metallic breath. Not knowing what else to do with her, and feeling like he was stealing something raw and rare, he'd eased her into the stroller.

"The Light of Jerusalem," Lenny said.

"Yeah, Jerusalem. That holy light. Like you wanna mess with *that* shit? Tell me what he said again, man, I gotta hear it." He reached up and ran a forefinger along the flank of Lenny's stump.

Lenny pulled his stump tight to his chest, edged deeper into the crease of the couch, away from trying to decide if he wants the same thing Raymond wants. How do you know for sure, until it's too late?

"I…I don't know. Something about…eternal flames. I think."

The light, motherfucker, the light. Gotta come from within. Lenny knew it by heart, but he didn't want to explain it all again to Raymond. *Why set all those young peepers on the miracle fires from afar, when we got light right here. Right here!* The priest tapping his chest, tapping his chest.

Raymond locked both hands behind his head. His *I'm trying to be casual about this* look.

"Right. Eternal flames. Crazy coot."

Now, the priest's face glows in the waxy candlelight as he bends to his work. He's mumbling, but Lenny can only make out his *motherfuckers* rising and falling with the seesaw cadence of his arms, one pulling a thread from the altar high toward the arched ceiling and the other pulling down the length of the thread to drop it into the basin and seesaw-seesaw back up with another thread. His yellow gloved fingers sliding down the entire length of the thread, coating it, the cords glowing gold just before spooling down into the baptismal font.

Lenny can't tell from the hollow of the alcove what, besides holy water, might be in the basin.

Bacteria, Buddo, his father would say. *Streptococci, coli bacilli, how would we know what's mixed up in our religious brethren's pots?*

While Lenny wishes Raymond could see the priest's preparations, the old man's yellow fingers all tripped out in crazy glow-water, he's also glad he can't. Raymond can't shut up about the priest, and about how Lenny needs to move out of the Rectory. But, just like Lenny has to remind Raymond not to leave Romey by herself at his apartment, or tool her around in his sports car with the top down, he has to remind Raymond, frequently, that their plans become much more difficult if the priest is angry and therefore watchful. And the surest path to an angry priest, besides learning that he's being filched from, would be for Lenny to move out of the Rectory, and even worse, move in with Raymond.

Eventually the altar is clear, as the braids of string find their home in the baptismal font. The priest puffs out each candle, cuts the gas from the Bunsen burner. Lenny eases deeper into the alcove as the priest stalks back down the aisle.

"Sneaks turn into cheats," the old man mutters, as he unlocks the doors, holds them open.

"Move it, sneak pants," he says. "Can't leave ye locked inside a house with so many Gods."

Lenny steps out.

"I didn't mean—"

"Don't matter," the priest says to the altar. "You just received a heavenly preview, son. A heavenly preview."

#

Lenny holds the barbed wire down with his stump arm and steps through a loose opening in the fence into the high weeds on the other side.

He's heading for the stolen boat, his pockets full of the priest's weed which he plucks from under the shed's burlap after the priest is settled each night. For once, Raymond came in handy and drummed up replacement panes for the shed window, which now, with a little shaving on Lenny's part, slides open and shut without busting glass.

It's unclear to Lenny that the priest would've noticed the theft, though, what with him being so preoccupied by prep for today's Anti-Miracle.

Lenny breaks into a trot. He's got to be back at the Block by mid-morning when the doors open for the main event. The breeze dries the sweat across his forehead, the center of his chest. Does the season never turn here? No wonder the harvest is left in the fields. It's looking to be summertime clear through winter into spring. Lenny pushes away an unexpected longing for the cool sense of hurry that the deadline of a mountain autumn brings to the farm back home.

He counts to what he thinks is the correct row of sorghum, turns down through the patch. Amber, amber, amber. Then blue. His boat lies hidden upslope in the third patch of blue spider weed. Three patches of sorghum in between each, a two-minute trot.

They can't keep plucking weed from the shed forever. At some point the theft will become obvious, and they'll have to wait for the Celebrants' next harvest to refill the wall. But so far, with Raymond's keen eye for clients, Operation Blue John has raked in over eighty bucks.

"Loving this gig, man," Raymond had said. "Are we long-term partners yet?"

Lenny is thinking maybe, but mainly due to that baby of his. *Vamoose goes Romey*. Is her mom, Shawnee, *stout and wild, man, stout and wild*, going to sell her? How else could you turn a profit with a baby?

But he's thinking maybe not, too. Maybe he'll take his cut from Operation Blue John, and his stolen boat, and head, well, elsewhere. He's trying to keep in mind the odd idea that for the first time in his life he's free to make choices. And the more money they make, the freer he gets.

Lenny stops to listen. With the sorghum so high, he can't see over the collar leaves of the stalks. Every so often he's spotted Celebrants walking up from the lower fields, trailing fronds of sorghum behind their skinny butts, bags of the grain over their shoulders. The priest says they'll use the plant for sweetener, or flat bread, or ferment for homemade beer. *Lots a ways to make that sucker work. Unspoken value, unspoken!* But Lenny's never seen Celebrants this far from the Rectory. Sure enough, the air is dead still. Nothing moving but his chest pulling and pushing air.

He jogs deeper into the fields, and the smell of earth and snake musk, leavened by the sweetness of the sorghum, fills his throat. Just as he hits the third spindly sea of purple blue, the air bends a little toward rotten.

Body odor rotten.

Then he's upon his boat, just as he'd left it, upside down and crushing a few yards of skunk weed. Just as he'd left it, that is, except for the boot up on top of the hull. Except for the man wearing the boot, arms folded across his chest, sweat dripping from his cap.

Basilios.

The air seems to grow even stiller. Basilios standing right there, gloating while trying at the same time not to look so out of place. He removes his cop cap, wipes his face down with his sleeve.

"Yep," he says, grinding the boat's hull with his boot. "If you want to find a missing boat, it makes sense to walk the shoreline. And if your boat's not floating in the water, why, it must've gone right up the bank."

The cop taps his temple with his forefinger. Nods, agreeing with himself.

"So, eventually, you find a trail. Around a field. And then, as a bonus, you discover a field of the prettiest and most illegal blue cannabis. Good god-a'mighty."

Basilios reaches for a fresh bud, snaps it from its shaft. Sniffs it. Glances down at Lenny's pants pockets bulging with the shed stash.

Lenny follows the cop's path in his mind, up from the lake, around back of the fields, through the sorghum from the other side. The shortest route from the lake, and a long way from the Rectory.

"You knew it was here," Lenny says.

"Son, as an officer of the law I take tremendous offense at any such notion that I might know the whereabouts of an illegal patch of pot."

The cop slides his boot off the skiff.

"Besides, what we're talking about here is a stolen boat."

Basilios flips the bud, arching it up and across the top of foliage. He adjusts his cap back on his bald head. An officer moving on instinct, but with purpose. Like when you feel a fish on the line, you've by god got to drop the rod low so the fish doesn't know you're right there on the other end. Lenny's seen this his whole life. Jude and his experiments. Not that Jude ever fished, but he flat out knew to wait, to feel the line, feel for when the fish swallows the worm. You never snap up and embed the hook until the bait is swallowed. Lenny's been in there. On both ends.

Basilios snaps his fingers at Lenny.

"Empty your pockets," he says.

Stems of blue spring out from the sides of the boat. Black, scuffed boots squared off beside it. The image presses on Lenny. Heavy. Like the busted dock. Like maybe how a fish feels when you hold it down by the end of the paddle. Hold it steady until you can gut it for dinner.

"That's it," Basilios says, watching the baggies of weed, Lenny's pocket knife, a few coins drop to the ground between them. "Back pockets too."

One bag from each back pocket.

"Yep, quite the find. Father Damien would be mighty surprised where you been, son. Yessir, that's what makes this such an outstanding discovery."

Basilios slips his gun from its holster. Eyes Lenny as he tucks the revolver under his arm, reaches deep into the holster and slides out a roll of papers. Pulls out a sheet, slides the roll and gun back into place. Settles down on the hull of the boat, chooses a baggie from Lenny's pile, rolls a joint. Lights up.

He motions to Lenny with the weed held between his thumb and two fingers.

"You and me, son" he says. "I believe we got a few business items to think ourselves through."

CHAPTER 9

BASILIOS TAKES ANOTHER PULL ON THE joint, holds it out to Lenny.

Lenny shakes his head.

"That's right," Basilios says. "That's right. But that'll change."

Lenny scrubs sweat away from his chin with his stump. If the cop's talking about smoking pot, then he's paddling the wrong way. Lenny's a river or two away from that shit.

"Now here's the way I'm seeing things." The officer reams a line-drive of smoke from his thick lips.

"Like we said, I'm seeing you as sixteen. A drop out. Cause you're sure not in school."

He laughs like a man who knows he's not funny but decides to plow ahead anyway.

"Caught stealing," he says. "Not *this* boat, we gotta return *this* boat. You know who this boat belongs to? Nah, didn't think so."

His voice eases off the pedal. "But maybe you're a shoplifter, a chronic type of shoplifter." Getting all thoughtful, like Jude and Frank in the culvert under the farm road. Jude never smoking the dope, but the weed's effect seeming to take hold of him all the same.

"Shoplifting, yeah. Maybe just across the state line, maybe down in South Carolina." The cop blows another stream of smoke toward Lenny.

"You ever been to South Carolina?"

Lenny doesn't want to talk South Carolina. Doesn't want to think about the Cooper River Bridge waiting for him in Charleston. Not with Basilios. Doesn't want to think about floating under that bridge, sliding under in his skiff as opposed to the roller-coaster crazy ride they'd taken over it as little kids, careening in the backseat, their mom laughing and flying them across. His dad in shotgun, eyes squeezed tight shut, trying to control his fear of heights. His fear for their mom. No, Lenny would just drift under, not even paddle, just let the current take him directly into the Atlantic Ocean.

So why didn't he leave *before* Basilios found the boat? He had enough cash to start. What's he been waiting on? *Go or hold, Buddo. Go or hold.* He chose wrong. But why?

"What is it you want?" Lenny says, trying for a voice less miserable than he feels.

Basilios doesn't seem to hear.

"Yep you've been, I can see you've been to South Carolina. Stole a lot a Coca-Cola down that way, did you? Gum?"

Basilios sucks deep on the weed.

"Kids'll start that way, once they get away with it, never thinking the store keeper is just taking pity on 'em."

Basilios throttling down into some kind of trance. Talking more inside his own head than to Lenny.

"Snickers and Heath Bars. Cigarettes. Stuffing a pack down inside your briefs. Yep. Cold cans of Coke down close to your chilly little pecker. You gotta get outta there fast, right? But you still gotta pull off casual. It's a trick."

Basilios recites to the ground, now.

"Then one day it's a beer. Or, three goddamn cans of beer."

He flicks the joint to the ground, tries to stand, sways slightly, sits back hard on the hull. Yanks a Virginia Slim from his shirt pocket, lights up. Lenny notices a pile of the trim cigarette butts on the ground near the boat, and wonders how long the officer had been waiting for him. Or, for that matter, how many days he'd returned to the boat, just hoping Lenny would show up.

"Not just one, but *three* beers."

The cigarette rests idle between the officer's puffy lips, wobbles as he talks around it. "How the hell did you think you could get away with three beers that day? Stupid little bitch."

Basilios glances up at Lenny like Lenny shouldn't be listening in, then drifts back into the safety of his own brain.

"Still it mighta been okay if the shop owner hadn't been off hunting that day. Yep, that mousy little fellow would of let it slide. Let it slide, all the school kids knew he would, those who couldn't afford a Coca-Cola. He knew our situation. But this punk substitute of a store clerk, he's all lit up. You didn't think about that, now, did you? Punk ass, pimply face all alert, juicy eyes side to side, side to side. You should of left those beers in the cooler and walked out, I told you, you should of just walked out empty handed."

Basilios drops his hands between his uniformed knees. The cigarette droops from his lips. Sweat rolls down his jaw to his neck and streaks down the collar of his shirt.

Lenny could back down the row right now and the officer would never notice.

"But you don't," the cop says.

"You don't, because your so-called buddies are waiting. Older kids. They want their beers. You already bragged it to them. Yeah, you the big-shot boast-king. So out the store you go. Pecker icy cold. Dumb ass bitch."

Basilios shakes his head saying no, no, no to the ground between his boots.

A breeze whips up from the lake below the field. The sorghum shuffles overhead in the distance, but the weed plants are too stiff to be bothered by the breeze. Lenny wants to stand on the boat to catch the cooler air. But he's not getting anywhere near the cop. The cop has hooked him—with the boat, with the pot.

So, would he be arrested? By a junkie cop?

Low odds. Likely Basilios wouldn't risk it, what with all Lenny knows about him. But low odds aren't no odds. If Basilios hauls Lenny into the city jail, it's a runaway's word against a police officer's. It would mean city services tracking down Lenny's identity and shipping his ass back to the family farm. His chest tightens, reminding him that he'd wound that spring until it nearly broke. Did break. Broke him right out onto the river. He can't go back to his brothers' experiments, back to his parents' inability to see what's right in front of their eyes, back to face a trusting Buford, the honest man's eyes full of floorboards freshly emptied of his life's savings. Back to face Glenna, who let him go when he needed to go. Encouraged him to go. *You had to leave. God, what you've been through. Your brothers. Remember?*

Never returning is a done deal.

And never being buried inside another pocket is also a done deal. For years, he'd been buried at the bottom of Jude's. Now he can see his own head peeping out from inside the cop's shirt pocket. The sight makes him want to puke.

But how to avoid it?

No matter what dirt he has on the cop—or on the priest—it's not going to be near enough. They will chase him down. His one-way ticket back to the farm.

That power surge he'd been feeling? Thinking he could paddle in their river? Chart his own route? Make his own choices? Slim chance. It's not the cop or the priest who are tripping him up. Or even Jude. It's hope. Hope is what he needs to escape.

"Popped those beers right up under the high school football stadium. Go Blue Panthers! Police cruiser shows up before you arrive at that cold third gulp. Goddamn pimple-head store clerk."

The cop's lips rapidly swipe his cigarette up and down, up and down.

"Then along comes Father Damien to save your ass. Gives you a job. Gives you a Latin name. *Positions* you."

When he cocks his head, sweat rolls sideways across his forehead.

"Likes his runaways to sound like family, you understand? He gonna name you Epicurus." The officer grins. "Or wait. Achilles."

He laughs, refocuses on Lenny. He drops the cigarette to the ground, rises off the hull of the boat and takes two quick steps to crowd up head-to-head on Lenny.

"Tag, you're it, you little shit. Old coot saved your butt, and now you gonna be his. Just one caveat, you gonna be mine too. You got that?"

His chemical breath pinpricks the inside of Lenny's nose and claws its way down his throat.

Lenny takes a step back, surprised to see that he's as tall as the officer. He guesses they've never been face-to-face.

"So that's your story. Happened to you down in South Carolina, where you *mighta* come from. That's what you tell 'em—not that you *did come* from *anywhere*, but it *mighta* been South Carolina. We got folks who'll send papers from down south. So, stick to that, if anybody should care to ask."

Sweat drips from his chin. Three drops, quick.

"You don't know much about Father Damien, now do you? What you've done? Shit. He finds out? Shit. What's your name?"

And there it is, the cop's ditch.

Lenny's whole goddamn life Jude's thought ditch was right there, waiting to trap him. You could run as fast and as far as you can, whether you were really running or just running circles inside your own head. And there stood Jude. There was never a way to just jump the hell out of that ditch.

"Yep, priest says you're not giving out any information. Well, that's fine for the priest. But an officer of the law, a person of authority such as myself, well a fellow's gotta have a name."

He wags his finger at the boat, then at the baggies next to it.

"A criminal *crossing a state line*, we could extradite your ass, like I say I got friends down there."

He looks Lenny up and down.

"You really are just a skinny nothing. I reckon that's a good thing. Juvenile Unit downtown don't pay much attention to skinny white nothings. But still. You get yourself an I.D., well now, just think what you might make happen. You cough up a name, we can shake all over this business deal. You and me.

"So, go ahead. Cough."

Lenny Boyer-Moore.

His only card.

The rest of the cards, his boat and his income, are over there, in the cop's hands. Lenny's big bet out, but also his buy in right back to where he absolutely will never go.

The breeze has grown bored and disappeared down the slope toward the Rectory. Again, Lenny swipes his stump at the sweat across his forehead.

He won't give up his name, but he'll play their game. He'll bluff until he can figure a way out. Which means, he'll need to find a way out where they simply *cannot follow him*, where the possibly of dragging him back to the farm *does not exist.*

That's the ditch he would follow. Jude's ditch. *Whatever it takes, boys, whatever it takes.*

Basilios points around the patch.

"Return that goddam boat. And that tackle and rod. Yeah, I already looked under the boat. That rod cost a lot more than what it looks. Belongs to the Mayor's little girl. You return all that shit. Except the weed.

"If you can pull all that off without getting caught, we'll go from there."

He leans down and picks up three bags of pot. Shakes them at Lenny, shoves them down the inside of his shirt. "I'm taking these as evidence. And you gonna keep the evidence coming. Every two weeks. For now, anyway." He again glances around the patch of blue weed.

"But from the looks of it, there's plenty of volume. Me thinking all this time the old man had a supplier. Hell, he's his own supplier."

Basilios turns his back on Lenny, heads down the row toward the lake at the far end of the fields, opposite the Rectory.

"Stealing from the church! Short-changing the law!" he calls out to the sorghum in front of him. "All indications of a one-armed boy in a hell of mess!"

CHAPTER 10

THE CROWD QUICKLY SHIFTS AWAY FROM the Block when the great doors start rattling, vibrating, shaking like maybe the priest is behind there, panicking that he can't escape, can't get to his flock.

From across the street, Lenny scours the Celebrants for flowy angel hair. He needs to let Raymond know what's up with the cop, warn him not to go back to the fields, back to the boat. And maybe let him know that following Shawnee to Raleigh, as Raymond had been hinting they should do, was not such a bad idea after all. She'd taken the baby, taken Romey, taken her *profit* scheme, and headed in that direction.

"What a relief," Raymond had said at the time. Then when Lenny didn't say anything, changed course. "Should we go after her? Raleigh could be our city, man. Plenty of action. Just say the word."

The Block doors swing wide and the priest steps out onto the stoop.

"Quickly-quickly," he calls, waving his arms, beckoning to the crowd.

Celebrants hesitate at first, check each other's confused faces for the okay, but when the priest continues to motion them in, they begin mounting the steps and filing through the doors of the Block, the old man standing to the side, clapping his hands, goading them on.

"To witness the Anti-Miracle you must be-quick-be-quick."

The Block fills to standing room only. As he enters, Lenny scans again for any sign of Raymond. He catches a glimpse of stroller handles over next to their usual window seat and his heart picks up a beat at the thought of *Romey safe*. But of course, the next few heartbeats thud back into their hopeless bucket when he confirms that of course it's not Romey's stroller.

He's surprised Raymond isn't at the Block today, given the show's billing. The Anti-Miracle. Such fertile ground for Raymond's swirly brain seeds.

Lenny winds through the murmuring crowd, hunting for the most advantageous viewing. He edges as close to the front as possible and backs into a space along the wall between two kids he gauges to be brothers about his age. His real age, that is. Fourteen. When they grin at him, all optimistic and goofy, he recalibrates across their smooth skin to slightly younger.

The priest enters the Block, turns his back to the crowd to fiddle with the doors, like they've become a complex puzzle.

The old geezer trots up the aisle, nodding at Celebrants on either side, although it seems he's passing everybody way too fast to recognize them. It's like his sermon is lurching up the aisle ahead of him, and he's trying to catch it. He manages to lasso it and attack, even before he arrives at the altar.

"Infinite light, motherfuckers! We ain't got time for nothing else! Infinite light! Do ye believe in that spontaneous flame on the tomb of Jesus? No matches! No tinder! Do ye believe in those holy fires of

Jerusalem? Holy Flame alighting its own self? Same day every year! All the way across the world. Masses, they do believe! And they do pilgrimage from afar just for a single, spectacular gander."

Above the altar hangs the kite string Lenny last saw sunk deep into the baptismal waters. Now the strings flow down in sheathes across metal trapeze-like rods hung from the cracked beams in the Block's ceiling. An opaque liquid drips from the ends of the strings, splattering across the length of the wooden altar. Drops fall from there to the concrete floor. The baptismal font is draped in a stark white cloth.

Lenny could swear he smells garlic.

"Holy flame! Blue light of the tomb-tomb! We gonna witness that same miracle, that same Infinite Light of the Tomb a Jesus, right here in *this* house, right here on *this* day! No need for Jerusalem pilgrimage. I been telling ye for so long now, witness only when your eyes be open! Witness only when ye heads be screwed down tight. Hadn't I told ye that much?"

The priest's arms emerge from his tattered robe to reveal his yellow-gloved hands. He reaches and strips the holy cloth from the baptismal font.

"Well screw 'em on tight," he says. "Cause we gonna witness that miracle of the holy light."

The priest shakes out his holy cloth, lets it settle across the altar. He turns, green eyes strobing, robed arms eagle wide, yellow gloves like withered flowers opening to embrace the Celebrants.

One of those yellow flowers sprouts a foot-long fire match from his paper-thin robe, holds it aloft.

"Eternal flame-flame! A fire so potent it needs no kindle. No kindle. Is your heart the same? Do your desires quicken at the thought? At the *miracle* of a self-lighting holy fire? Do ye draw closer-closer to that flame? Yes, yes. Ye do! Like moths. And ye do not hover in solitude above those god-ignited flames. Nay, the entire world gaggles at the matchless eternal fire of Jerusalem."

The old man's yellow flowers drop to his chest, the match protrudes between his fingers toward the Celebrants. He gazes up at the dripping string. A few strands now gently twist, and, even more oddly, start turning color. From bright yellow to a pale gold.

The priest licks his lips. His teeth chatter for a few seconds, like maybe he's caught a chill.

"But why? Why such grand pilgrimage? Why the waste a footsteps when flames burn more brilliant right here in ye own chest?"

He thumps his chest for emphasis and calls out, "Yes-yes. No-no. Ye must decide! From where does your flame ignite?"

He lifts the match like a choir director and thrashes it three times at the Celebrants. "Nay, hear ye hear ye hear ye motherfuckers! We gonna bust that match, unlit!"

He crushes the match in his yellow hands and sends splinters skittering across the floor.

Lenny glances around the sanctuary. Entranced faces, except for a few, who, like Artemis, look concerned. The smell of garlic, Lenny is sure now, drifts in waves from the altar. His eyes sting a little.

The priest glances up to the glow-twisting strings, yellow deepening to pure gold and a few now bordering on burnt orange.

"Though the match be crushed, ye *will* behold flames."

The priest's flower hands glow brighter. Yellow spots appear in drips down his brittle robes. His voice becomes a hoarse, chattering cry.

"Listen up! Ye must think past these holy fires, think past these so-called miracles that do not ignite within your own heart. I have told ye, no faith without thought! No thought without reason! For every miracle, there is an Anti-Miracle. And that Anti-Miracle is *blind faith.*"

The congregation stirs, sort of uneasy, still sort of enthralled. One of the boys beside Lenny, rubbing his eyes, leans over and whispers.

"His hair."

Sure enough, the sparse tufts along the old man's skull flicker. Lenny takes a closer look. Liquid from the strings are hitting sporadically across the priest's skull.

A child near the back shouts out.

"His head's smoking!"

The priest is taking notice too. He shakes his head. Then shakes his hands. Tries to recover his grip on his sermon, his voice rising with the smoke from his temples.

"Now I say to you. I say—What? What do I say? Tell me, tell me!"

The yellow spots on the priest's robes have turned amber and start to smolder.

Several Celebrants shout *Amen!* A few shout other words like *Watch Out!* And *Hey!* Lenny thinks he hears Artemis's voice, her *Good God Damien*, but he can't make himself turn away from the priest, now caught in some sort of a battle with himself. Like maybe he's lost control of his own Anti-Miracle.

There's a whoosh from the baptismal basin as flames spontaneously burst across the surface of the water.

The priest stares at it, clearly surprised.

"Well behold, goddamn it!" he shouts out, but immediately he's distracted by his own glowing yellow flowers, rising, rising. His green dragonfly eyes follow his smoking hands as his arms fully extend above his head.

Then, as if in benediction, both yellow-gloved hands burst into flames.

Celebrants sitting, half rise. Celebrants standing, jump back.

The priest's chest heaves as he lifts onto his toes, trying to catch up to his sizzling hands. Still, he attempts to corral his sermon.

"Look ye at these…*god*-ignited…holy fires. Tell me—"

Above the priest's flaming hands the twisting strings catch fire, one after the other, like blazing inverted dominoes.

Smaller fires kindle along the altar.

"We're locked in!" someone shouts from the back row of pews.

Several Celebrants charge for the doors and start trying to hack or pry their way out.

The priest pulls his flaming hands down and frantically slaps at his smoldering head, now haloed from ear to ear in a golden glow.

Celebrants toward the front cough, rub their watering eyes, and cover their face against the smoke and chemical stench. But they can't seem to turn away from the priest. Men and women at the back slam against the locked doors.

"Tell me…this matchless…holy shit…fire…is some earth shaking…miracle?"

The priest attempts to wrap his hands in his robe and violently shakes his head as if trying to rouse enough breeze to blow out the embers, which only makes them glow brighter.

"Ask yourselves!…a matchless flame?" Somehow, his voice grows stronger, like when a worn out fish, eased close to the net, finds energy to bolt.

The priest waves his hands, attempting now to throw the gloves off.

"Anti-Miracle… blind faith…negates…miracle…I'm a giving ye the *real* miracle…*goddamn phosphorus. White phosphorus*! Just like in Jerusalem, ye innocents. Same in Jerusalem."

The priest twists his neck as if it might be possible to separate his head from his body. Garlic fumes rise from his robe. The fiery flowers glow dark and appear to melt into the old man's skin. Lenny can't decide whether to run forward to help the priest or run back to help with the doors. But there's no time to think that through, because at that moment, next to the burning altar, under the blazing strings, the priest's brittle robes combust.

The old man screams and falls to his knees as flames lilt heavenward from his shoulders. Still on kneeling, just before face-planting in concrete, he gives one final fizzling effort to tie off his sermon.

"What they don't tell ye…*science*…the true miracle…embrace *science*…only then…do ye know miracle."

Amid screams and shoves, Lenny pushes his way in stinging blind confusion to the altar and grabs for the white holy cloth to smother the flames rising from the priest, but the cloth disappears beneath his fingers. Artemis, her own eyes streaming, flutters the wool down over the old man. She kneels and presses on all sides. The cloth steams as it suffocates the flames. After a few minutes, she pulls the cloth from the priest and smudges out the remaining glow spots across the old man's grizzled skull.

"Good God Damien. Good God."

As the phosphorus-coated strings burn themselves out, as the fire dies down in the baptismal font, as the seared altar settles without collapsing, the Celebrants finally manage to ram the doors open. The smoke begins to clear and the harsh garlic sting of the white phosphorus begins to fade.

Artemis, eyes and nose dripping, rocks back on the concrete floor beside the priest and begins patting down any wayward chemical bead not quite finished with its staged role.

"What, Damien?" she says. "What's your point? White phosphorus self-ignites? Is that your point? The monks proved that eons ago. And do you think Jesus's tomb is tuning in here at our Block? Eavesdropping from way over yonder in Jerusalem? Did you intend to stop the pilgrimage?"

His dome is charred, his hair singed crisp. Lenny can barely look at the old man's hands. But the priest's eyes flicker, and he manages to croak out his point.

"Pilgrimage my ass."

CHAPTER 11

STANDING BEHIND THE SCREEN OF THE second-floor porch, just off the front of the Rectory, Lenny can't see who's persistently rapping the door beneath him. But after a few more attempts the knocking stops and sheaths of bright red hair appear directly beneath him. Then a skull cap. Both backing away in unison from the Rectory door and looking up at the windows.

Artemis, spiked hair ablaze in the sunlight, and Elias, slim as a rake shadow. They catch sight of Lenny on the porch. Elias lifts a hand. Artemis places her fists on her hips.

"Father Damien!" she calls up.

From Lenny's vantage point, her swaying chest beneath her cotton sheath hides her feet. That's really all Lenny can see. Face engulfed by flaming arrows of hair aboard an ocean of boobs.

"He sleeping in?" she says.

Elias edges away, hands behind his back, to examine the thick green and white leaves splaying every which way lining the Rectory's front walkway.

"Yes," Lenny says. "I mean, no, he's down the Block way. The coat drive, maybe? Well, the coat drive's today."

She glances over at Elias who's ambling out of earshot. Then back up at Lenny.

"Recovered, then, I guess."

"Yes ma'am. Mostly. Well, maybe not so much his hands. Or his head. But, mostly."

"Mostly, huh." She puckers in thought, then grins. "Well, then, I guess there *is* such a thing as a miracle."

Her hair spikes shimmer as she laughs.

"Should've gone straight to the hospital, though."

Lenny checks Elias, primarily in an effort to pull his mind from the swinging chest beneath him.

"Yes ma'am," he says. "Maybe so."

"Well, aren't you just a whole lot of maybe and mostly. Listen here, I don't think he's down the Block way. I don't think he's coat driving. You want to come on down? Save my neck from all this craning heavenward?"

Lenny jogs down the stairs and opens the wooden doors of the Rectory, steps out into the sunlight. Artemis sits on the front step. Elias has disappeared.

Even sitting, she's tall enough to go eye-to-eye with a small child standing.

Lenny eases down on the step below her, making her seem even taller. Strangely, from below, her blunt nose and light blue eyes appear miniature, almost like a doll.

"I never asked you about that arm," she says.

Lenny glances down at his stump.

"That's alright," she says. "You can keep your secrets. For now. I expect we'll get to know each other much better, shortly on down the road."

He holds in his *No ma'am*. There's no *on down the road* here at the Rectory or at the Block. *On down the road* is just that.

She flutters her long fingers, dismissing whatever might be inside his head.

"So. The good Father Damien may have *started out* for the coat drive, but I seriously doubt he *made it* to the coat drive. More likely he's down at the station. I expect the police have picked him up by now. I was hoping to get to him first."

The police.

Lenny thinks of the weed in the priest's shed, of the blue patches hidden throughout the Block's sorghum, the Rectory's cash crop. He thinks of all the pot that wasn't under that boat when he flipped it over that last time, and of Raymond, who hadn't been around since before the holy fire Anti-Miracle. Which makes him think of Romey in Raleigh, or wherever, which makes him just not want to think at all.

"You're mighty quiet," she says.

"Well," he says. "The police?"

"That's right. You can't go locking people up in a church and then setting fires to the altar. Miracle back fire, if there ever was one. Am I reading relief on your face?"

"No ma'am. I mean—"

"Though, technically, it's an open question among our fine congregation as to whether Damien set those fires. Can you believe that? Some, and there may be an officer or three among them, seem to think we've been visited by the almighty holy divine. Just plain missing the science point, among a few other things."

"I guess," he says. "I guess it's not all that surprising."

She cocks her head.

"Hmm...yes...I expect at some point in your short life, you've spent more than a few minutes in a church."

"Yes ma'am. What will the police do with him?"

"Damien? I'm not sure. Not my area of expertise. Supposedly Basil...Officer Basilios...is working it, in his own meandering way. I may need to step in and deploy a different skill set."

Lenny waits, but she doesn't explain. He recalls Miss May at the Market with her Sunny Family, and her thoughts on Artemis. *That's a fine friend to have. Handy. And tall!*

Elias emerges from under a row of trees along the drive, starts back in their direction. Hands still behind his back.

Behind him, a police cruiser slides into view, winds its way up the long stone drive.

Basilios hangs his arm out the driver's window, thrums his hand along the door as he pulls to a stop in front of the Rectory.

"Marva," he says, pointing at Lenny. "I see you got yourself one of my *vagrants*."

Artemis steps down to the drive, leans over to peer into the backseat.

"Where is he?" she says, standing back up to her full height.

The cop eases out of the cruiser, opens the back door, and pulls out Raymond. Handcuffed.

"I got more important matters at the moment."

Basilios glances up at her. "But don't you worry, Miss Marva, you'll get your priority."

Her hair seems to grow redder from heat rising in her face.

"My priority? You seem to have forgotten a few things, Basil. I know where you came from. I know *exactly* where you came from. My priority should be your priority."

Artemis swings around to Lenny, talking like there's a word per minute record she needs to break.

"The good Father Damien will be returned to the Rectory this afternoon by this officer of the law, and when he is safely returned without issue—*without issue*—please tell the good Father that I will be back tonight, and that we will have much to discuss."

She turns and strides down the drive, her long legs eating up the pavement. Elias hurries to catch up.

It takes a few moments for Officer Basilios to remember Lenny and Raymond. He pushes Raymond around, unlocks the handcuffs.

Lenny edges back up onto the top step.

Raymond stretches his arms, fake yawns.

"About time," he says to the cop. Then to Lenny, "Adventure, man. You missed it."

Raymond's voice checks into Lenny's ears as tired, maybe even unnerved.

Basilios goes into full cop mode, directing traffic with his hand, first toward Lenny, then toward Raymond. *Keep going, straight. Go straight through the intersection. You there, left turn.*

"Seems to me you young fellas got some sort a side business," he says. "Seems to me, I done warned a boy, age sixteen, about to be bumped back to fourteen, name of Lenny Boyer-Moore, not to be short-changing me on crop."

Lenny Boyer-Moore. So there it was. The last card, solidly in the cop's hands.

"Yessir." Basilios taps his temple. "I been in an investigative mood lately. Funny how when people start searching for their young feller, it don't take all that much investigating. Not that it appears they did all that much searching. You understand?"

Searching for their young feller. Why does he care whether they searched or not? He's not going back, so why does it matter?

Lenny tries to steady his voice.

"Nobody short-changed you," he says.

Raymond looks from the officer to Lenny.

"That's your name?" he says. The information seems to rev up Raymond's missing energy. "For real? Lenny? Like Lenny Bruce?"

Basilios stares at Raymond as if Raymond just turned into empty space, leaving behind only twinkle dust.

"Seems to me," Basilios continues. "Seems to me I could march a one-armed thief down to the station, real quick." He tries snapping his fingers, but they're too sweaty and just slip past each other.

Which appears to top off Raymond's renewed battery charge. He snaps his own fingers, perfect connection.

"Lenny Bruce, as in counter culture? Man, give me more."

"I never shorted you," Lenny says. "I never missed one tax payment."

"Timeliness is for school, son. We're not in school. Now come on down here where I can see you."

Lenny drops down the steps to street level, but keeps his distance from the cop and the cop's cruiser.

Basilios pulls his cap off, swirls it on one index finger.

"One, you never told me about your little collaboration, about your main man, here." The cap flies off his finger, but he catches it, shoves it up under his armpit.

"You two young bucks, *if* that's an accurate description, appear to be taking liberty with all kinds of laws. Laws against the state, plus, just maybe, what some might call laws against nature?"

Raymond leans back against the cruiser. "Not that you would know anything about it," he says. "Man, have you *ever* been laid? This way or that?"

The flush starts in the cop's neck, grows clear up to his temples. He swivels his sweaty head toward Lenny.

"You best talk some sense into your man. Because here's the deal. He just got busted. You notice that? Smarmy little sports coupe just overflowing with weed. *The priest's weed.* You know how he gets caught? The beat Sergeant smelled it from a block away, goddamn nosed it out like a dog. Six uprooted plants crammed under those creamy little bucket seats."

Basilios wads his cap in his hands. Wrings it out one direction, then the other.

"Just lucky I was there to pull him out by the thin yellow film of his teeth. You understand what this means, Mr. Short Arm?"

Lenny thinks he does. He also understands, now, why Raymond's been missing in action.

"Taxes skyrocket, that's what this means." Basilios slaps his cap against his thigh, switches hands and slaps the other. He pops the wrinkled cap back on his bald head.

"I don't know what you're running from. Don't care. But you quit producing—or you squeal to our favorite scaly priest—it's homeward bound for you, son, homeward bound. And, if I'm not mistaken, that would be all the way up to the western end of this slender state. Western North Carolina mountains. Am I right?"

"Man oh man, I can't believe I missed the holy-rollie fireworks. So, if an Anti-Miracle backfires, then that just leaves us with a Miracle. Am I reading that right? Miracle down the Block way."

When Raymond opens his refrigerator, the door spans the width of his tiny kitchen. He fans the door a few times, guzzles milk from an open bottle.

Lenny props his feet on the TV table in front of the couch.

"You pulled weed from the field."

"Hazards of the trade, man, get used to it." Raymond swings the refrigerator door closed, steps out of the kitchen, bottle in hand, milk dripping from on his lower lip. "But I sold shit too. Raw and uncured massive profit. We got cash. Let's jet. I just can't believe I missed the sparky fireworks."

He saunters over, pushes Lenny's legs to the side and sits on the table.

Lenny stands and walks to the window.

"You pulled fresh weed and put it in your car."

"Well, *obviously.*"

"You got busted."

"Obviously, again. But! That car belongs to my Pop. And my Pop's flush in green. We're talking banker green. Connections green. Cops need green."

He holds his wrist toward Lenny. "Voila, no cuffs! So…Dream Boy…second chances are cheap. *If* we jet right now. Pop's ultimatum. I gotta split. Raleigh here we come?"

Lenny flips on the window fan, puts his face up close, feels the whir spin his brain.

"Is Romey in Raleigh?" he says.

Raymond clanks the bottle of milk onto the table.

"Man. I'm starting to think you got a unnatural thing with that baby. And I gotta ask, you gotta thing?"

Unnatural? Lenny tries to fit his feelings for the baby, for Romey, into some unnatural category, and comes up blank.

"Is she?" he says. "Is she in Raleigh?"

"Okay, okay, Mr. Surprise, that's cool. Yes, she is. She's in Raleigh."

Lenny flips the fan down one notch. So, Raymond needs to split. And Raymond's got the cash to split. And the car. *And* permission.

Also, Lenny needs to split.

Which seems like a flush dovetail, except Lenny *cannot split.* Because of the cop. Because of the cop plus the priest. Because they will find him and they will send him home.

Unless…Lenny cranks the fan down another notch.

Unless…they can't.

He stares out the window, peers through the churning blades at the low lying buildings, paved sidewalks, concrete parking lots. Would he ever get used to a city? Would he ever like the dry, mountain-less heat? At least, living with the priest, he'd had the green, the Rectory gardens, the big fields.

Like back home.

Would he ever stop thinking of home as back home?

He turns from the fan to face the heat of the room, to face Raymond.

"You think you can stay out of the cop's way? Just…let's say, five days? Stay away from the Block? Don't go near the priest? Can you steer completely clear of the Rectory? Can you wait that long to… to leave?"

Raymond stands up, takes a step toward Lenny.

Lenny puts up his hand to stop any advances.

"You have to keep your head down, Raymond. No selling weed, no coming around. Five days."

"Holy-moly, if it's not Mr. Absence-Makes-the-Heart-Grow-Fonder. Sure. Any game you name."

"Okay then. Sunday morning. If it's not raining, if it's a calm day. I mean, if there's not much wind. Okay. Have the coupe packed. *No weed* Raymond. *No weed* or anything else illegal. You got that? If we're going to Raleigh, if we're going to Romey, we're going to go clean. You got that? Sunday morning, if the weather's right. I'll let you know exactly when and where."

Raymond grins. "You kill me, man. You kill me."

The priest enters the kitchen through the Rectory's back door, pulls a jug of uncorked Communion wine from the pantry, paws it and almost drops it from his bandaged hands, takes a swig, hauls it to the table. Drags out a chair, sits.

Lenny's swishing soap in dirty dish water at the sink, rinsing, swishing. Given his choices, he might as well be pinned back under that boat dock, holding his breath against the wakes, hoping the silt building against his head doesn't spill over and cover his face. He grabs a dish towel from the rack and dries his hand, runs it over the end of his stump.

"I was thinking," he says, turning to the priest. "I mean…well—"

"Thinking, are ye? Some brilliant awe-inspiring relief, that thinking."

Lenny leans back against the kitchen sink.

"I was wondering about…well, about Officer Basilios—"

"Me too, I been wondering about Basilios. About our strong arm of the law. About what took him so long to swashbuckle down my cell way this fine, sunny afternoon. About what piddle-shit I been doing on this God-given day instead of handing out coats to the poor, instead of feeding the souls of the lonely. Get in my way motherfuckers."

His two gauzed hands grip the wine jug. The blisters from the white-phosphorus fire have evidently broken and a greasy yellow film shows through.

"And you, you little pecker hole. You want to aim your brain toward mine and guess who I mighta seen down the station way? Guess-guess."

"Well…Raymond. You saw Raymond."

"Ah! You little shit-face liar. Yes, Raymond. Busted on shaggy plants, approximately six hefty pounds of the finest medicinal in the state of North Carolina. You tell me now. Whose pot?"

"Medicinal?"

"Never occur to you people need that shit? And now that boy-boy a yours, Mr. Glitter, now he's got the long arm a law, one Officer

Basilios, thinking he's hot shit. Thinking he can skim us dry."

The old man takes a slow draw on the jug.

"Disturbing the equilibrium's, that's what your boy's got going. So, you, Mr. Whoever You Are, you gonna make it stop. Folks just a wondering where Mr. Raymond got those plants. Those plants just jumped up into his topless sports car? Raw…sprung-up…plants! Who would do that? Spilling pheromones all up and down the street. Jesus keep me. And you leading him around by the thinnest of cock hairs. Shit what you absolutely do…not…know."

"I just—"

"You don't know shit-shit. Let me lay it out on you. Big turd that you don't know? They bust my ass over the tiniest little spit fire smoke storm flaming up inside the Block? Hell, small shit like that? What you think they'll think up to do once they go digging into god's Mary Jane up on my hill? Bust my head directly through my ass, that's what. You got it yet? City fathers? Unable to wrap their pinheads around a Catholic priest thinking outside a their skinny lines? Just *waiting* on an opportunity to jail me up good and tight."

He tips the bottle and the wine gurgles down his throat.

"And how would a thieving dilettante pot hawker like Raymond Freeport rate first dibs over me on sashaying out of his jail cell? You tell me. I'm waiting."

"Well—"

"Well what? That boy's bringing problems, that's *well what*."

"Well, his dad I guess."

"Uh huh. Uh huh. Now you showing some smarts. His banker dad. Screwed in deep and firm with all our civic-minded City Fathers."

The old man shakes his white phosphorus-singed head and his eyes drift through Lenny and head off some other place.

Lenny waits. It doesn't take long before the priest returns his focus.

"All I done for you. From hell. I pull a one-armed dead boy directly from hell. And end up heading for hell myself. Shit. If it weren't for Marva, Jesus keep me. Jesus keep me and you both for that matter."

Lenny folds his arm across his chest, hooks his hand onto his stump. Pulled from hell and dropped right into the old man's robes, right into the cop's pocket. The thing about growing up under Jude's rule? You get plenty of practice living inside that pocket. Lenny just wishes he'd known back then what he's beginning to understand now. It doesn't really matter what threat hole you're dropped into. It only ever matters that you don't lie there staring up at the man who dropped you.

"I've been thinking," Lenny says again, and has to rush on when the priest parts his crazy smooth lips to interrupt. "I've been thinking that Officer Basilios was a runaway just like me."

The priest cocks his head, pushes the jug away.

"Uh huh," he says. "What would you be knowing about that?"

"Well...that maybe...maybe Officer Basilios was a thief? Out of South Carolina? And that maybe he's got some other name. Like, well...like not Basilios."

"Uh huh. You got a point to make here?"

"No. No, sir. Just wondering."

"Wondering," the priest says.

Lenny tries to loosen the grip his hand has on his stump, but his fingers aren't listening. He pushes on anyway, trying to squirm out from inside the pocket, out from under the dock in the lake.

"Yep," he says. "Just wondering. Also. Well..."

The priest reaches and gives the jug a half turn, squaring the label to face him, but remains silent.

"Well…how many boys there's been. I mean, even if there's only been two, what, umm, what's the penalty?"

Lenny pulls in air, fills his chest tight, tight, hoping his lungs will press his heart into slowing down. The skinny priest is like rabbit sinew, tense, and even when dead and exposed by a thin skinning blade, seems ready to spring. Go slow, go slow.

The old man turns the jug another quarter turn.

"Penalty?"

"Well…what would be the penalty for harboring…a runaway? Or two? Or more?"

There. This threat is out, taking up more of his chest-space than he'd imagined possible. Still, there's more. He's got to push on. If he doesn't push on, and afterward if the priest doesn't let him go free and clear, then he'll have leave on different, more desperate terms.

"For keeping them away from families," he chokes out. "Families who might be searching."

He closes his eyes against that thought, knowing it's not true, not for him. Likely it's not true. Otherwise, they would've found him by now, right? And probably not for Basilios either. And maybe the priest knows all that, that no one cares about them. But still, Lenny has his threats to throw out there on the wind, and back-up threats too. Please, please let the priest listen.

"For showing kids the drug trade," he continues. "Illegal drug trade. And would it be like…like delinquenting a minor, practically, or something."

"Contributing to the delinquency of a minor." The priest says this like it's a confession he wishes he wasn't making.

"Well, yes, what would be the penalty for that?"

"You full of shit," the priest says. But his eyes are quiet, almost landing on an emotion, sadness maybe, that Lenny hadn't anticipated.

Lenny's face flushes, heats deep in a surprising embarrassment. But he's got to push on.

"Well, I'm just wondering. If a boy, a minor boy, fourteen, were to find somewhere else to go, leave town even, not telling anyone anything…well, where I come from, that would be a deal."

There, all the words were out that needed to get out.

"Where you come from." The words drop softly, but the green eyes flash. "I'm gonna lay down my bet you not wanting to get sent back to *where you come from*. Penalty this? Penalty that? Sha…you wanting to get sent back?"

"Well, no. I just—"

"You just not thinking. Maybe one day, one day you might be growed up enough to walk outta here, I could maybe trust that. But you leave now? You going straight back to wherever. I'm guessing you'd rather just stay put. But don't think I won't find out where to mail your butt."

The priests looks Lenny over like maybe he's turned into one of the seven deadly sins.

"What exactly happens to Miss May without me?" the old man says. "What happens to her blond babies and all them other rag-tags, with zero revenue coming in from the fields? Without that sweet sorghum? Without that tobacco? What that is? Money makers for folks with no money. They making it without the Market? They making it without the clothes drive and *everything else* up that a way? You think you thinking?"

"I just—"

"No, you not riding outta here on a threat, you little ratter. We building something here, something better than what's outside a here. You a part a that? I am."

Lenny pushes off the sink, not wanting to think about what the priest is saying. Not wanting to understand that the priest is exactly right. That if he carries out his plan—and he can't think of any other way out of everybody's goddamn pockets—his actions, even if he can find a way to somewhat control them, will affect every single Celebrant.

Well, the Celebrants will just have to fend for themselves, like they always do.

Lenny stares at the priest and the priest stares right back. Two boats sinking. The priest just doesn't know it yet.

#

Lenny starts to back out of the Rectory, but just as he gets to the screen door, it squeals open and Artemis swings her boobs into the kitchen.

"Good god, Damien. Here I am checking on you, making sure you survived your admittedly short brush with the law, and here you are all a fluster, punishing this boy here with a lecture on sorghum and tobacco and Celebrant life. Is that what I'm hearing?"

She snags a juice glass off a high shelf, pours herself a splash from the priest's jug, then another splash, sits at the table.

"Get over here," she says to Lenny, tapping the chair between her and the priest.

"I got to—"

"You got to get over here." She thumps the chair. "Right here."

Lenny sits.

"Now tune your ears," she says, looking from Lenny to the priest. "The both of you. We've got a real issue down at the Block."

She points at Lenny.

"Your friend, Raymond Freeport? On the verge of bringing down our reputation, closing down our church. Don't you agree, Father Damien?"

The old man considers her, opens his mouth to speak, but

Artemis breezes in, now pointing at the priest.

"Not that *you're* not," she says. "Good god, Damien, setting chemical fires. And just look at your hands. Look at your face. Between you and that Freeport boy, well, how much more can the Block withstand? Are you thinking on that? Are you thinking on that at all?"

She turns back to Lenny.

"Okay, where did your buddy get the cannabis?"

Lenny holds her eyes. It never occurred to him that she wouldn't know about the priest's side business.

He shakes his head.

Artemis examines him, then nods.

"You have given me no reason to do anything but trust you. And we are all taking quite a liking to you. Glad you turned up. But he is *your* friend. So. If you *are* lying—"

Why would she trust him? Buford had trusted him. Glenna had trusted him. He stole from one, deserted the other.

"I don't really know him that well," Lenny says.

She nods again, turns back to the priest.

"Root it out, Damien. Root it out. You know my history with the drug scum. Nobody should have to travel down that path. *Nobody*. Lock them all up, I know you agree."

She shakes her red hair which has darkened to amber in the yellow kitchen light.

"You have a special place down at the Block," she continues. "A sanctuary in the true sense of the word. But a sanctuary that we both know a few non-ecumenical type folks around this sorry town would love to shut down. So. We are not going to let drugs—*or white phosphorus fires*—shut us down, are we? Find out about the cannabis, Damien, root it out. If you don't, I will do it myself."

The old man rises, grips the table, his knuckles white, his eyes glinting. But not so much at Artemis as at Lenny.

"I'm a rootin Marva," he says. "I'm a rootin."

CHAPTER 12

LENNY LEANS AGAINST ONE OF THE Block doors, propping it open with his back. The two kids who help him sell corn prop open the other, brown eyes hopeful, as usual, for a dollar each. Lenny feels in the pockets of his cutoffs for cash, but today there's just the two plastic baggies necessary to carry out his plan in one pocket, and two quarters in the other. The quarters will have to do.

He checks the watch he'd borrowed from Raymond. Service starts at eleven, Raymond meets him at noon. That gives him only one hour, only one hour.

Celebrants meander through the doors, like it's just any other Sunday. He needs a full house today. He needs every Celebrant who might otherwise be over at the Rectory, or worse, back in the Rectory's fields, to be spiritually moved and church-ward bound. He doesn't want to get caught, for sure, but also he also doesn't want anyone hurt.

Artemis and Elias pass through the doors. Separate, of course, but not too far apart. Elias focuses on his Old Testament, already open in his palms. Artemis scrutinizes Lenny, but nods.

Man, nobody crosses that woman, unless she wants crossing. Raymond answering Lenny's questions on how the priest busted out of jail so fast. *Why? Goddamn Mt. Vesuvius, that's why. And she can't be bought. Why? Because nobody has anything on her. Pious Amazon woman runs the town.*

Not for the first time, Lenny wonders what religion Artemis leans toward. Maybe Christian. Maybe her spiky red hair is some kind of Christian-hippie halo.

The coat drive committee is all accounted for, the shoe drive committee too, as well as the folks who show up to clean the Rectory and harvest the tobacco, tend the kilns. They all make it through the doors.

Lenny half expects to see Raymond, but so far, he's been true to the plan. Hasn't turned up down the Block way, nor the Rectory, since his arrest. Strange behavior for Raymond, doing what he's told. Lenny guesses the Raleigh gig must be pretty motivating.

He checks the watch again, scans the sidewalks for the Sunny family, Miss May, June, and July. They need to be safe inside. And these corn kids, waiting for their pay. He wants them all behind the heavy closed doors of the Block. Listening to today's homily: *Religion Don't Gotta Hurt!*

Lenny's almost sorry to miss it. But he can't start counting up all the things he's going to miss. Like the geezer's concave chest heaving from his makeshift pulpit, panting and pulsing in the effort to keep his words riding smooth against his crazy, intermingling, brain waves. He's going to miss the priest dropping ideas like lures, sinking them down into his congregation, the old man just waiting to see what might be snagged.

Lenny's hardly missed a service since the priest pulled him from under the collapsed dock. He hasn't missed a tax payment to Basilios. Icing on the cake if Basilios sleeps in today. He doesn't need the officer showing up over at the Rectory, nor the Rectory fields. Lenny can't think about that. He'll just have to work fast and hope for the best. Luckily, Basilios has already done most of his work for him.

The corn kids squeak their door back and forth, back and forth as Celebrants pass. Still no sign of the Sunny family. He can only give them a few more minutes.

If the cop hadn't found his boat, would he be half way to the Atlantic by now? He'd like to think so, yes, he would. He would've been gone. But it's just as likely, well, with the Raymond development, which you can't really call a complete development, not yet, well, if they hadn't been caught at Operation Blue John, it was just as likely they'd be deep inside the selling shit business. And then what? Eventually everyone gets caught. And what about the baby? What about Romey? Lenny doesn't know why he even cares, doesn't know if he'll ever see her again. Who knows what her mom will do when they get to Raleigh. Shawnee. A wild card for sure. But still, he doesn't want to sell drugs. He doesn't want to be like his two brothers. Not Jude. Not Frank watching Jude, always watching, always doing whatever Jude tells him. That's not his route. He'd veered off that route then veered right back on. Time to stop the goddamn veering. So, it's almost lucky Basilios finding that boat, catching him in the weed. It's a chance to start over. Again.

He just needs to pull off today. He needs to trust that the Celebrants will fend for themselves. They always do, they always do.

Lenny checks up and down the street. Empty, except for the elders setting up their chess boards along the rock wall across from the Block, their dogs settling themselves underfoot.

Lenny pulls the two quarters from his pocket, holds them out to the corn kids.

"No playing church hooky for you two today," he says. They

look disappointed, but take the coins and step inside.

Lenny hesitates, takes one last look down the aisle of the Block. The priest, on his makeshift pulpit, raises his bandaged hands above his head in preparation to release a most likely startling version of truth intended to tip his congregation toward salvation.

Just before Lenny closes the wide wooden doors, leaving himself on the outside, the old man's green eyes glint as sharp as the stained glass in the little chapel back home.

Lenny runs through the lower fields behind the Rectory then up the slope toward the burnished autumn sorghum. Brittle tobacco leaves swipe at his knees. He pulls to a stop at the crest to catch his breath and sight down the long fence line before wedging himself between the barbed wires. Once through, he jogs along the dirt path next to the fence, counting rows and ducking eye-level fronds, their pollen pushing heavy against the back of his throat. He turns down at row number seventeen and soon arrives at the first blue patch of skunk weed. The musk is thick, a good indicator of just what he needs—a windless day. He crosses into another block of sorghum, runs through the second pot patch, cuts down three rows and pulls to a stop in the third, where the little skiff was hidden before Basilios made him return it. He drops his good hand to his knee, air churning through his lungs. Glances at the watch.

Fifteen minutes. Faster than his practice run from the street south of the Block, just out of view of the chess players, to the weed patch. He figures it'll take him an additional fifteen minutes in the priest's cash crops, then another fifteen to swim two coves up Lake Norman where Raymond should be waiting. All giving him fifteen minutes of slack time before the priest releases the Celebrants.

Lenny fights off the urge to run through his schedule again.

There's no time, but the repetition calms him. Different from when he'd run away from the farm. Back then, except for his dad's often-recited word map outlining every single river and tributary winding its way to the Atlantic Ocean, there had been no plan. Just take Buford's money, grab the gear, untie the boat, row like hell.

Hoping they'd search for him.

Hoping they wouldn't.

They'd find him.

They wouldn't.

Of course, they didn't. Had they searched?

Someone would search this time. He knew too much for them not to. They would search…unless they couldn't.

Lenny picks among the stalks and spidery leaves of weed until he locates the spot where he'd hidden the cop's gift: a tiny pile of his signature slim and trim cigarette butts. Covered in cop fingerprints. Thank you, Basilios. Smoked right at the scene of the crime. And of course, there's the roach. The golden evidence, tossed to the dirt, the cop feeling all god-a'mighty, standing directly over Lenny's skiff, trying to weasel out Lenny's name, exacting his tax. Just for good measure, shielding his own fingerprints with tissues, Lenny's collected extra cigarette butts from wherever Basilios had blown his smoke across town, wherever he could recall seeing the cop making someone's life miserable. Lenny pulls a baggie from his pocket and sprinkles the ground with all but two of the sleek butts, which he returns to his pocket. If they survive the fire, the butts place Basilios inside the patch. If they don't survive, he's still got insurance butts in his pocket.

He peels off a thin leaf of skunk weed from a nearby plant, balances it across the fingers of his good hand, uses that to pick up the roach, and, rolling it between his fingers and thumb, wraps the little fatty tight inside the leaf, shielding it from all but the cop's fingerprints. The leaf tears a bit, but mostly it holds. He wonders if the cops down at the station, or the feds for that matter, if they ever called the feds around here, would even hunt for fingerprints. *But still. You gotta take care.* Jude's voice rising right there inside his head. Would Jude be impressed with this plan?"

Lenny brings the covered roach to his mouth and bites a tiny hole in the leaf at the end of the roach, swallows the bit of leftover weed, *no evidence left behind, Jude*, and lets the leaf-encased joint hang between his lips. *No lip prints either*, just in case there is such a thing.

He pulls the other baggie from his pocket, sets it open on the ground. Twenty-five loose matches. Hopefully that's enough. He selects one and strikes it on the zipper of his cutoffs. Lights the roach, chokes a little. It's been a couple of years since he'd smoked, down under those porch steps with Jude and Frank egging him on. Such a kid thing to do, thinking that would lead to some sort of truce. Lenny places the burnt match carefully inside his back pocket.

Lenny sucks in and sparks the joint, then bends to tilt the red tip toward a low-lying leaf. But before the plant can catch fire, he pulls back. All his mental gymnastics somersault back on his brain.

What if the community fire department doesn't notice smoke until it's too late? What if the entire years' worth of sorghum, and maybe all the Rectory's tobacco, burns to the ground? What would become of the Celebrants? What if the Rectory itself catches fire?

Of course he'd been through all of this in his head, over and over, the past few nights. And every night he'd managed to tame those thoughts. The Rectory buzzes with Celebrants after every service. Hell, he wouldn't be swimming past the first cove before they sound the alarm. And by the time he reaches Raymond at cove number two, fire fighters would have these fields soaked. That's what fire fighters do, right? With no wind, even if they get a late start, the fire would consume maybe less than a quarter of the crop. Leaving plenty to keep the shoe committee and the coat committee and whatever committee in business. Most of the crop was harvested, anyway. They would be replanting again come spring. Sure they would.

Lenny examines the joint. Decides it wouldn't hurt to take a long draw.

He'd also worried about how suspicious it might look disappearing so soon after the fire. But who besides Basilios, the priest, or Artemis would even notice his absence? It's not like he's in school, or on the radar of anyone important. And if Artemis ends up suspecting anything, she might just let it ride, since she'll have her hands full with the now drug-exposed priest and cop.

Anyway, what choice does he have? He needs a clean break, and he needs the priest and the cop behind bars, at least for a while, and unable to come after him. The key for them is Artemis. Will she be so angry at the marijuana business growing right under her nose that she lets them rot in jail? Or at some point will she work her Amazon magic and break one or even both of them free? He hates to think about the priest rotting in jail.

Lenny takes another toke, glances around the pot patch. He wishes there was a better way out. He wishes he could've dug a fire break around the patch, like the farmers do back home. Swailing, they called it. But that for sure would give him away.

Swailing. Controlling their burns, hoping to keep wilder fires at bay.

Hell if that wasn't just exactly what he's doing right here. Swailing.

Lenny relights the joint, deposits that match in his pocket, and quickly, before his drifting brain can catch up with him, circles the patch, lighting plants low to the ground.

He runs the roach down the row to a spot that's hopefully out of flame range, but close enough to serve as a final piece of pot-patch evidence.

Half-assed plan, if I've ever heard one, boys. But half-ass can sometimes work.

Shut up, Jude.

Lenny lets the joint drop from its leaf shield to the ground. Eats the leaf shield. *You gotta take care, boys, you gotta take care.*

The spiky plants around him gently smoke their own dope, but they aren't exactly aflame, as he'd expected. Not true of his chest and lungs, not to mention his brain, and all other organs he can't take time to think about, gone skittery and heaving, his nose and throat full of the sweet stink of his own sweat and the priest's *best goddamn medicinal.* The plan has taken longer than expected, if he's reading his watch correctly. Probably, he's not on time. He gazes at the watch, then peers at the ground, fighting off the urge to lie down. Lie down, float some cloud shapes across a cloudless sky. Somehow, to Lenny, that sounds like the wrong thing to do.

He focuses on the open baggie of matches on the ground, which helps him recall the right thing to do. He strikes another match on his zipper, lights several nearby plants, blows the match out and stuffs it into his back pocket. Peat and repeat until only ten matches are left, which he shoves into his pocket in case the fire doesn't catch.

He swerves back out of the pot patch and through the sorghum rows to the fence line. Up on this side of the fields, he can see the Rectory wavering down there in the valley, surrounded by rippling rows of the priest's gardens. The fields running down to the Rectory, golden, blue, golden, blue. His mother would love this land. She would run her long fingers along the tops of crops, like she played her piano, blessing every key. Cursing every key, too. Don't forget that. Cursing with her eyes hidden under her long, curly hair.

He lifts his hand and blows a whistle of hope toward the sky. Hope for the sorghum, hope for the tobacco, hope for the Celebrants. Takes one last look at the Rectory.

Tries to hold it in place.

What would the priest think? What would Basilios do? Lenny could go back to that patch right now, he could still smother those smoking leaves. But he can't. He sure can't. He just can't let himself care. Get rid of the problem. Get out of town. That's all he can afford to think about. Concentrate on the task. Same as rowing away from the farm. Row. Then row again and again. That's all. What will he tell Raymond? Nothing. Absolutely nothing. Except that they are clean and clear and they are heading for Raleigh. Heading for Romey.

He needs to finish this now, not only to beat the Celebrant crowd, but just to finish. Before he has any more second thoughts. The Rectory is looking much steadier, the garden rows straighten. Lenny closes his eyes to fight off the beauty of the fields, and the anguish. But only for a moment. He needs to keep rowing.

He drops the last two slim butts at the fence line, just about two inches apart, just about like a man would drop them if he were standing there contemplating his next move. To Lenny's mind, it doesn't matter whether the fire is judged an accident or arson. Either way, Basilios is placed inside the fence line, and hopefully inside the patch of weed. The butts are weeks old. The first question anyone would ask, is why hadn't the cop reported the pot crop to authorities when he first found them? Basilios will have to explain that. And Artemis, Marva, would Marva just stand by and let the cop off free and clear? Lenny's betting not. He's betting on her anger, he's betting on her passion to save the Block, the neighborhood, hell, the whole world from drugs. Sure, it's not a fool-proof plan. He knows that. He's betting on catching luck. *You've tied your knot, Buddo. Whether it holds, well...we'll see.*

Lenny steadies himself against a fence post. By now, the priest should've gotten his homily out of his system. He runs his stump across his face, surprised at the sweat, surprised at the heat on his back.

A sharp snap, then another, sends him ducking low along the fence line.

He turns back toward the patch. Flames snap and whip along the fringe of the blue skunk weed. Smoke billows low across the auburn fronds of sorghum, then rise, its black cloud roping against the blue sky. A breeze has picked up. He estimates a matter of minutes before those sorghum fronds catch too. It would only take a few sparks. Lenny glances up, stupidly hoping for rain. But all he can see is a bright dry day at the end of a bright dry autumn.

A high-pitched screech rides the heated air currents. He's heard the farmers rave about the uncanny spirit of a fire on the move. He listens closer.

Is that the fire? No.

"Birdie-Birdie-Birdie!"

A woman's call, and he's pretty sure he knows the woman. Lenny zig-zags down the sorghum, looks down one row, then darts across the plants to look down another.

"Birdie-Birdie-Birdie!"

She's standing in the sorghum, her rope trailing behind, with just one sunny kid holding tight. The end of the rope, where second kid, July...where July should be...trails along the ground.

"Birdie!" Miss May calls when she spots Lenny. "He were here."

She looks at the older child, June, now twisting her portion of rope in her small hands. "Weren't Birdie here? You tell him Belle.

Birdie were here. Just now."

Belle and Birdie. June and July.

Miss May follows Lenny's eyes to her apron pockets, which are full of weed.

"It just…it just helps," she says.

But Lenny's mind is not on her pockets of weed, not on the smoke rising upwind of them and now drifting over their heads. It's on the possibility of endless rows of sorghum between them and the littlest Sunny kid.

Lenny coughs. Little Belle's eyes are reddening and starting to run. She wrinkles her nose and lets out two discreet huffs.

"Come on," Lenny says. "You've got to get out of here."

Miss May doesn't move. She glances around, then pulls the rope and Belle toward the weed, toward the fire.

Lenny trots down the row, grabs the end of the rope and tries to pull the two of them toward safety. But Miss May yanks back hard enough to saw the rope into Lenny's hand. He momentarily loses his balance.

"Birdie!" she calls out, still backing away, still pulling Lenny and the girl toward the smoke.

Lenny winds the rope around his chest, clamps it tight between his stump and his ribs, anchors it in his clenched fist. The smoke, growing closer, slams its hostile, heated warning against his eyes.

"Come on!" he yells.

But the mother's frantic strength is too much for him, and she drags him and Belle further toward the crackling skunk weed.

Keeping tension between them, Lenny unwinds the rope from his chest, then quickly releases the rope, knocking Miss May and Belle off balance. He uses his advantage to run forward and grab the little girl by the elbow, twist her arm to pry her loose from the rope. Her mother screams, terrified evidently at this unexpected and additional breach of her family's rope code. Coughing now, Lenny pulls the girl, pulls Belle, down the long row to the fence line, clear of the smoke and the path of the flame.

"Stay here," he says.

He watches her for a moment, then braces her between his good arm and his stump and lifts her to the other side of the fence, drops her on her butt. Hopes the barbed wire deters any advances.

"Stay here," he repeats.

He catches up to the mother, who's flailing her way toward the crackling plants, toward the high flames, the rope still trailing from her hand.

"Birdie-Birdie-Birdie!"

Lenny reaches and grabs the end of the rope and whips her around. They both hack smoke. The high flames have not yet caught the sorghum, but it feels as if they are licking Lenny's neck. His cutoffs are flat-ironed against his legs. His hair caps his head like it was just pulled from an oven.

Lenny jerks the rope and this time she loses her balance long enough for him to whip the rope around her body and wrap her arms to her sides. Her eyes frenzy around the field, and she manages to shimmy one slender arm loose and swing at him, catching him hard in the lower lip.

He grabs her arm, twists it behind her back, pushes her down the row toward the fence line.

"I'm sorry, I'm sorry," he yells. "You gotta stay with Belle."

She stumbles back against him, off balance but still standing. He catches his own balance, continues plowing her down the row.

"I'll get him," he yells. "I promise I'll get him."

She falls to her knees gagging when they reach the fence line. She shakes loose of the rope, turns and leans back into the barbed wire, her apron torn, weed spilling out and catching across her shift.

"I'll not just sit here," she pants out. "I'll not."

Flames crack closer now, and smoke wavers out toward the Rectory. Lenny glances down to the house and its gardens, thinks he sees movement, but his eyes sting so he can't be sure.

He points down the fence line.

"Then run up and down this path. Look down every row, and call out if you see July…I mean…Birdie. But, look," he points to the girl, who's standing now beside the fence post. "Belle needs to keep you in her sight. Okay? Otherwise, she'll be scared…" He looks at Belle and recalibrates. "Otherwise, we might lose her too. So don't get out of her sight. Okay?"

Miss May scrambles to her feet and trots away down the path, shedding spikey leaves of pot as she goes.

Lenny jogs back toward the flames, now consuming the sorghum in gargantuan bites.

He pulls to a halt, retraces his steps.

Belle is churning her mom's rope through her hands.

Lenny squats down close to the barbed wire.

"Where did Birdie…where did he let go of the rope?"

The blue of Belle's eyes ring a yellow globe, and her breath comes cool through the wire fence.

"In the sand," she whispers.

"The sand?"

Lenny stares at her.

The tobacco fields are sort of sandy, but they're way down slope. Surely May would've noticed Birdie's absence long before she reached the fence line. Hell, she could not have crossed the barbed wire without stopping to help him through or over the wires.

The only other sand he knows of blankets the edge of the lake. And, now that he thinks about it, the lake side is the only access point without barbed wire. Just that wooden gate, which he'd only ever seen propped wide open. They could've strolled right though that gate with the rope dragging the ground and the mom never feeling any loss of tension.

Lenny reaches through the wire and shakes Belle's elbow. "Can Birdie swim?"

Belle nods, softly at first, then so vigorously she has to stop her head by dropping the rope and placing both hands under her chin.

"Miss May!" Lenny calls down the fence line.

"Mama," Belle calls too.

Another high-pitched wail speeds along the air currents. A siren. Maybe two.

Lenny catches the mother's frantic eyes and motions the opposite way toward the lake, then he turns and runs down the short path, away from the heat of the fire toward the water.

He races through the gate, down the embankment, hesitates, then sprints out onto the beach. The sand runs empty north, and empty south. Reluctantly, Lenny widens his vision to the flat water, empty too, save for a stick-up of driftwood.

Which is not driftwood.

Poking straight up in the lake, face to the sky, arms treading the flinty water, is the littlest member of the Sunny Family. Birdie. July.

Miss May kicks up sand, her skirt flapping around her knees as she sprints past Lenny on a dead run for the lake.

She splays into the shallows, swims out and pulls a dripping Birdie into her arms.

Belle passes Lenny too, but stops a few feet short of the lake's edge, rope trailing.

Lenny wipes the sweat from his forehead, his temples, and his chin. Tries not to wonder about Miss May, Birdie and Belle, *fending for themselves* in the months to come. Wills himself not to second guess again. The plan is burning its way to completion.

With his good hand, he feels in his pockets to make sure the baggies, the used and unused matches, are all there. That there's nothing he's left behind that he didn't intend to leave behind.

Miss May stops in front of him, both kids now reattached to the rope.

He wants to tell her that the kids aren't going to hang onto the rope forever, but he guesses she's already realized that for herself. So instead, he points his stump toward the fire on the hill.

"You can't go back that way," he says.

She steps in close, puts a hand on his shoulder. The kids bunch up behind her.

"Naught can you," she says.

The wail of sirens grows closer.

Her hand slips from his shoulder and she turns to lead her kids south down the lake toward the access road. Soon the Sunny Family will step aside for the fire trucks to pass. From the sound of it, more than two. The fire fighters might ask her questions once they get things under control. Eventually, they would. With any luck, any luck at all, she will not have an enormous interest in answering those questions.

Lenny watches the flames lick at the blue, cloudless sky. The Celebrants' crop burning to the ground. Talk about a holy shit fire. Out there against the sky, and inside his own heart.

Go or hold, Buddo. Go or hold.

Lenny turns and wades into the water. When the surface of the lake reaches his waist, he dives forward and swims with his lop-sided stroke—arm-stump, arm-stump—north toward the second cove. Toward Romey.

He hopes Raymond is on time.

BOOK II

CHAPTER 1

THREE BROTHERS, JUST GODDAMN KIDS. GODDAMN boys up on a barn's roof. One gets shoved off the edge, loses his arm. What did the other two lose? Or gain?

And for God's sake why would the one-armed brother, supposedly now a man, drive a little girl, Romey, directly back into the land of his brothers? Rumbling along in his pickup truck, tracking back into land he'd sworn he'd never set foot on again. Never in the history of ever. The very act was to compromise the idea of Romey, the one, the only pure thing in his life.

"Where we going, Lens?"

Romey's frizzy head startles out of her eleven-year-old dreams then droops back against the truck's cold, fogged window. Outside, the gloomy November afternoon and its gloomy decaying landscape passes them way too rapidly in the opposite direction.

He's plucked her out of danger on the city streets only to toss her right back into danger on the farm. Catch and release. Hadn't she been through enough?

Romey riding away from her demons, directly into his.

Why?

His mother and his brother out riding horses. Goddamn grownups. His mother doesn't make it back. So, a memorial service, five days from now. Was it an accident? Is anything an accident when his brother, Jude, is the witness?

Jude had been on the barn roof when Lenny lost his arm. Was Jude saddled up beside his mother when she lost her life? From what he's heard, Jude swears not. Jude swears that by then they'd separated on the trail.

Lenny could hope Jude is a changed man. Lenny could hope Jude is telling the truth. Yep, he could. But he's so sick of false hopes. Where's it ever gotten him?

Also, there's his mom-dream. Looping back at him. His mom-dream, resurrected from childhood, welling right back up to sting his adult eyes. Looping, looping. His mother rouses herself from her stupor, or from whatever it was that seemed to veil her from seeing her kids clearly, her husband clearly. Whatever. She awakens, finally. She rises, long curls shimmering. Her head clear, finally. Her voice clear, finally. Strong. On a mission. Calling. Calling for a reckoning. A God-trembling, devil-quaking reckoning.

That's what reels him back to the farm. His childhood mom-dream reels him back into what he'd left for good ten years ago. Had her death been an accident? Or had she called Jude out so late in the game? Hell, inside her own erratic, twisty thought garden, it would not have been too late, not for her, and certainly not for Lenny.

Had she finally, finally challenged her eldest son, Jude?

Had she given terror his name?

What about those rope burns on my youngest child's neck, Jude? Your little brother, Lenny? All those years ago? Rope burns on a nine-year-old? And, how exactly did an eleven-year-old go flying off the barn roof?

Who else was up on that barn roof, Jude? Explain. Explain that to me right now.

She could've gone on and on, salve soothing Lenny's heart, she could've enumerated all of the "accidents" throughout their childhood years, "experiments" Jude called them back then.

And then what?

Once his mom's accusations were out there floating in that open country air, how would Jude have reacted? What would Jude do? What *did* he do? That's the question needling him now, the question he's returning to answer. He's heading home to finish his mom's reckoning.

She calls, even though she's gone.

Yep. When word came of the accident, he'd taken just enough time to pack Romey's bag and nab her from the school bus line. He would've done that eventually, anyway. Yes, eventually he would have snatched Romey from her own nightmares. His mom's unexplained death only escalated that timeline. Romey had been in need of a rescue for as long as he'd known her.

So he's rescuing her.

Most folks would call it kidnapping.

But one goddamn kid up on a ledge. What you gonna do? Just leave her teetering?

#

"How many heads you got, Lens?"

Romey. Age nine. Asking the question that eventually cleared Lenny's mind, eventually pointed him in the direction he should've been navigating all along. It took years for Romey to refine that question. But she did, finally, sending him in the direction called *Out*. The direction called *Anywhere but Here*.

"I got one head," he'd said. "Same as you. Sorry shame, but just the one."

"Nuh uh," she said. "You don't. You got two. You only got one arm, but I think you got two heads."

"I've got *two* arms," he said, trying not to read too much into her meaning. But easing toward distracting her, just in case. "Maybe only just the one hand and one elbow, but I do have two arms."

He lifted his stump to rub its rough scar edges across her smooth forehead. She'd loved that as a little kid, back and forth, back and forth. It was still his most reliable tool to soothe her.

But her mouth puckered and she moved away.

"Well, anyway," she said. "I'm talking about heads. I've got two. I think you've got two, but I can only see the one."

"I don't want to talk about it."

#

"That's what Shawnee said you'd say, Lens."

Romey, age ten, refining her point. Persisting.

Lenny eventually unable to resist.

"What is it with you and the two heads?"

"I didn't say heads," she said. "I said…*mind*s. Girls have got two minds."

"A lot more than two," Lenny said. "And what's Shawnee, what's your mama, got to do with it?"

"She said it's a subject that men won't want to talk about."

#

"Here's the deal, Lens. Do you know what in-utero is? It's Latin."

Romey, age eleven. One week before he took her from the playground.

"You're studying biology? *And* Latin?"

"Shawnee says we've got two minds. Our mind-mind, and then our in-utero mind. And it's that in-utero mind that is our womb, and it turns out you were correct, you don't have one."

"Well, right."

"And if we're not careful with our in-utero mind, it turns into a wandering womb. You ever hear of a wandering womb, Lens?"

A wandering womb.

"It's Greek, Shawnee says it's Greek. You ever hear of it?"

"Well—"

"Shawnee calls it that Separate-Creature-All-of-Its-Own. She says Hippocrates, he's Greek too, Lens. She says Hippocrates said so."

"Hippocrates."

"Yes, Lens. Listen now. Hippocrates said that even from a very young age," Romey, as usual, patiently lecturing, like he's one of the slower students in class, "Even from the age of eleven like me, we have to exercise our in-utero mind or else it gets real, real, real unhappy. And if it gets unhappy, it could just wander off. Just leave town. Me, though. Not you. It could just up and take on a life of its own."

"What the hell does that mean?"

"Shawnee says it means I've got to keep it happy. I've got to keep my Separate Creature from wandering off without me. Soon, she says, soon I'll have important responsibilities, all related to my Separate Creature, Lens."

Responsibilities. So that was Shawnee's profit scheme? She hadn't planned on selling the baby. She'd planned on hustling the girl?

"She gave me some smell-good lotions to rub down there, in case my second mind should take a hike. And Lens, if it does happen to desert me, the smell-good lotions make it want to move right back in again. She says there were some ladies back then who went absolutely nuts if ever they forgot to take care of their Separate Creatures."

He'd plucked her directly off the Shawnee ledge. Grabbed her from the school bus line. Drove west.

Any fool would've taken a kid out of that situation, right?

Here's the thing.

From the moment Raymond climbed through the priest's shed window with that stroller full of baby, full of Romey, from the moment Shawnee set fierce, drug-rimmed eyes on him, they were all linked, all four of them, like fish on a stringer. No connection to each other whatsoever except what was killing them.

CHAPTER 2

ROMEY STIRS IN THE PASSENGER SEAT, ducks low to peer out his window at the twin peaks bracing the west side of the river valley. Their shadows stretch across the fields, darkening the farms here well before the sun sets on the other side of the range.

"Rosy Face and Chub Ridge," Lenny says, pointing toward the mountains.

"Uh huh," she says. "Are we stopping soon, Lens? I gotta pee."

"Yeah, soon" he says. "We're stopping soon."

Everything is soon, now. Soon, soon, soon. That phone call yesterday? That was the starting gate. No *ready*, no *set*. Just *Go*! And now they're barreling toward the farm. That call. After all these years, Glenna out of left field. How had she found him so fast?

Your mother...An accident...A horse...Lenny I'm so sorry.

A horse? Wait. His mom?

Glenna? Oh...well...did you say a horse?

Yes. Jude found her, Lenny. I'm just terribly sorry. All of us are just so sorry. You know how everybody loved your mom.

They did? All of us? Who the hell is all of us?

Wait…I mean…Glenna? How the hell did you find me?

Well, your church group. You know, that lady? Marva?

Church group. Marva…the flaming red-haired Amazon Artemis. He hadn't heard from her in years.

Lenny? Are you still there? It's just all too much of a jolt. Lenny?

What about Marva?

Well, she answered the phone. I called that same Rectory, the one you told me about. Remember? You called me from there? That one time, and I get that, that's what we agreed on, but, well, what could it hurt? She answered. I'm really sorry.

Glenna eventually stopped apologizing and got the story out. Artemis expressed condolences about Lenny's mom. Artemis asked Glenna to write down a banker's name. Artemis said the banker most likely would put her in touch with Lenny.

Well hell yes. Raymond's father, the banker.

She especially wanted you to know about the priest, Lenny. The priest at the Rectory?

The priest. Of course, the priest.

She said to let you know the priest was out? That doesn't sound right, but that's what she said—out.

Good old Artemis. Glad, certainly, to have the illegal cash crop burned to the ground. Glad to get the cop off the streets. Not happy about the priest, maybe, but not too unhappy either. Probably opened the door for her to take over the Block. Legitimize it. Make it what it should've been.

She was adamant that I put it that way to you, Lenny. She said she was absolutely positive the priest would also contact the banker. She was particular on that point, Lenny, and she asked me to be, well, particular.

So that was that. A priest connects with a banker who's connected to a charmer. Raymond. The one person outside of the farm who knows about the farm. The one person Lenny allowed through that window into his past. Unless you count the cop, Basilios, which Lenny doesn't. Basilios will rot in prison. According to news accounts. A cop in dope, no hope. Precinct gone up in a cloud of cannabis. Not even Artemis could throw that in reverse.

But the priest walking free after ten years, not a surprise. Lenny will take a guess: good behavior. Or maybe just too annoying to keep behind bars.

"What's the joke, Lens?"

"Nothing. Nothing."

Who else would Raymond yammer to? Shawnee? Yes, most likely. But what was she going to do, call law enforcement? No way, not with her record.

Shawnee. Was she already on the road, chasing them?

Lenny downshifts as they approach Buford's car shop, just a one-armed kid's ten-minute bike ride from the family farm. He wonders if Buford still stashes his life's savings under his floorboards. He wonders if Buford is even still around. He wonders if his own embarrassment over Buford will ever fade.

"Right there's where I learned to clean a carburetor," he says.

"Why do you know their names?"

"Whose names?"

"Rosey Face and Chub Ridge." She points out his window, where the mountains seem to ride right along beside them.

"Yeah, I don't know…I guess…well, I guess they're kinda like family."

Romey presses her scuffed white go-go boots into the floorboard. "I've really got to pee, Lens. Shawnee always pulls over when I need to pee."

Shawnee.

Lenny pulls to the side of the road and Romey hops out on a

dead run for the woods, her bell-bottoms tucked inside her boots, white fringes swinging.

Good god, Shawnee.

It took her a while to warm up to him, if you can call it that. Eventually, though, she seemed to find him more reliable than Raymond, and once he and Raymond split, he saw more and more of Romey.

Starting the day he opened their apartment door in Raleigh to find Shawnee, biceps and thighs like a yearling bull, blocking it. Thick hands out in front of her, like she might be expecting a quick punch to the chest.

"So. If you can cook my ex's stringy noodle, you can change diapers."

Romey, a chunky toddler by that time, disconnected from Shawnee's trunk legs and marched through the door, black eyes fierce, diaper hanging heavy to her stubby knees. Kinky amber hair a bouncing halo.

Shawnee crouched low and grabbed Romey back, reached into the soggy diaper and shook out a bag of what appeared to be pep pills. Dropped Romey, her little legs churning for Raymond's back bedroom.

Shawnee's face, always cutting from worried to more worried. Followed by angry.

She wiped the plastic bag on her jeans and shoved it into her back pocket, urine scent permeating. Stared at him like he was challenging her mothering instincts, which he guessed he was.

"Uh huh," she said. "Talk to me about it when you come from where I come from."

Then, not looking at him, more like she was looking through him, "Romey! I'm leaving your sorry little ass with this cocksucker. You hear me?"

Like she'd yelled it afterwards for years and years. Years and years before it finally dawned on him that his door might not be the only one where she was dropping Romey.

Romey climbs back into the truck, Lenny eases them back out onto the road.

Years and years, figuring Romey out.

Where exactly his mind had been before that, he couldn't say. Where had his mind been?

Lenny slows as he turns off onto the gravel lane leading up to the farm. A decade. How long would it take the priest to locate these pot holes, these leaning fence posts? How long would it take Shawnee?

Romey pulls her book bag up onto the seat between them from where it slid to the floor while she slept. Romey, always preparing for whatever comes next.

CHAPTER 3

"WHERE ARE WE, LENS?" ROMEY WHISPERS, more as an accusation than a question.

"It's hard to say," he whispers back, and she nods, serious. Still young enough to seek his true meaning, rather than worry with his ironic one.

Her cool slate eyes take in the farmhouse from the truck window. He's just outside her window, attempting to steady his legs against the gravel drive. Last time he stood in this spot, the drive had been dirt. Dirt he'd kicked up a little, delaying his departure. God he'd been so naïve. Fiddling there, hoping his mom would come to the door, or just drift by the window. Just to wave.

Well, she wouldn't be waving now.

Lenny's unsure whether Romey will step out of the truck. The farmhouse is obviously not what she expected, and it's not what he expected either. Sure, the road leading up to it had hardly changed, but everything else seems new. Freshly painted. Not a warped plank in sight. The lowering sun is slick against varnished porch steps. Why would anyone varnish porch steps? And a varnished ramp—a ramp?—rounding up the side. Has the farmhouse he knew turned into a goddamned Gentleman's Ranch? Nothing like he remembers. The house narrower somehow, and now pastel blue for god's sake, reminding Lenny of a giant Easter egg. The windows bigger, staring at him. Glaring. Purposefully directing the last of the evening sun into his eyes. He shades his face, squints at the glass. Rosey Face and Chub Ridge, the elderly twin mountains behind him, back across Buford's pastures, appear from this angle to be standing guard inside the house. A goddamn pastel blue farmhouse with mountains inside.

Lenny swings the passenger door open and Romey drops from the cab, her go-go boots touching down in the gravel beside him just as the front door to the house swings open.

"You need to move, I know you can move."

A man charging out, talking to, Lenny now notices, another man back in the shadows of the porch. A man in a wheelchair.

"There's nothing wrong with you. Anybody can see that. I can see that."

A man charging out.

That would be Jude. That gait, that cocky carriage. Same long, black hair, now tied up in a bun.

Doesn't exactly hesitate when he spots Lenny and Romey and the truck in his drive. More like recalculates. A rightward thrust of the upper body and he's veering from the man in the wheelchair to the top step of the porch.

"What!" he demands. Then, "Christ. Lenny?"

Of course Jude compresses the silent years like they haven't passed. Cements over a decade worth of yawning gaps. Seizes the reins. Applies pressure. Cues direction.

"Father, look," he calls back over his shoulder as he descends the porch steps. "Little Lenny's back. Little Lenny's finally decided to come home." He pauses on the bottom step, points at Lenny. "They all thought you were dead. All but me, of course. What can I say? I knew it! What do they know? What…do…they…know?"

Father? Dad?

The wheelchair eases into the evening light. His dad's face turns toward the gravel drive.

"Lenny?"

Jude seems to startle at the sound of their father's voice.

"Lenny…your mom…" His dad's voice trails off, his arms disappear into the folds of a moth-eaten blanket draped onto his sunken lap.

Jude stares at their father. "Suddenly you can talk?" He takes a second to recover himself, then resumes his advance. His hand stretches toward Lenny, crosses over to Lenny's stump.

How many years would have to pass to forget your brother is missing a body part?

Lenny's stump stays reliably still at his side. Jude's outstretched hand drifts into a question mark.

"Remarkable, all these years…I knew it, I just knew it. Dead? Ha. Lenny's back!"

Romey reaches into the truck for her backpack. Bought new for sixth grade. No idea that she's not going back. No idea that he's removed her completely from her shit pile to his.

"And look, Father. He brought a…a girl. Lenny's back and he's got a girl."

The slate in Romey's eyes drops several degrees. Just a whiff of a kid, staking out the tough-guy corner for herself. Lenny knows the position inside and out. But he's never owned it like Romey. Romey possesses something else, something Lenny could only name as Surprise. And she possesses enough of it to completely stay Jude's unwanted welcome. She side-swipes him on her way to the porch steps, her jacket too big, the shoulder seams drooping close to her bony elbows, and too long, the tail dropping almost to her knees, the fringes of her boots tic-tacking.

Whatever the hell Jude thought he was doing dissipates into the brisk November mountain air as he follows Romey onto the porch.

At some point, Lenny would need to side-swipe Jude too. However, Lenny understands what Romey cannot—that they're playing chicken with a man who makes up rules as he goes.

Instead of side-swiping, maybe he should just go along with Jude until he can figure things out. But going along, he'd proved over and over again, had never worked as a kid. Nothing he'd done back then, no level of compliance, no level of appealing to Jude's better self, if there were such a thing, no amount of trying to win over his other brother Frank to his side had ever worked.

Besides, he's already losing ground. They are moving fast, the three of them, and Romey is disappearing, disappearing like in that quicksand of his childhood dreams, where his mom is unable to pull anyone to safety.

Almost horizontal to the porch with the effort, Romey is pushing his dad's wheelchair across the threshold and into the house. Jude close by, his hand oddly protective on their dad's shoulder. Lenny checks that Jude is not touching Romey.

Jude calls out, "Lenny, you've got to see what all we've done to the place. Father? He's got to see the barn, right? He's got to see the horses. All new. Everything new!"

What all we've done to the place?

Lenny commands his brain to ignore Jude and commands his legs to get moving. Move.

It takes forever, but finally he catches up and follows them into the pastel blue house of frozen memories.

The hardwood floor of the farmhouse creaks beneath their combined weight.

CHAPTER 4

SURE, IT'S HIS IMAGINATION. BUT STILL, Lenny can see the two horses, cantering side-by-side down the back slope to the river, splashing through the sparkling shallows and heaving up the opposite bank. Yep. He sure can visualize those riders. His mom smooth and solid with every jittery sidestep of the new white-face mare, the new mare Jude had bought for her just the week before the "accident". Jude upright and awkward, kicking and kicking his gelding to stay abreast of his mom. The two of them so close at times that their legs touched, then separated on the horses' forward thrusts, then touched again.

Three beats, then a rest. Three beats, then a rest.

Why would a horse with four legs drum out only three beats? His mom tried to explain it many times.

Watch the legs, Lenny, watch the legs. Don't look at the big picture, the horse itself. That right back leg? That's where the trick is. Can you believe that skinny leg supports 800 pounds of horse?

Lenny knew she was explaining this to her one-armed son for a reason, and he appreciated that. But he was more interested in the horse.

Watch now, that one beat anchors all the rest. That's the first beat. The other three hooves just dance useless in the air? The second beat? Left back and right front hooves land precisely at the same moment. Then the left front finishes the third beat. Just watch them.

The faster the horse goes, the longer the suspension after the three beats. He could hear it in his head, he could drum it out on his bed. But it happened too fast for him to parse out the actual beats by watching the horse.

It doesn't take much mental exercise to see what happened that day. The horses heaving and shiny with sweat by the time Jude and his mom reached the trail flanking up to Chub Ridge, her long curls swishing in concert with her horse's mane. Jude's chest heaving.

That's how they rode, sure they did, as far as the land would let them. As long as the trail was wide enough for the two of them. Up the goddamn slope until the overhang of the hemlock grove engulfed them, until the trail turned into a slim ribbon between Chub Ridge and Rosey Face with nothing but open air and mountains spooling out like ocean waves to either side of them. They rode like that until the trail forced them to pick their way across the blade of the ridges, single file, Jude close behind his mom. Close behind. Three beats slowed to a walking four. Nice and easy now.

Lenny knew this next part like you know the back of your missing hand.

All you need is a short section of curtain rod. Wire from Old Man Buford's car shop would work. Cork from one of Dad's wine bottles. And—the tricky part—the capacitor from Mom's stereo. Feed the wire through the curtain rod, punch it through the cork on one end and attach the wire to the capacitor on the other end to complete the circuitry. Don't nod off in seventh-grade vocational class, and you've got yourself a cattle prod.

Years and years ago, Jude had tested his invention on the barn cats.

Dad, impressed by the power of the spark. Mom, sore about her stereo. Neither acting like they knew about the cats.

That was then. This cattle prod would be shiny and new just like the skittish mare his mom was riding across the blade. In Lenny's mind it glinted in the sun when Jude pulled it from his saddle bag. His mom up ahead wouldn't see, wouldn't have any idea. Jude stretching way, way out over his gelding's head to reach just ahead of him to the mare's hind quarters. Knowing Jude, he'd most likely practiced the move with his gelding for days and days, the shiny prod flashing past the old gelding's eye and shooting its crazy sparks backwards on the pull of the trigger. No need to practice, though. The gelding never startled, not once. He knew his job and that job was to keep his gait until Jude's knees prodded him elsewise. Jude would take pleasure in the practice, though, testing and testing the gentle gelding's faith.

There was just one more thing to imagine. Lenny could hear it. Jude shouting when he ignited the prod, burning it into the new mare's haunch. Jude shouting *Snake!* just as insurance. Just in case. Cause it wouldn't do for his mother to hear the zap. What if she heard the zap and the mare couldn't buck her off? What if she didn't break her neck?

Snake!

Yep, that's just exactly how it would work.

Lenny could imagine.

Lenny could imagine it all.

CHAPTER 5

LENNY WANTS TO ASK HIS DAD why he's in a wheelchair.

There's plenty of other *Whys* he'd like to toss out on the waters for examination.

For starters, *Why didn't you look for me*? Or, *If you did, why didn't you try harder? Why didn't you find me?*

But his mom's death sits square and solid between them, further widening the silent gulf carved by Lenny's ten-year absence.

He's not sure he wants to know the answers anyway. It's all he can do to try to keep up with what's right there in front of him.

Jude setting out goddamn crystal glasses, silver spoons, satin napkins on a smooth oak table. Where did it all come from? Who's paying for it? What happened to the worn, cotton blue-checked tablecloth their mom loved? The mason jars for water glasses? The chipped plates?

Could the ten-year gap completely swallow his past?

He's also got to keep up with what's not right in front of him. Romey.

Lenny gauges his distance from Romey. She's out of sight, but he can hear her rummaging in the hall closet angled up under the steps leading to the second floor. She's already pulled out two baseball mitts and a bat. She's directly through the wall, maybe fifteen yards from where he stands at the kitchen sink.

Romey's safety quotient.

The distance between him and her, the numerator. Always too far. The denominator? The heat and range of her curiosity. His task is to keep the numerator small as possible because that denominator is goddamn huge.

Jude rolls their dad to one end of the kitchen table, takes his place at the other end. Indicates an open chair.

In expectation of what? A family dinner?

Lenny leans back against the sink.

When their mom started taking her meals by grazing in the garden, his dad started cooking. Who's cooking now?

Lenny calculates, recalculates, trying to track Romey, who's moved from the closet to the front porch, from the front porch to the yard where he can see her pitching a large rock into the air, catching it with her mitt. Jude drones on at the table about the new wine racks, the new root cellars, the new brick infill on the barn.

"Keeps it cool in there for the horses. Not like you remember it."

A new stable of horses.

"Three of em right, Father? Mother's big white-faced mare and two little dark-faced fillies. Lenny! Including the foal of the foal of that crazy Tovero you liked as a kid. Remember that black-faced mare with the crazed blue eyes? You called her Moon Knight. You loved that nag."

Words form in Lenny's head, but they seem so old compared to all the changes that surround him. Old and worn out words. From worn out times. His mind is shifting on him, trying to keep up, keep track, seeking new words, unplanned words that could finally make a difference. As a kid, he'd stood right here at this same kitchen counter willing words to surface that would change something. Anything. At least shift something in his favor.

"Lenny, you couldn't have forgotten that nag."

New words simmer in Lenny's brain. Strange words. Words unlike the shadowy words of the past, the words that tried to accommodate, tried to line themselves up behind Jude, words searching for a safe place. No, these words cut corners.

These words swung for fences.

"Jude, do you happen to recall what happened to that mare?"

Even saying that name…Jude…feels powerful. But strange, too. Lenny cannot recall ever having said it, unless pleading it.

"Jude?"

Jude's fingers trace the swirly wooden grain of the table. He edges up in his chair a bit, cocks his head.

"Well, Lenny," he says, his eyes fading back into their past. "Yes, I do recall, I believe I do." He nods his head slowly. "That old nag passed. All things have to pass."

Lenny had loved that Tovero. And, yes, it died—unexpectedly. Foundered. How would an old, foraging pasture horse get access to so much grain that it foundered?

Jude tips back in his chair, a movement so solidly entrenched in their childhood that Lenny feels the awkward balance of his brother's chair pull at his chest. Jude tips an inch further, just past the point where most people fall.

"I know you wish you could've arrived earlier. Wish Mother would've lived to see this. To see *you*. Lenny home? Father? Mother would've loved this, right?"

Jude's fingers pulse now against the wood, signaling he's done with this distraction, done with whatever direction Lenny is taking them.

"What the hell happened to Mom, Jude?"

Not as subtle as he'd hoped, but there it was, out on the table. The reason he returned to the farm. New words. Punches. But punches thrown in the wrong direction. They broke Lenny's voice. His mom, his mom. He concentrates on the sudden sting behind his eyes. If there's one thing he knows, it's how to keep that sting in check. Even if he's out of practice.

Just as Jude gathers himself to say whatever Jude would say, their father stirs in his wheelchair. Panting, wheezing.

Who is this man who was so animated ten years ago? Sitting anchored at the opposite end of the table from Jude. His father, always so curious about his own intention, not caring so much about where it got him, just that it launched him.

Now moored.

"She died," he sputters. "Your Mother. She's dead."

The information is offered earnestly. An honest answer. As if Lenny's question to Jude had been honest, straight forward, without malice, without threat. His father. Eyes glassy with his loss, with his remembering. His eyes full of his Lizzy.

Lenny swipes at his eyes with his stump, walks to the kitchen window to watch Romey playing catch with her rock. But he turns back when Jude drops the front legs of his chair to the floor and strides down the length of the table to stand behind their father.

Their dad's hands fidget relentlessly along the braided edging of his satin napkin. His father's face. Long suffering? Humiliated? Simply restrained?

"Me?" Jude says, massaging their dad's shoulders, shaking them a little too hard for Lenny's liking. "I'm by his side 24/7. But *you*? The family runaway? The *deserter*?"

Jude releases his dad's shoulders, pushes away.

"Our father no longer speaks. Then you show up, and suddenly he finds words? Always the favorite. Little Lenny. Always the favorite. Even when you were dead."

#

Romey squirms beside Lenny on the porch swing, crowding his stump. His dad's wheelchair crowds her knees. Her sixth-grade math book lies open atop his dad's blanketed lap. Night had fallen quickly, as night does in a mountain valley.

Jude sits alone and finally silent, the porch light silhouetting him through the screen of the open kitchen window. By Lenny's eyes, his brother appears not much different from a rotting stump in the forest.

She's not your granddaughter.

Lenny wants to warn his dad, but doesn't, not yet, because for the first time in years, Lenny hears his dad's voice again. Not like old times. Not like Mr. Articulate, tossing out the odd theory, testing it through his verbal thought puzzles, his ever-hopeful meanderings as they fished the river, hunted the woods. His endless scientist's curiosity. *I'd like to know why, Buddo, I'd simply like to know why.*

Now, it's as if his dad is practicing one word at the time, thinking he will soon form sentences.

So, Lenny doesn't say much, tries not to get his hopes up.

Romey's determined to get her homework done before tomorrow. Not yet understanding that they're not going back.

Lenny has to tell her. But what's he going to say? That they've left absolutely nothing behind, nothing that was worthwhile? That he could find landscaping work anywhere? That there's plenty of math classes out there along the road?

Does she want to go the Atlantic Ocean? Once he's figured out his dead-mom puzzle?

Her yellow No. 2 pencil, twined between her skinny fingers,

bounces up and down the lines of her composition book in mathematical ecstasy. No eraser. Worn that sucker to a nub.

His dad's forefinger taps the math book in his lap for a few seconds. Then points toward Romey.

"Um-no," he says.

His eyebrows lift in expectation of Lenny's understanding. When Lenny does not respond, his dad tilts his head back to stare at the yellow light dangling from the porch ceiling, his Adam's apple working up and down his throat.

Rehearsing.

His dad tries again, and this time manages to push it out.

"Un…own."

He waits for Lenny.

She's not your granddaughter.

Lenny has to tell him.

But first Lenny has to breathe. That's all. Throw some unreliable hope in there on the exhale.

"Un…known?" Lenny guesses.

His father nods, points to Romey. His father giving him an opening. A life raft back to old times. The idea settles Lenny.

"Oh, oh yeah," Lenny says. "Yeah, you got that right, she's a bit of an unknown."

His dad stares at him like his youngest son could be the twin to the flickering yellow bulb above them.

Romey pauses her pencil.

His dad's Adam's apple races. He laboriously lifts both forefingers into the shape of a cross and pushes them toward Lenny, like he's warding off Dracula. His father holds the cross there for a few seconds before dropping his hands back to the math book in his lap.

Now Romey peers at Lenny like he's quickly fading from view.

With exaggerated patience, she slides her pencil between her lips, lifts the composition book and flips the page to face Lenny. At first, her figures are too loopy to decipher. Like math could be done in cursive. He squints where her finger is tapping, but her patience ebbs.

"X," she says around the pencil in her lips. "X, Lens. It's an *unknown*."

His father's eyebrows go up and down in affirmation. And there it was, that scientist grin of recognition, of insight, of a theory conjured and played out. Positive or negative, it didn't matter. Just the joy of a puzzle solved, no matter how simple.

Lenny ignores their satisfied faces.

"Well, yeah," he says. "I guess so. I guess I can see that now. X. And, well, there's the Y. So, you're learning equations?"

His dad leans back against in his wheelchair and Romey goes back to working the page, pencil heaven.

Lenny tries swallowing, but for the second time in the few hours he's been home, something has pushed tears to his eyes. This something having to do with how Romey is never going to turn in that math assignment. And something else, too, crowding his airways. Lenny has no idea where they are going. Just that they're not going back, and they're not staying herc.

He tries to breathe. He searches for something safe to say.

"So," he finally manages. "So…who helps you with math? You got a pretty good teacher, right?"

Her pencil twirling.

"My mom," she says. "Shawnee."

Romey gives the pencil a rest, taps it against her forehead. "Shawnee knows everything about unknowns. Shawnee says math is the only safe place because it's the only place where you can always come up with the correct answer."

Lenny tries to let this new information seep into his brain

without letting his incredulity seep out. Yes, Shawnee the dope peddler, the man slayer, the child neglecter. The Hippocrates scholar. The woman has scary power and scary intentions. But Shawnee the math genius?

Romey's sincerity convinces him though. He's never known her to entertain anything but the solid, unadorned truth inside that frizzy-haired head of hers.

The distant grind of tires on gravel pulls at Lenny's attention. Lenny glances at his father, whose face has become warped in puzzlement. But not at the car making its way down the farm lane.

His dad's attention is focused back inside the house. Through the kitchen window.

If his dad's not curious about the approaching car, then the approaching car must be someone he's expecting.

Frank. Has to be. Jude's boyhood henchman. His flunky. The kid in the middle.

Catch him, Frank. Don't let him loose, Frank.

The car is excruciatingly slow against the gravel. It's taken on the cadence of Lenny's memory of its driver.

"No…no," his dad mutters, still focused on the farmhouse kitchen.

Romey edges slightly closer to Lenny's stump, her eyes still jumping a bit from her calculating, but mostly watching the headlights approaching from the south. The farm's only entrance and the farm's only exit.

Lenny reaches and steadies Romey's math book where it's in danger of sliding from his dad's agitated lap. Too late. His dad lurches toward the door leading back into the farmhouse, Lenny reaches to grab him and the math book drops to the porch floor.

Jude barely avoids colliding with them as he strides through from the kitchen and out onto the porch, shotgun cocked across his arm.

"Coyote!" he yells, as the screen door bangs twice behind him.

Jude takes the porch steps two at a time and disappears into the dark edge of the yard, seemingly heading for the barn.

The truck swings up close to the front walk and Frank opens the door, eases out.

Sniffing the air, just like when they were kids. Two quick audibles, sniff, sniff, before heading up the walk.

A shot rings out, makes its way clear across the valley, echoes off Chub Ridge, meanders back to the porch.

So here they are, Lenny thinks. Here they are.

Frank sauntering across the front yard. Jude shooting blindly in the dark. And Lenny, wondering where the hell he's from.

Frank pauses on the top step, looks Romey over before focusing on Lenny.

"I thought you were dead," he says.

CHAPTER 6

THERE'S A LOT LESS OF FRANK now than Lenny remembers.

Tie his hands, Frank.

Flip the rope around his neck, Frank.

Let go the wheels, Frank.

Same biceps stretching out the sleeves of a faded red NC State t-shirt. Now wheeling their dad away, back into the depths of the farmhouse. Less neck, less chest. Less front lineman. More clarity at the center of his eyes, though. More quarterback?

Both his brothers seem smaller. Not something he was expecting, to have outgrown his tormentors.

"Goddamn hip shot, no time to aim."

Jude sitting at the kitchen table, chattering into their silence. "Still hit him. Sucker went sidewise real quick."

Evidently Jude had decided the wounded coyote was not worth seeking out, not worth putting out of its misery.

Lenny leans back against the sink, guessing this will be his spot. He's sure not sitting at a table with Jude.

"Off to bed old man."

Frank steers their father toward what used to be the mud room. Had Jude expanded the house, built a goddamn new wing? And what all is involved in getting his dad to bed? Does Frank brace him at the toilet? Brush his dad's teeth? Is this the routine? It sure feels routine. It feels like maybe nightly Frank arrives to ease his dad out of his wheelchair, settle him into bed.

Lenny glances out the kitchen window at Romey, who's nodded off on the porch swing. Math book completely covering her thin chest, pencil lodged deep into the thick kinks corralling her forehead. Fringed go-go boots braced and ready, as if even in sleep she might need to spring her trap and run.

She might.

But for now she's right there. Perfect risk quotient, the tiniest fraction.

Jude's forefinger traces his soft internal rhythm against the table. Sitting there, staring outward but peering inward. A goddamn sipper of port in front of him. Port? It had been a while, but as Lenny recalled, nobody between Chub Ridge and Rosey Face could afford a bottle of port, or would want to, for that matter. Two empty wine glasses reflect sparkly light from a dangly fixture overhead. Jude's invitation to his brothers to sit.

The eldest brother. Lord of their parents' house? Or now, Lenny reminds himself, just his dad's house. One down, one to go?

Frank rounds the corner from the back, opens a high cabinet, feathers his fingers across several glasses, chooses a plastic sports cup. Wolfpack football. They'd all had them as kids, one for each school. Frank's was State. Lenny UNC. Jude, Duke, for god's sake. Lenny realizes he's been gone long enough that both his brothers could've achieved their collegiate dreams. Gained jobs, likely more elevated than landscaper. What did he know?

Frank tilts his plastic cup toward Lenny. Code from their childhood. He wants the sink. Lenny edges over. Does a man ever forget his boyhood code? Frank pours and drains the cup of water, sets the cup in the sink. Thinks better of it, rinses it, dries it, returns it to the back of the cabinet. Pulls a chair out from the table, but doesn't sit. He looks over at Lenny, hesitates. Maybe he wants to say something to his kid brother. After ten years. Maybe there's something to say. Or maybe he's waiting on Lenny to say something. They talked to each other as kids. Little kids. Lenny remembers. But then they just started reacting. Reacting to Jude. And Frank went silent. A silent pawn.

Frank's grip on the back of his chair tightens and he drags it away from the table. Away from Jude. Away from Lenny. He sits, rocks the chair back against the wall. First focuses on Jude, then Lenny. Folds his arms across his chest.

"So, you came back. From the dead."

Lenny stares at his brother. There's just no end to all the *new* around here. Frank not waiting on Jude's cue? Speaking out of turn, going his own direction, in control of his own line of thinking? It was too much to be true. But there it was. A slow dawning swirls inside Lenny's brain, that maybe, just maybe, Frank had done his own running away from their boyhood, without ever leaving home.

"Our Little Lenny was not dead, Frank. That's a fact that I knew all along. And I knew he would return, and if anyone had listened to me they would have known too. I keep telling you, Frank. Mother and Father? Not all that bright. Just adept at keeping the neighbors fooled."

"Dad's a scientist," Frank says quietly. "Mom's a doctor. Are you off your meds?"

Meds? Fun house mirrors and crazy mazes. That's where he's

landed. Just like the state fair the priest shepherded the Block kids through whenever he could afford it.

Jude white knuckles the table. "Father's a doodler, Mother's a shrink in need of a shrink," he says.

Lenny can see that if he's going to stick around long enough to figure out what happened to his mom, he's going to have to fight off every urge to sink back into his own silence, into reliance on his boyhood survival kit. *Appease Jude. Avoid Frank.* All designed to accomplish exactly what it *had* accomplished. Survival. But he'd sworn off survival as a plan of attack. Steering your own life, even at extreme risk, was a different thing altogether than surviving in someone else's.

And he didn't by god intend to go backwards.

He takes a deep breath. Whatever is going on, he's going to have to charge ahead to stay ahead. Fight off the urge to watch, to wait, to survive.

"Dad's in a wheelchair," he says into the space between his brothers. "Mom's headed for a goddamn oven. Exactly why is that?"

Jude shakes his head at the ceiling like he's told it time and time again not to be up there.

"Father is faking," he says. "Am I the only one with the wherewithal to understand? I have told Frank, I have told Mother, I have told the doctors. Clear as day."

Jude looks to Frank, as if for confirmation.

Frank nods.

"Yep, you are indeed off your meds." Then, "Dad was a drunk. Now, he's a depressed drunk. That is, according to Mom. He's numb. The numbness of depression. Look. It's been like this for over a year. The doc says nothing is wrong with him. Physically. So, Mom tried working her magic. As you can imagine. Or maybe you can't imagine, not anymore."

Lenny tries to settle his mind, sort through this information, but Frank, the new take-charge Frank, butts in.

"So, what's with the kid?"

"What's with Mom?" Lenny shoots back. He is not going to talk about Romey. And he's not going to let his brothers talk about her, either. "She was an expert rider. What's with the sudden *accident*?"

Frank grins, lets it linger. Like he's discovered something unfamiliar and of high interest.

Jude presses his palms flat against the table, fingers spread in opposition to the grain of the wood. "Expert riders fall off their horses, Little Lenny" he says.

Lenny looks from brother to brother, trying to steady his own mind by concentrating on this dynamic between them. It's going to be more difficult to stay ahead of them than he thought. Who are they? It's like that game they played as kids, Night Tag. Played in pitch dark, so you never knew who was "it" until it's too late, until you'd been caught.

Frank shifts in his chair.

"So, Lenny, if you're not going to be dead, what are you going to be?"

But he doesn't wait for Lenny to stumble his way into an answer.

"What time will Freta be here in the morning?"

"Day off," Jude says. "Mourning. Grieving. The whole dead-neighbor extravaganza." Then, "We are late on the apples, but the tractor seems to be back in order. I see no reason we can't pick them."

"Jude," Frank says. "Let's get through Mom's service, first."

"Wait," Lenny says. "Freta? You mean Freta Hatmaker? Buford's wife?"

Frank shrugs.

Jude strums his fingers impatiently against the table.

"Yes," he says. "Buford's wife. So, you remember her. Well, tomorrow she will be joining Mother's swarm of uncivilized grieving patients. Do you have any idea how many patients a country shrink accumulates? No, you don't. Because *you've…been…missing*. Well, I will tell you. Enough to trample all Father's flowers into the ground. Cannot walk a straight line, none of them. Bringing in all kinds of pies and casseroles." He gestures toward the refrigerator. "Not an act of kindness, hiring Freta, I'll tell you. Mother…"

He pauses. Drifts into silence. Lenny cannot ever recall Jude drifting.

Frank picks up the story.

"I'd agree. It was more like…well, like a reformation. The same day Freta walked out of county jail, Mom put her on payroll. 'Therapy in action', is what Mom called it."

"Therapy my ass," Jude says.

Pilgrimage my ass. The priest, all those years ago, after the Block fire. Is Lenny trapped in just one big circle?

"Just my opinion, it was an act of desperation," Frank says. "Those two women were devoted to each other. Mirror images."

Mirror images. Lenny grabs at the concept, and it sticks. Freta, to his recollection, travelled down tracks mostly headed for derailment. So did his mom.

"Dad thought it would be a good idea," Frank says. "To hire her, that is. For both Freta and for Mom."

"Freta Hatmaker was in county jail?" Lenny tries to imagine Buford driving his wife home from the county jail, the two of them on his tractor. Freta's long skirt billowing in the breeze.

Frank runs his hands down the legs of his jeans.

"She was," he says. "Swine flu. Hit the hollers here something awful. Did the swine flu hit wherever the hell you were, Lenny?"

Jude knuckles the table, tunes back in.

"Freta smothered her little boys," he says. "I've said that from the beginning. Our mother, in all her psycho wisdom, got her off."

"Some thought that," Franks nods. "But Mom would never have done that. She was up there the day the Hatmaker boys died. It was swine flu. Sheriff Fletcher wouldn't have done that either. Freta wasn't in lockup but two days."

"And they *hired* her? Dad thought *hiring her* would be a good idea?"

Frank drops his chair to all four legs, leans forward, elbows flared.

"You're shitting me, right?"

Lenny startles at the suddenness of Frank's anger. He glances at Jude, but Jude is watching Frank. Not like Jude watched when they were kids. When they were kids, Jude would simply wait for Frank to make a mistake so he could pounce on it. Now it's like he's more wary than anything.

Frank stands and takes a step toward Lenny.

"You take off. You take off on some leisurely, candy-ass, latrine break. Ten years, Lenny. Leaving Mom, leaving Dad."

His hands fly between himself and Jude, once, twice. "Leaving me, Lenny, leaving me. Now, you decide to drop back in? Bless us with your presence? To what? To judge? You can only be shitting me."

The kitchen table seems longer than it had earlier in the evening. Narrower. Jude seems further away. Frank magnified.

Lenny tightens his grip on the counter, pushes off to his full height.

"Leisurely break?"

Lenny wants to throw every last excruciating moment of his boyhood back at them. He left on a dead run from the two men right there in front of him.

But something in Frank's angry eyes stays him.

Anguish? Pain? A pleading of some sort? Is that possible?

A gully forms right down the center of Lenny's plans. A vein opening. Are these the men he left behind? He needs to breathe. He can't afford to lose track, to be swallowed up again.

If you're gonna steer, you can't disappear, Buddo.

But he'd disappeared at every opportunity his entire life.

He turns his back on his brothers, to the kitchen window where Romey stirs on the porch swing, tugs his dad's wool blanket over the math book on her chest and up close under her chin. At some point, she's kicked off her fringed boots and they lie askew on the wooden slats of the porch beneath her.

She should be in bed. Her own bed, in her own home, with her own parents who should be safe parents.

Why does the air have to fit so tight and heavy around a kid's fuzzy head?

Lenny had sworn that, once back on the farm, he would not allow the suffocating air of his own childhood to empty Romey's lungs.

But why had that air been suffocating? What had he wanted back then that if he'd tried harder, he could not get? That's the thing. Could he have tried harder?

Jude's laugh pulls Lenny back. Jude pushing back from the table. Pointing out the window.

"That kid doesn't look much like you," he says. "It may be 1985, Little Lenny, but mixed mutts still don't do too well up in these parts."

Just like that. Mixed mutts.

Romey's bare foot dangles off the swing. The yard beyond is deep black, accentuating the soft yellow cast from the light above her.

Just like that. Breathe in, breathe out.

"Well, Jude," he finally says, his voice sounding a lot more even than he'd expected. "I guess we're just going to have to change things *up in these parts.*"

Jude nods. "I am just saying, it could be rough around here for a child like that."

Lenny takes two steps forward and slams his good hand down on the smooth hewn maple. It stings all the way up his arm and shivers the nerves across the shoulder of his stump.

"*Like that,*" he says, leaning into the table toward Jude. Even more in control than he could've hoped. "She's here, Jude. And she is going to be here. With me. Until I leave. And she is going to be safe."

Jude stands, pushes his chair into the table, brushes his hands across the smooth back rail.

"No, Lenny, she is not," he says. "You know why? Because no child is safe. Not any child, not anywhere. I would think of all people, you would have learned that lesson."

Frank is suddenly up and leaning into the table alongside Lenny.

"And I thought we'd stopped with the lesson shit," he says to their older brother.

Jude bites down on his lower lip. The three of them standing there in the bright light of their dead mother's kitchen.

Franks steadies himself. Half turns to Lenny.

"Why'd you bring her?" he says.

Lenny has two, maybe three inches on Frank. Even more on Jude.

He smiles, surprising himself. And it occurs to him that his brothers might not know he can smile. Did he ever smile as a kid?

But the answer to Frank's question, the oddness of his own reasoning—what other reaction can you have? It's laughable.

"Goddamn," he says, shaking his head. "To protect her."

Hard to believe, but that's as true as true can be. He'd brought Romey here, to this place, to this farm, to protect her. Has he lost his mind?

His brothers' expressions say the exact same thing.

Maybe he has. Lost his mind.

Where the hell you from?

Goddamn priest, all those years ago. Asking that one question which he still can't answer. *Where the hell you from?*

CHAPTER 7

LENNY WAKES LIKE HE'S BEEN JUMP started. He listens for what may have startled him, then realizes it's the quiet of the room, the lack of breathing. The lack of Romey.

She's not in the bunk beside his where he'd tucked her in the night before.

He swings out of bed, dresses. Last night, after he'd finally… what?…grown exhausted in the effort to understand his brothers? He'd roused Romey from her slumber on the porch swing and helped her to bed. Listened to his brothers' vehicles grinding down the farm lane, away, away. It was only a moment that he'd wondered where they were going, then the silence of the farmhouse lured him into a rock-solid sleep with only that wounded coyote pacing through his dreams.

She's not in the bathroom.

She's not in the kitchen with his dad.

"You seen Romey?"

Lenny's father motions with his eyes toward kitchen windows that overlook the front yard.

"Out," his dad manages to say. "Early."

Lenny walks down to the farm lane. Nothing but dusty gravel all the way out to the main road.

The early morning fog hangs just above the fields on the other side of the road. Soon it will clear halfway up Rosey Face and Chub Ridge. Twin waves of haze just racing each other up the peaks, heading for a perfectly clear finish line by noon.

Jude could attempt to change every single structure on the farm, and trade every single animal, but he couldn't change the farm itself, the essence of it. He couldn't change those mountains standing guard, nor the angle of the sun's command of those shadows. He could not shake Lenny's foothold on the farm itself. Nor by god match it.

Why hadn't he thought of this as a kid? Would that have kept him home? Or was it the actual leaving that made it true?

Lenny scans the fields for any sign of unusual movement, like a girl's fuzzy head, just for starters.

The horses amble at the far end of the pasture, the air rising in short bursts from their nostrils. Gentle snorting, not agitated like maybe an eleven-year-old curiosity had recently cut through their territory.

He heads down the hill for the barn, anyway, glances at his watch as if it will read Romey's safety quotient. What's her distance from him right now? And really, what's it matter when measured up against Romey's white hot curiosity?

Lenny strides through the barn doors and down the alley, checking the horse stalls as he goes. The back doors stand wide open, but that's not unusual, as he recalls. He walks out as far as the corral gate. Nothing but dirt clods and cattails running down to the water. The dew is heavy in the autumn grass. If she'd been that way, he would spot her slush path.

Lenny returns back through the barn and trots up the slope toward the farmhouse, squinting into a sun that's rapidly harvesting steam from the slope.

He reaches the yard to find his dad in his wheelchair out on the farmhouse porch, and, hovering over his shoulder, stands his mom's ghost.

Lenny pulls to a quick stop on the walk. Takes a closer look.

Buford's wife, Freta Hatmaker. There's no mistaking her. Still skin and bones, maybe even the same dress hanging at its odd angle, like someone dropped the hem for a taller woman, but just on the one side.

Not like his mom at all, so where is the confusion? Frank's words from last night rumble through his brain. *They were devoted to each other. Mirror images.*

The woman points at Lenny with both hands raised above his dad's head. Her fingers jab in Lenny's direction.

"Dead man," she says. "Dead man."

His dad stirs, shakes his head, but she continues her jabbing.

"You oughtn't to be here," she calls out. "She oughtn't get one back if I can't. She oughtn't. Even now, even now. Getting her own way. Not fair, not fair."

She slips into the house, her thin sheaf of lacey dark hair floating like a miniature wedding gown train behind her.

Lenny climbs the porch steps.

"Jesus, Dad, she's supposed to take care of you?"

His father isn't listening. He's grunting in an effort to speak, raising his eyebrows, pointing with his whole forehead toward the porch swing.

Lenny follows his dad's indications and there, propped on the swing, sits Romey's backpack, zipped up and ready for school. Something he'd missed on his way out earlier.

Of course. She would've been expecting to go to school today. No idea of his own plans. She would've been up early and ready for a front row seat in math class. She should've been waiting right there on the top step. Waiting for Lenny to rouse himself and drive her to school.

What could've distracted her from her mission?

"Where could she be?"

His dad's face mirrors Lenny's question right back at him.

The familiar grind of a tractor on the lane saves Lenny from traveling too far down that dark thought hole of inadequacy, of wondering whether he's any better guardian of Romey's life than Shawnee, or even Raymond, for that matter.

The tractor pops gravel as it lumbers to a stop in front of the farm house.

Buford. Same tractor, same ball cap pulled tight to his sweaty forehead, same skinny kid hanging off the tractor's running board. Only it's not. It's Romey.

She hops off the running board like she's been doing it her whole life, hits the ground in a determined trot before Buford can cut the engine. She makes a bee line up the porch steps and through the screen door, like nobody's standing there wondering where she's been.

Buford slides off the tractor, nods at Lenny's dad, swings the cap off his head in a wide arc, and points it directly at Lenny.

"I sure am hoping you brought back from heaven that whole bunch of money you stole off me," he says. "You been dead long enough to bank beau coups interest."

Lenny's dad opens his mouth. Then shuts it. He looks at Lenny, clearly confused, and likely thinking that Lenny couldn't possibly have stolen anything, especially not from Buford. His dad's hopes and wishes, Jesus.

Lenny wants to say yes, yes he's brought all the cash he'd taken. Every single one and five and ten he grabbed the day he ran away.

But it's not true.

And he wants to ease his dad's mind, say he never stole anything from anybody. Never committed arson, never took a kid from her parents.

And there it is—his own bag of hopes and wishes. Jesus.

Buford's laugh brightens his pale freckles all the way down his forearms.

"Nah, now, Richard," he says. "I'm just funning." He props a boot up on the bottom step, slaps his cap against his thigh to shake loose the dirt. "We both know this boy pays his debts."

He fixes his cap back on his scrubby head, peers out from under the bill at Lenny, the freckles back to pale.

"One way or another, he does."

Romey trots back out of the house, slamming the screen behind her. She slows at the porch steps, balancing a bowl overflowing with corn bread in her small hands, a dripping quart bottle of milk stuck under one arm.

Freta appears behind her, inside the screen, hands knitting, knitting, but yarnless.

Romey picks up speed down the walk.

"Hey, what." Lenny calls.

What? Why can he never form effective words around Romey?

Buford grins. "Hold on now," he calls. "I thought that corn pone was payment for your palatial ride on my farm throne."

Romey keeps her eyes on the bowl in her hands.

"I'll be right back," she calls, taking a sharp left from the drive onto the lane.

Lenny descends the porch steps two at a time.

"Hey, now. Wait."

He starts down the walk, but she turns on him.

"I don't have to wait and you aren't my boss," she says. "This is… this is *my* thing."

"Well…your what thing?"

How much of an eye do you have to keep on an eleven-year-old?

"I found…"

She half turns back toward the lane.

"It's like…like…I found some kittens. Lens, please? I'll be right back. Have you never heard of Fading Kitten Syndrome? Those kittens might *die*. The percentage who do is staggering, Lens."

She doesn't wait for an answer, which Lenny doesn't have anyway.

Down the lane a short way, she turns again to make sure he's not following her.

Then she steps off the gravel road and disappears into the low woods that eventually run up Rosey Face.

CHAPTER 8

LENNY CLIMBS THE PORCH STEPS, TAKES a seat on the cedar bench. Puts one boot up on the split rail. Bench, rail, floor planks, wood so new you could still smell it, harsh and sweet and clean right into the upper reaches of your throat.

He's warned Romey to stay clear of the river, but otherwise he's giving her some rein, mainly to keep her mind off school. He's pretty sure she's checking on her kittens way more than necessary, but since she hasn't mentioned missing math class for the entire day, plus reporting back in with a satisfying frequency, he's letting her have "her thing."

Frank sits opposite him on a matching bench, leaning against the farmhouse in his sock feet, methodically massaging saddle soap into one of his boots with a scrap of cheese cloth. Circling, circling, deepening the copper color of the leather, smoothing it out to the soft outer edges and into the crease of the sole.

His mom's parade of early afternoon mourners has disappeared back down the farm road in their cars, or on foot, slow and easy, like on holiday. Lenny guesses maybe that's exactly what it's like.

An hour stolen from routine. Might as well take your time. What would his mom think about this formal procession of grief, the solemn condolences of her patients and neighbors, her townspeople? She wouldn't notice them, he'll take a guess. She'd look right past them, every one of them. Even family. She'd be thinking on the next thing. He imagines her up in heaven—*heaven, wherever the hell that is*, she would often whisper in church. Question marks all over her face.

What's next, what's next?

Frank sets aside one boot, picks up the other. He's whistling, low, barely audible. A harsh, off kilter tune just for himself. Lenny can never, ever recall Frank whistling. Who is this man? Where is the boy of brute force he left behind? Frank, the keeper of all Jude's nasty promises.

Lenny plucks an angled splinter from the porch rail.

"What happened to Mom, Frank?"

Frank's whistle fizzles. His fingers pause, then continue their circuitous route along the boot wedged between his knees.

"Well now, little prodigal brother. First off, good morning. Second, it's no big secret. She fell off her mare, busted her neck. Jude found her."

Frank repositions the boot for a better angle down the shaft.

"And just so we're clear, and even though Jude thinks he's King Knowledge, I never fell for Dad's 'dead story', either. Dad just made up that 'dead son' shit."

"And why would he do that?"

"He hardly even looked for you, Lenny. Almost like he was… giddy? Sure, once he saw the skiff was missing, he trotted out the drowned-son story, but you could tell he didn't believe it. When they called off the search? He seemed more than relieved. So, yeah…his favorite son…why indeed?"

Lenny's not liking the turn of the conversation. But he has to admit, his long-ago escape from the farm had indeed seemed too easy. He thinks back to his dad's word map, the river route, told to Lenny over and over as the two of them fished the waters surrounding the farm. Their big adventure to the Atlantic, via the French Broad, the Swannanoa, the lakes near Charlotte, him repeating every single portage, over and over. Eventually, floating under that Copper River Bridge.

Had there been more reason to his dad's word maps than he'd realized?

Was inviting your youngest child to leave for good the only clear survival path a father could dream up for his son? For himself? How long had it taken his father to create such an enticing word map? How many fishing trips had the two of them dreamed their way down rivers and lakes and tributaries and sailed directly into the Atlantic Ocean before his plan finally took hold? Before the way was paved for his son to escape? Like some fathers worked three jobs so their kids can finally head off to Ivy League.

Lenny rolls the splinter between his finger and thumb.

"Jude was with her. When she fell, right?"

Frank pauses to consider Lenny.

"Nope, nope, that's where you're wrong, little brother. Jude *found* her. She never came back from her ride across the ridge that afternoon. Freta kept on and on about it, your mother this your mother that, your-mother-your-mother-your-mother, just how Freta does, until Jude finally rode out to have a look for himself. Doc said she'd been dead a while."

Snake! Lenny attempts to back his cattle prod story out of his mind. *Jude reaching, reaching for the mare's flank. In the underpass of the hemlock grove.*

How would Frank know whether Jude was there or not?

"Just how long is a while?"

Frank slants the boot shaft down, takes an end of the cloth in each hand and begins a rapid back and forth buff across the toe.

"I don't ever recall you being so inquisitive," he says. "In fact, there were times I thought you'd been birthed without vocal chords."

Lenny flicks the splinter over the porch rail toward the yard.

"I could say the same for you."

Frank nods, as if a truce has been reached.

"Maybe four, five hours," he says. "Doc Holloway guessed most of the afternoon. Must've spooked the hell out of the mare. Horse was gone for hours."

"For hours? How many hours? You'd think the mare would beat everybody back to the barn."

Frank stands the boot next to its mate. Drapes the rag over one knee, leans back on the bench, rests his head back against the farmhouse wall.

"Yep. Weird, huh? Came back without her saddle, and from the looks of her flank, probably rubbed it clear on a tree, or a post, or whatnot. She was a bit torn up. Her barrel raw. Spooked by death, just like the rest of us. I'm just guessing though."

Frank cuts his eyes to Lenny.

"Maybe you should've stayed put here, Lenny, or stayed put there, over in the big city."

"You mean…I mean—"

Frank leans forward, forearms on knees.

"I mean Jude. You escape, right? You get away. Do you understand what this means? This means you'd *won*. You *won*, Lenny. Having never won a goddamn battle in your short life, you *win the war*. And Jude was *pissed*. So, it was my fault. For a while. Yeah, my fault."

Frank lifts his hands to stay any rebuttal.

"He accused me of helping you escape. Once Dad started acting all thrilled-weird about you disappearing, that is. Sent Mom off her rocker, even more so than *before* you left, I know that's hard to believe. Charging up and down the valley knocking on doors, obsessively saving people by day, cutting herself up by night. If you get to the morgue before the cremation, check out her arms. Dad drinking himself comatose. And what the hell, now you *show back up*? All shiny and new, dragging yet another kid behind you? I'm guessing you expect us to take care of her too?"

Another kid?

"Come on, Frank…you know why I left."

"But you *left*. And yeah, I guess I do know. What I don't know, and what is most interesting to me now, *is why you came back*. You escaped, Lenny. You escaped. Why the hell would you come back?"

"I came back to find out what happened to Mom. That's it. Once I'm straight on that, I'm out of here."

"And you are starting with Jude? Look, he's medicated. Or at least he *was* medicated. Thanks to our maternal shrink, at least until she fell off her horse, he *was* gaining control. *Had* gained control. I guess with her gone now, who knows?"

"Well, maybe Jude didn't like being medicated, Frank. Maybe Jude didn't like seeing things clear and shiny just like Mom *prescribed* for him. And by my eyes, this place doesn't look like the work of the level-headed. Who refurbished the farmhouse? Paved the walkways? Replaced the fence lines? It's turned into a goddamn gentleman's ranch, Frank. Did Dad want all this? Did Mom? Did you? Did Jude pay for all this? Was this house Jude's new toy? Was Mom? And now that she's gone, is Dad?"

Frank slips the rag from his knee, winds it around his hand, unfurls it. Repeats.

"Okay, yes, Jude pays for all of it. I don't see what's so bad about that. It's not like it's hurting anything."

"And how does he pay for it?"

"Pharmaceuticals. Even you should've guessed that. Makes a boat load of green, and everybody up and down this valley loves him for it. Or hates him for it. Because he has exactly what they need. Or what they wish they didn't need. But what the hell? Everybody's getting their healing."

He pauses, then drives his point home, although it seems to Lenny he's more resigned than agitated.

"Of course, Lenny, if you'd stuck around, it's possible things would be different."

"And it's possible that I would be dead. You never considered leaving?"

Frank lays the cloth aside and wipes the tips of his fingers down his pant legs before massaging them into his temples.

"That girl of yours is a bit wild-assed," he says. "But you'd know that, I'm guessing. And you'd know, I'm guessing, that even hungry kittens probably are not eating leftover beans, right?"

Lenny hadn't paid much attention to what Romey was dragging out of the farmhouse kitchen. He'd just been glad of her new focus. Maybe it was time to find out about those kittens. And try a new distraction. Teach her how to track. And shoot. And ride.

But he's got one more line of questioning for Frank.

"So, Glenna Rader," he says. "She's still in this general area?"

Frank picks up the disk of saddle soap, tosses it into a bucket. Follows it with the rag.

"Oh, yeah. She is. Working her dad's farm. He passed a few years back, before she married Max. You remember Max?" Frank laughs. "Maybe Max? You remember those lane kids?"

Maybe Max. Of course, he remembers Maybe Max. Always asking questions that nobody ever wanted to answer, so they'd just resort to the answer that might shut him up: *Yeah, maybe Max.*

Max's questions had a way of roughing up Lenny's thought patterns, but in a good way. Like the time they were down back of the barn after one of those days-on-end mountain deluges. The rain had cleared, so they were down at the bloated river, watching a bloated cow float by. Huge, dead, hide stretched to peeling.

Maybe Max observed that cow with its hooves reaching out to them, toward shore, its head submerged. Lenny thinking what all can happen to a farm in a flood. Maybe Max's mind running off sidewise.

"Full of gas, ain't she," he'd said.

Lenny thought a moment, then nodded. Eddies caressing the hide no different than they would a canoe.

"Well, now" Maybe Max said. "You reckon that gas could be useful? Reckon we could harness such a thing?"

Useful? A cow full of gas?

Lenny had thought about that for a minute, then said, "Maybe Max."

But he'd really meant it, *maybe Max*.

Evidently, Glenna, too, had found intrigue in Maybe Max's offbeat brainwaves.

Lenny smiles, surprising himself that it's a real smile, not a cover, but also not knowing whether it's the sudden memory of Maybe Max or the thought of Glenna marrying Maybe Max that brings it on.

A pleasant pain? An entertaining hurt?

"I do," he says. "I do remember Maybe Max. And they work the farm?"

"Yep. Glenna does. She works that farm. Along with that kid of hers."

Frank holds Lenny's eyes. "A boy. All grown up now. Just about the age of your girl. Name's Richard. Ricky. Yep, kid's name is Ricky."

Frank's focus broadens to scout the lane behind Lenny.

"Well, well," he says. "Speak of the she-devil. Looks like your little wild-ass finally decided to bring her kittens home."

CHAPTER 9

ROMEY'S SMALL HAND IS TUCKED INSIDE an ancient claw attached to an ancient lizard walking on two legs. The two of them, hand in hand, make their way down the road toward the farmhouse. Romey, soaking wet. River water hesitating along her fringed cutoffs before dripping down her bare legs.

"Stray picking up a stray," Frank murmurs. He tugs on his freshly polished boots, reaches under the porch bench and slides out his .22, hefts it onto his lap.

Jesus couldn't've planned it better. Jesus, Jesus.

Romey, who, okay admit it, he'd kidnapped yesterday and who's stitched solidly across the entirety of his heart, is latched onto the old geezer out on the farm road, latched to the priest, to Father Damien, the scaly-ass reptile scrambling and practically skipping along the lane trying to keep up with Romey's short legs.

Talking. The two of them, talking.

Or, now that Lenny's focusing, it's Romey doing the talking, while the lizard's sharp green eyes scan the landscape, sure at any moment to catch hold of the one-armed man on the farmhouse porch. Lenny feels himself rising, expanding to goddamn gargantuan proportions. Jesus. Rising into the clouds clear above the farm like a giant B-Wing Fighter ready to strafe flames over the whole goddamn mess.

He tries releasing as much air from his lungs as possible, then lifts his one good hand to stay Frank who's shifting into a half stand and shouldering his rifle. Frank's movement sure enough connects the priest with the farmhouse porch, with Frank, then with Lenny's stump.

Never a hitch in the old man's trot, never a falter of his ancient ear inclined toward Romey's lilting chatter.

"She's no stray," Lenny murmurs back at Frank. But really, would those words ever be true for Romey? Or, for him?

Frank eases over and leans his hips into the porch rail beside Lenny, wedges his rifle under one arm, barrel down.

She's no stray, she's no stray, Lenny repeats to himself. His legs kick into gear and he's down the porch steps and headed for the road, as Romey's slender fingers pull away from the old man's claw. It takes her longer to disengage than Lenny would like. Skipping forward, still connected, her arm lifts the priest's arm so that they make a perfect arc. Finally free, she runs toward Lenny, her hazy wet kinks romping around her eyes. She slows as she nears, both palms toward him like a shield.

"I know, Lens, I know. You don't have to say. I lied, that's all."

The priest stops out on the road, his fingers spinning air loops at his waist, skinny hips rocking forward, back, forward, back.

A man fresh from prison. Sizing up the farmhouse. Sizing up Lenny. Calculating.

"It's not kittens, Lens, I know, but it's even better. *Better* than *kittens.*"

"What the hell have you been doing?" Lenny says.

"Please, Lens—"

She stops, her slate eyes catching on that he's not talking to her. She glances back at the priest. Lenny's heart pulls toward her as she wedges her fists into the pockets of her cutoffs and solidifies into the wary but practiced stone camouflage.

In three quick strides Lenny closes his distance to her.

"What the hell?" he says again.

The priest's fingers stop their air knitting, flutter a moment before drifting to his chest in prayerful concentration.

"Think ye on this!" the old man calls out, all preacher-mode like he's expecting crosses to sprout up from the dirt at his feet. "Just shy a ten year. That's right! Just shy a ten year, we been held in the righteous arms of our Lord's all-knowing enforcers of institutionalized behavior."

Frank stirs, treads light as he descends the porch steps.

"You mean prison," Lenny says.

His brother's presence, so sudden and so close behind him, sends memories sliding into the farmhouse yard, distracting Lenny, interrupting his defensive intentions. Frank hovering. Frank close at hand whenever shit went down.

"Think ye! So much time to ponder. Ten years! Ten brain-contorting years!"

The old man's hands unfold to display the height and length of Romey's thin frame.

"Until behold. One vision, one small yet powerful vision-vision appears afore ye!"

The geezer's crevassed brow smooths clear down through his grizzly jaw. His voice drops. Like he's got secrets to tell.

"Angel saved my cock-eyed ass, that's what. Ask her, ask the heavenly savior afore ye."

The priest's voice splits into an empty gargle.

"She's not shy! Ask her but what she saved my ass."

Romey's clothes cling to her. She pulls her hands from her pockets to wring water from the tail of her t-shirt. She releases her shirt, which continues to drip onto her bare feet. Her fuzzy hair sparkles, her face shines clean and taut from the sun toasting her skin.

Lenny closes his eyes for a second. Too many tangled neurons to pull straight.

"Why are you soaked?" he finally says. "I told you to not to go near the river."

Romey stands on tiptoe and whispers, "I been practicing. I'm getting better at it. I wanted to surprise you, Lens. And I'm sorry I lied about the kittens."

Practicing. Lenny lets the word weave in and out among the twisting maze of his brain. Dive down into this synapse—does this make sense to you, buddy? No? Climb back out, dive into another.

"I told you to stay away from that river."

Her thin hands fan out, fingers gently wiggling skyward like she's calling for rain.

"I haven't been in the river," she says. "Lens. I was—"

"You're soaked, Romey. It's kind of obvious where you've been. Can you even swim?"

For a moment she appears confused, then regains her edge.

"You did tell me, Lens, you did. And I haven't...well, whether I was or was not in the river, I didn't think you'd mind. Not for the practicing part. I'm really good at it. Mr. Damien was right there; he was right next to me the whole time."

The priest spits to the side of the road.

"Right there the whole time, motherfucker," he chokes out. "Repaying an angel's kindness. I'm a firm believer in the God of Debts. Aren't you a fan of the God of Debts, son?"

Practicing.

"I'll ask you one more time," Lenny says to the priest. "What the hell have you been doing?"

The priest unties his rope belt, re-cinches it high and tight, causing his pants to balloon out from his skinny waist. His pockets disappear beneath the rope.

"Been doing like I always done, son. Wandering the goddamn wilderness. Forty days-forty nights."

He cocks his head, peers at Lenny.

"Just like you? Yes-yes just like you. You been a wandering too, I do know that much. Yes, I do surely-surely."

Romey steps away from Lenny.

"Lens, please, this will take care of everything. I won't have to worry no more about…well, if I practice hard enough, you know…"

She drops her voice. "You know my separate womb creature… well, it won't run off—it won't go wandering. And that means I won't have to chase it up and down city streets like Shawnee says I might. *Please.*"

"What the hell." Frank breathes the words in from behind, connects them just at the base of Lenny's hairline.

"Angel's making sense," says the priest. "Better listen up, *Lens.*"

"Practicing *for what*, Romey?"

Lenny's afraid that if he looks at the priest now, he'll have to wrestle the .22 out of his brother's hands and shoot the old man. He keeps his eyes steady on Romey, watches her skinny fingers find his stump to nip at his elbow seam.

"Romey," he says.

She stops her stitching and holds firm to his stump.

"Baptizing, Lens. He's going to baptize me."

When Lenny doesn't respond, she repeats herself.

"Baptizing. You know about that, right? He's a qualified baptizer!"

Qualified baptizer.

Baptize Romey? Snatch up her eleven-year-old trust? Shove it under water? Restrain it there? Make her hold her breath *and* her faith *and* her hope—her hope that anyone can vanquish her nightmares, her goddamn womb demons?

Romey's fingers slide away as Lenny lifts his stump to point at the priest. It's been a long, long time since he forgot there were no fingers there to finish the job.

The priest takes a small step backward, off-balance. Suddenly unsteady.

Not something Lenny expects, or remembers, the priest off balance.

Lenny can't think about that right now. He can't think about what prison might do to a pious lizard-man already flush in decades.

Jesus, what he did to the priest. What he did to the old man's land, his Rectory, his church. What he did. You can never win a fight after such a thing. Sure, he'd been young, just fourteen, and convinced there was only the one way out. But nobody deserves what he'd done to the priest.

And now? Now, whatever he does to the priest, must run through Romey, or through Romey's faith in him, or a thing like faith, a thing he didn't know he'd been asking for, but had only recently been given. Or, not given. More like allowed to test. Her faith in him.

The priest seems to sense his hesitation. Like a deer you're not going to shoot, a deer finding it's balance, front hooves fanning the air, turning, bolting.

"Just repaying her kindness," the old man croaks. "Just repaying. Teaching her the ways of the wilderness. So to speak."

Yes, the old man can smell it, Lenny's guilt, and cranks up his preacher volume.

"She pretty up to speed on those streets. You would a known about that, right? You would a known all about her and those city streets. But come to find out," hitching his pants even higher, "come to find out, she ain't never been baptized! I been. I been baptized! By both water and *by fire.* Son? You ever been *baptized*?"

By fire.

What he did to the priest.

Frank breathing behind him, like on the barn roof, breathing, waiting, waiting for the *Go*.

Romey edges closer.

Lenny drops his stump to his side. "Don't…take her…into the water."

The lameness of those words, the lameness of his authority. But he presses on.

"Get out…just…go."

Romey again takes hold of Lenny's stump, shakes it harder than he imagined her capable.

"You can't talk to Mr. Damien like that," she says.

She shakes him again, then whispers, "Ain't you been baptized, Lens."

The thing is, she's not asking him. She's telling him, and he's not sure he's capable of sorting that out.

Lenny reaches with his good arm to pull her head in and the water from her hair soaks cold through his shirt and against his belly.

"Since when did you start with the 'ain't' shit," he whispers.

Had he ever been baptized? And what would that buy? A new life? A free pass to commit any sin of his choosing?

Then yes, maybe. Maybe his whole life up to now was just one baptism after the other.

Fail, run, fail, run.

Would he fail Romey? And if so, would he run?

Romey tries to look at him but has to squeeze her eyes shut against the low, evening sun behind him. In just minutes, that sun will drop behind the mountains and ease the valley toward dark.

"I'm sorry you ain't been baptized," she whispers.

The safety flicks off Frank's rifle, barrel still low, and he steps up beside Lenny.

"Get on out, old man," Frank says. "We're done here."

The priest shakes his head, spits again.

"Can't do that, big brother. You're the big brother, right?"

He points at Romey.

"Girl wants a baptism. Ask her your own self. Heavy responsibility done been laid upon these shoulders. All debts shall be repaid."

He nods toward the farmhouse, and his voice rises.

"Fight fire with fire. *All debts*!"

Frank turns to Lenny. Questioning. Willing logic. But all Lenny can do is return his brother's confusion. Whose side will you be on, Frank? Where will you land? Where does a brother land when both sides blow shit? That's always been the question.

Had Frank been asking himself that same question? Had Lenny, consumed with his own pain, not taken care to notice Frank's?

Frank suddenly refocuses over Lenny's shoulder, the confusion in his eyes shifting to cold determination.

Lenny pulls Romey away and ducks as his brother swings the shotgun up to his shoulder and goes still, long barrel aimed for the woods behind them.

"There he is," Frank whispers.

Lenny turns toward the woods and sure enough, through the web of scatter-leaved November branches, ears back, half-crouched, a coyote paces. Its gait ginger, newly sore. So. The same coyote Jude shot and missed badly the night before. Circling back.

Lenny peers through the leaves. He'd seen it before.

A wild animal, wounded, knowing, yet circling back toward the source of its own misery.

Pausing there in mid-stride, ears up, paw up, head squared off to face a twitching trigger finger. Hell, if that wasn't the way of the wounded.

"Do it," Lenny says.

Frank fires and the coyote leaps upward and takes off in a crouched, sidewinding run through the thickets parallel to the fence line.

A miss.

Without looking at Frank, Lenny reaches for the rifle and Frank puts it into his hand, no hesitation. Like maybe there's not such a wide gulf between them, not as wide as Lenny had always thought. Like maybe there's a connection stronger between them than just their two hands now momentarily connected by inches of heated steel.

With his good hand, Lenny jams the rifle butt into the crease of his stump shoulder and fights those thoughts, those hopes, back down. That's not why he's here. Frank was never on his side.

Romey's hands fly up to cover her ears, and once again Lenny regrets all that she's been through, all that she understands, all the crap to which she is clearly resigned.

Lenny scans right for a clearing in the brush and waits for the coyote to squib into it.

He can't recall the last time he held a rifle, but the motions learned as a one-armed kid aren't easily forgotten. His good hand settles underneath to steady the barrel, his thumb slides up against the trigger.

Always a trick shot. Folks loved it back then.

Lenny sucks his breath in, fires, and drops the coyote. A clean shot, straight through the ear.

He waits for movement, starts toward the fence to make sure.

Then remembers the priest. Then remembers Romey. Her hands still up over her ears, eyes wide, staring at the empty clearing in the woods.

She turns to Lenny.

"That was so fast," she whispers.

Lenny nods.

Yes. Yes, it happens fast.

Frank reaches for the rifle and heads for the woods, but freezes as the priest recovers himself.

"God almighty!" the priest calls out. "Another debt paid!"

The old man turns his back to them and slowly unfolds his arms toward the mountains, tattered sleeves exposing bony elbows anoint the fields across the road; quivering wrists praise the pasture running down to the river; warped fingers swoop out and up the slopes of Rosey Face and Chub Ridge. He rocks his withered head to the sky and lets his words drop easy. Just breathing words. Just letting the mountain air preach.

"Yea, we gonna wash her sins clean in those *forever* waters, eye for eye, like all saviors, little girl gonna pass through that gateway to the holy-holy spirit, she gonna set all our sins right, original and personal, a rebirth outpouring, water gonna run *dee*p over that head a hers, yea, when debts weigh heavy, the good Lord, the Angel of Mercy, the Maid of Heaven. Whoever. They do provide."

Lenny thinks he hears, *Atonement's coming, son*, as the old man scuttles back down the road, the sun shimmering him into a silver mirage.

CHAPTER 10

LENNY'S CHEST TIGHTENS. THE PORCH IS too crowded with pulsating grief, faces like faded memories, recognizable but locked in their past, immeasurable. Mourners, those constant reminders of your most vulnerable heart space, those ghosts you wager will rip the gash wider but could just as likely stitch it up neat, drift into the farm yard.

How'd all these people connect to his mother? The banker, Sam Vaughn, his graying hair curling down inside his pressed collar. Black jacket, black shirt, black tie. A business relation? Social? Or was he a patient? The Lowells certainly were. They'd had that one son, the one who fell from the Gorge Bridge. Jude, Jude, your unmatched ability to witness trouble, that scene too. Buford brought his father-in-law down from Rosey Face, a long haul, Old Man Roberson now talking gibberish to anyone who will listen. It had taken some minutes before the old bear lumbered over and practically choked Lenny. Buford behind him, shaking his head, still jostling him, *You ain't dead—you ain't dead which means you goddamn owe me*, but then growing uncharacteristically solemn,

Your mom always listened, Lenny. Always. I guess I never thanked her enough.

His mom the shrink. He'd known that families up and down the valley counted on her. But all these connections? Swarms of concerned eyes, of careful hands setting out their casseroles, just as Jude said they would, their pies, their warm bread. The porch rail, the kitchen counter, gradually engulfed in live plants. No cut flowers for his mom. Only fauna from hard tilled soil that could be re-planted, re-birthed. Note cards piled up on the telephone table underneath the stairs. City and valley folks alike wiped their palms down their pants and skirts and kicked dirt from their shoes as they touch their neighbors to file up the porch steps, put a hand on his dad's shoulder, pull Jude aside to talk in low voices, shake hands with Frank.

Lenny tacks from the knot of shared sorrow. He doesn't want to talk about his mom, not to townsfolk, not to farmers, not to anyone. For sure he doesn't want to be the focus of their conversations. *Is that you, Lenny? Lenny! Son, what the hell?* But eventually eyes will quietly shift to his shaved off elbow and it will betray him. How many one-armed men would you find on this particular porch? Mourning this particular woman. Mourning Dr. Lizzy.

He thinks, not for the first time, that wishing to disappear should make it so.

He needs air.

He'd slept restlessly last night, unable to drift the priest back down the farm road and out of the valley. Evaporate him, make him just a wisp of a bad dream that dissipates before you can grasp its true meaning. He could come close, if it weren't for Romey insisting the old man would be back to deliver on his promise.

"You'll see, Lens. It'll work. Maybe you should practice, too. We could practice together."

And on and on.

Romey has retreated to the porch swing with her trusty No. 2 pencil and her math book. Working ahead. He's going to have to break the school news to her. Eventually. If he can breathe for just five minutes. Breathing around the farm is proving more difficult as time passes. The mountains seem bigger, but everything else has shrunk. The driveway is shorter, the front yard a patch compared to his memory. Did he and his brothers, Glenna and all the lane kids, Max and his sisters, really play Night Tag in such a small space between the road and the house? Ten years. Does each year forward shrink the year behind you?

He rounds the corner of the yard and heads for his mother's garden, wondering if it's still there, wild and out-of-control, his mom's hallowed ground.

Lizzy's Therapy Dirt his dad called it.

It's still there. And growing right out of the center, right there in the brilliant midday sun, stands his mom. Dead center of her little plot. Where he'd seen her a million times, long skirt billowing, curly long hair restless even without the slight breeze blowing her way.

But of course, it cannot be his mother. So instead, it's Freta Hatmaker.

Before he can turn and head another direction, she spots him, freezes him with her frantic arms. Beckons him. Or maybe she's just waving to the gods in her head. It's difficult to tell.

Unable to shake off the mores of his childhood, even after all these years, or more likely out of respect for Buford, he heeds her call.

The garden is enclosed by a truncated wooden fence, no more than a foot high. Jude's work? Has to be. His mom had been satisfied with just enough chicken wire to keep the rabbits at bay. Only

Jude would think of a miniature picket fence, and then paint it goddamn white.

Lenny steps over the barrier, reaches low to strip a handful of coarse foxglove seeds from their stalk, lets them float ahead of his approach to Freta, her arms still a slow-motion windmill.

"I done seen you," she calls, her voice hoarse, like maybe it's not yet warmed up for the afternoon. "You not dead. You the littlest boy, a tadpole. That's right." Her arms drop to her sides, hands smoothing the off-kilter dress tight to her legs, then releasing. Smooth and release. Smooth and release.

Lenny stops a few yards away. The garden has gone to seed, but the beds are still defined, the burdock, the yellow dock, the sarsaparilla, his mom's continued attempts at medicinal root healing, he guesses, now dying back. Probably the garden had been tended this past summer. Probably his mom tended it. For enjoyment? For therapy? He'd never know, there was no bridge back.

Lenny glances down. His mom's garden brings to mind the shed behind the priest's Rectory. What had happened to that shed over the years, with the priest in prison? Were the Celebrants still sweating, summer after summer, over the flat pans of peas and sliced tomatoes, okra, the assorted beans and bags of basil, oregano? Who would orchestrate? Artemis…Marva? Had she replaced the cannabis with legitimate crops? Or had his juvenile pyro rage burned all that hope to the ground?

Freta Hatmaker's bare legs. Bare, dirty feet. His own pants legs covered in hitchhikers.

"Mrs. Hatmaker," he says.

She stares at his stump, her smile frozen where a real mouth with a real expression should be. What on earth could Freta Hatmaker possibly accomplish for his parents?

"I remember that." She points to his stump. "That weren't no accident, either, I'll say it. I'll say it again and again, I will."

Lenny studies her frozen lips. His parents had clung to the story of his stump being accident, and he'd never expected to hear anyone say different. It surprises him that he doesn't much like the sound of it being said different, not out loud by anyone who wasn't there.

"I remember you with my little boys," she says. Her face lightens, thaws a little, but still a face that could crack if you touched it. "You remember my boys?"

"Yes," he says. "Yes, I do." Though he can only remember the heat from their bodies, snuggled close to their rangy dogs, heat radiating from under the Hatmaker's broken porch anchoring their broken farm. As kids, he'd hid under there with them, waiting for his mom to tend to Freta.

Her eyes, still light, suddenly drain tears. Like someone's slowly dripping water over a plastic happy mask.

"Your mother left me," she says. "I loved her. Almost as much as your daddy loved her. Almost. You hear about that? You hear about my boys?"

"I...yes ma'am," he says. "I'm...I'm real sorry."

She peers at him, eyes swimming.

"No, you ain't," she says. "You don't know sorry."

She glances again at his stump.

"Well, maybe you do, some. But you don't know truly sorry. Buford's got that suspicious head, mighty suspicious, and once somebody's grow'd suspicious, there's nothing to do about it. But your mother, she know'd *everything* all along. Took all my sorrows onto her shoulders. And she took all my sorrows directly to her grave."

Her tears finish off in a quick drip from her chin to her chest. She dabs the salty drops with her apron.

"I just hated your mother. Did you know about that? What was your name again?"

Lenny glances around. Wouldn't Buford stay close, ready to gather in his wife?

"Lenny," he says. "My name's Lenny."

"I know that. Don't tell me things I know. Just like your mother."

She ducks and nods her head, like there's something on the ground between the two of them that she intends to keep an eye on.

"Little Lenny this, Little Lenny that. Your mother never stops. Never, never, never stops. I could just not get her to stop."

Freta glances up at him, her hands holding on to each other like maybe if they let go, her body would split and fly off in opposite directions.

"I help," she says. "Your daddy pays me."

Lenny thinks he hears her giggle. Slowly she releases her hands from their grip on each other, lifts the sides of her dress, high steps to the edge of the garden then over the miniature picket fence. Before reaching the road, she turns back to him.

"You find that saddle?"

Her ragged voice even more tattered with distance.

Saddle? Lenny, not wanting to appear impolite, not wanting to just stand there and gape at her, shrugs.

"Well, you will," she says. "Just like she found my boys. You will."

From the corner of the house, Buford, as sturdy as ever, trots to catch up with his wife before she swirls up onto the running board of his tractor. Buford climbs up behind the wheel. With one hand he cranks the engine and with the other he holds his wife steady.

CHAPTER 11

ROMEY WADES RIGHT INTO THE RIVER. No hesitation. No looking back to see if Lenny would stop her. Directly up to her thighs, the eddies swirling and cutting dark over the fringe of her shorts. The boy wades in behind her, her darker skin like his shadow leading him across the river, his hands in his pockets, sure of himself, steady in the current. They move together, now sidestepping against the gentle updraft. Like they know each other, which they don't. Like they know the capricious nature of the water tugging at their knees, which she doesn't. Like they think the land stretching out on the other side of the river is theirs, and the mountains, Rosey Face and Chub Ridge, even in their glare, belong to them.

From where Lenny stands atop the hill leading down to the river, Romey and the boy should be dots on the landscape. But they are all he can see.

Sure enough, Romey lurches in the current, loses her footing, but the boy reaches to steady her. How would she know how to swim? It's not like they teach freestyle along the back alleys of the city. He tries to imagine Shawnee or Raymond signing Romey up for swim lessons. Doesn't track.

The boy turns, his long dark hair catching sunlight. He hops on one foot, kicking into the reeds that grow out from the bank. He lets his bare toes do most of the work but eventually bends and digs from the mud what appears to be a washed-out pop bottle. Romey's curiosity is caught. The boy holds the bottle high to dump its sludge into the river between them. She reaches for the vessel, then pulls back, her hands out and imploring the boy to wait. She wades toward shore, tipping this way and that, and once out, runs halfway up the bank to where she'd dropped her backpack.

Romey does not look up to where Lenny waits on top of the hill. Maybe she doesn't realize he's followed them, although he's been behind them from the moment the boy's family car rolled its slow mourner's pace down the farm lane and into the drive. The boy bursting from the backseat, then the woman emerging from the front passenger side, the woman he could not let himself recognize, not yet, and forget all that anyway, because Romey immediately zeroed in on the boy and they were gone. How do kids do that? Fast friends on first sighting. Lenny had waited there, watching. Waiting for the woman to look up to meet Lenny's eyes, but she didn't and he'd turned and followed the kids across the hillside until the land bent toward the shimmering water.

Romey sits in the dirt of the bank, pulls out her trusty No. 2 pencil along with her composition book. Writes, book propped on knees, like maybe she needs to break the pencil. It's possible she's completely forgotten Lenny, the way kids forget their parents until some surprising but urgent need arises. More probably, and he and Romey have this in common, the two of them, and likely it's their draw to each other: she just doesn't expect anyone to be watching.

It doesn't take her long. She rips the page from its mooring, folds it into a tiny square, tucks her pencil and composition book back into the pack, and trots down into the water where the boy is dunking the bottle through the ripples and hurling ropes of clean river through the air.

Romey and the boy confer, then he hands her the bottle and trudges back against the current until he hits the mudflats and a shank of cattails. He understands the river, sure he does. Lenny's own memories nettle the boy into sharper focus. His straight black hair reminds him of Jude; the easy shoulder set, of Frank. The boy pulls a pocketknife from his cutoffs and slices a small plug from the thick burnt-amber sausage of a cattail. He examines the plug, discards it, cuts another. When he's satisfied, he grips the side of his shorts and slices denim to encase the stamen plug, then rips the rest of the sturdy plant from its mud bedding. Jaunts back downstream to Romey, letting the current push him toward her, the long plant winding past him atop the water, racing him downriver.

The buoyancy of cattails. *Submerge that sucker for a hundred hours, Buddo, it'll pop right back up. Can't be sunk.* Growing up, they'd built rafts with the plant, devised tiny floating battleships that his mom then used for table displays. The fluff, his dad swore, had insulated vests and filled bellies toward the end of WWII.

Romey shoves her folded note into the opening of the bottle then plugs it with the boy's offering, as if this were a process long memorized and ritualized for great purpose between them. Romey holds the bottle horizontal over the water while the boy pulls apart the plant idling around their knees and wends thin strips to encase the vessel, knotting them off at the neck.

Of course. A note in a bottle.

Anyone out there?

Cast it out. What river kid hasn't dreamed it? He could've tried that a million times himself.

The boy takes the bottle and again examines his work, holds it out to Romey. She shakes her head quickly and gestures to the river. Without hesitation and without ever looking into the bottle or asking any questions the boy cocks his arm and flings the bottle in a high arc so that it lands dead center of the river, sinks, bounces back up, and rotates bottom forward to begin its pilgrimage downstream.

What's the message? Did she tell the boy the message? It takes Lenny a few moments before he realizes that he's letting his mind tack. He's steering to avoid the head wind. The real question is, who's the message for? Who would Romey try to reach? Surely not Raymond, a father who takes better care of his pressed shirts than he ever did Romey. And any kid could figure out Shawnee. That couldn't be more obvious. But, when he thinks about it, has he ever heard Romey say one negative word about her mother?

That's the sorry thing about kids. Compelled to dream up hope. He'd bet Romey is sending a message to Shawnee. That's how kids think. If you have a plan, then the plan should work, right? Inside her tousled head, she's figuring furiously that she will surely re-couple them, Raymond and Shawnee, and then—she'd be a part of that re-coupling, right? An inseparable bond. The ribbon that wrapped up their family package. Dear Mom and Dad.

What the hell. Why not?

He wishes he could tell her…what? That she's the only one of those three interested in a golden dream package? That family packages, like Santa, simply don't exist? Or, if they exist, you don't want to be getting all possessive and certain? You don't want to rely on bows staying tied? Bows don't stay tied. Bows get ripped off. For sure, you don't want to go trying to *be the ribbon.*

Lenny doesn't notice the kids heading toward him until they are running past him, heading for the farmhouse. He doesn't follow them. Hell no. She certainly wasn't tossing a message in a bottle for him. He's not following them, to hell with that.

Which is why, when Romey falls from the barn roof, *a thump and a crack*, Lenny isn't there to catch her.

CHAPTER 12

He'd peeled off from the kids as they merged into the loosening knots of mourners in the yard, peeled off, away from the possibility of running into Jude or Frank, his dad or Buford.

Or Glenna. Mostly Glenna. Who was for sure that same woman stepping out earlier from the front seat of the boy's car. Who was for sure the river boy's mom. Who was for sure the girl he'd never called back after that one time from the priest's library. The girl who'd held firm to their pact. Their stupid pact, is how she'd probably thought of it, likely angry at him, fed up with such a fool who'd make a firm decision then wobble all over the decision line.

She emerged from the car, back arched to support what appeared to be a belly full of baby.

So, in steering clear of Glenna, his past, he flat out missed his chance to rescue Romey, his future. He'd abandoned the safety quotient, so he never saw Romey and the boy heading for the barn, never saw them skirt around the corral and scoot up the ladder to rise over the rafter tail and brace themselves against the steep roof pitch. He hadn't considered that, it never occurred to him, even though he knew, knew by heart the draw of that barn roof, god you could see clear up and down the river from there, you could think you were staring directly into the face of Chub Ridge. You could look down at dusk and see cows like mice, and you could roll off that slant in slow motion until you got fast and close to thinking you might fly.

Yep, he knew, but instead of keeping his eyes on what he knew, he's down slope where the river turns away from the mountains and heads south to eventually commit itself to the French Broad. Last time he stood here, feet on the edge, it was launch time. Escape time. It had been a powerful, scary feeling. And it still is.

So when Romey falls from the barn roof, he's studying the goddamn river.

But something makes him turn. Could it be that weird paternal radar, surprising him again like it had been surprising him since Romey was an infant? That connecting instinct, even though he's the only one doing the connecting? More likely the boy called out, or the slate of the roof vibrated when the boy went down on his belly to scramble head first in an effort to reach Romey. Did the boy call out? Did Romey? Lenny turned, twisted just in time to see her slip on the new tile, which, had it still been rusty like in his day, her feet would've held firm. But no, Jude tiled the goddamn roof, and she slipped, and he sees it, and he sees the boy grab for her, sees him go down flat in a desperate attempt to snag her, snag at her hair, he may have grazed her halo, sees him slide to the edge himself, braking with his hands only after he's missed.

A thump and a crack echo around his brain, like maybe Romey falls, hits the ground over and over.

There's a scream from the yard that he recognizes, ten years older but so familiar from when the two of them sat in her car watching the older high school boys careen across the mountain ridge drag racing. She'd screamed just once then asked him to take her home. It was one of the last times they'd been together. He wonders if she'd screamed…later. But he wouldn't know because he wasn't here.

At some point during her long, drawn-out but extremely quick drop, Romey manages a mid-air half twist and saves her own life.

CHAPTER 13

"NO HEALING-HEALING, WE DO NOT DEIGN to elevate that mighty prayer."

Underneath her thin smock, Romey's chest rises, then shutters back down into place.

"No purgatory be all we ask in the essence of this crooked waif lay low in the dirt afore ye."

Lenny has no notion of when the priest showed up, no idea for how long he's been standing there staring at Romey. Glenna is at Romey's side, and he can almost feel the familiar intake of her breath, her urgency.

Or maybe that's the boy breathing heavy above them, still stretched belly flat along the barn eave, watching, arms dangling.

Romey in the dirt. Again, where the hell did he get off thinking he was any better for this kid than Shawnee? Or Raymond?

"Although we do stoop low to beg-beg from deep within our heart-hearts."

Lenny worries he may clock the priest next time the old man opens his dried-up pie hole.

But someone has him tight by the upper portion of his stump, someone with a we-don't-have-time-to-discuss-this-shit written across his face. A face Lenny knows like he knows the faces of his brothers. Maybe Max. Of course, Maybe Max would have climbed out the driver's side of the car, but Lenny had been focused on Glenna.

There's nothing Maybe about Max now. He releases Lenny and drops to his knees with a purpose, checking Romey's pulse, palpating her right arm which lies at an unholy angle next to her thin frame, and appears to be swelling rapidly.

Beneath her fuzzy kinks, Romey's eyelids flutter.

She'll be okay, she'll be okay, Lenny says to himself, at least he hopes it's to himself, as he waits for her sharp slate eyes to open and accuse him of hauling her into a god forsaken land where little kids can lose their arms.

He was just her age, just exactly her age.

Lenny looks skyward. The boy has disappeared from the barn roof.

"I don't think Corker and the guys can get here quick enough."

Maybe Max reaches to feel Romey's pulse again. Practiced, professional fingers running along Romey's neck and up to her temple.

Corker and the guys. So, the volunteer rescue squad is still intact.

Max rocks back on his heels and looks up at Lenny, a mix of wariness and sympathy and warning. Right there in the dirt by the barn, right there looking up at him and him looking back like they'd done throughout childhood and into their jumbled-up teen years. Max a couple of years older, both trying to avoid the same dangers and rarely succeeding.

"No telling what all's busted, Lenny. Think you can put together a body splint?" Max gestures toward the barn.

"Maybe," Lenny says before he can pull the word back. A grin quivers between them. Lenny starts for the barn but the priest's gargling stops him.

"Ye behold, ye behold…"

Lenny swings around to silence the geezer but then sees what the priest sees.

Romey's eyes are wide open, and she's sitting straight up, flecks of sawdust and dry autumn grass speckling her amber curls. Her right arm drags along the ground and for a moment she doesn't seem to register the pain.

Max quickly reaches to steady her swollen, off kilter pendulum. As he makes contact Romey's face crumples.

"Hold on now," Max says, reaching and pinning her between his arms. "That was a helluva Wonder Woman move you just pulled off, goddamn gold medal dive, but we still gotta check you out."

Max turns to Lenny. "I've got my kit up in the car. I could jerry-rig a splint, then meet you at the office. Your girl's crook is going to take an x-ray, and a bit of straightening."

Lenny glances at Romey, not just to gauge her pain level, but also so gauge whether she's registering being called *his girl.* If so, she isn't giving anything away.

The boy shows up under Glenna's arm. Black hair falling past his brows but not low enough to hide dark, steady eyes, a little shy maybe, but alert, intent on his dad's fingers running up the scale of Romey's spine.

Glenna pulls him close up to her swollen belly.

"Your kit," Lenny says.

Max looks at him. No checks or balances. Just a man who knows where he's from and where he's headed.

"Yep," he says. "Doc Halloway's retiring. Medical hole needs filling." Max shrugs as if that was the only possibility, for him to fill Doc Holloway's shoes.

The boy shifts under Glenna's arm. "Graduated medical school," he says, eying Lenny, challenging him to debate the point. When Lenny doesn't, he drops his eyes to examine Lenny's stump.

"My daddy says you could wield an ax. Fell a good-sized sapling, with just one swing."

Glenna pulls him closer, shushing him, but the boy locks in on Lenny, questioning the truth of his father's words.

"Used to," Lenny says. "Yeah, I guess so."

Romey strains against Max's probing fingers, tries to stand, but her head falls back and she squeezes her eyes shut against a pain that connects directly to Lenny's chest. A pain Lenny understands.

"Christ-a-mighty," she whispers.

Lenny looks around to see if the priest will echo that sentiment, but the old man has disappeared.

Is he dreaming the priest onto this farm? Or, like the old man's rescue mission under the dock so many years ago, does Lenny just think he's dreaming? Hell, maybe he dreamed up every single one of those intervening priest years. He wishes. What he would give for the burning fields to be just a bad dream.

Glenna and the boy turn away, arm in arm. It's difficult to tell who is the anchor.

It takes Lenny a moment to wonder why he's standing there kicking up dirt. Max, carrying Romey, her wayward arm braced by his large hand, has already headed up the hill toward the knot of mourners watching from the yard.

Romey's face is crushed into his Max's shoulder, most likely the only tactic she can think up to keep from crying.

CHAPTER 14

LENNY PLUCKS A THICK MAGAZINE FROM a shelf in the physician's reference room just down the hall from Max's office. Max had wisely deposited him in the small library once Romey was settled on a gurney.

"Just a precaution," he'd said. "Bone reductions aren't fun to witness, and believe me, it's hell to try manipulating a kid's arm when the dad's passed out on the floor."

The dad.

Lenny thumbs through several slick, text-heavy journals, one bright with yellow syringes and blood-red test tubes catches his eye. Something about a freakish so-called "polygamy of multiple diseases." Evidently, diseases that act like gang members, making them even more evil than a single disease could ever manage by itself.

Lenny sets the journal on the table. Max estimated forty-five minutes to reduce and cast Romey's arm.

Once her bone is set, they could leave. And they could keep right on driving. It's not like there's anything they'd be leaving behind. That is, with the exception of seeing his mom laid in her grave. With the exception of explaining her death. Could he do that? Could he just cut and run on his mom? Again? Could he leave his dad in Jude's hands? Not knowing for sure Jude's intentions? Leave him unprotected? Could he run without setting things right?

Well, he'd done it before. Twice. First leaving the farm. Next the priest.

So yes, he could. He could just head right on down to the Atlantic Ocean. Cross the Cooper River Bridge. Just like he'd promised himself years ago. He could take Romey, teach her to ride waves all the way into the sand.

Or. Actually. He could take Romey right back to school. Right back to Shawnee.

What the hell has he been thinking? At what point is Romey going to call him out?

He's not my dad.

Nothing about her belongs to him. Not her frizzy halo, not her flat stub nose, not one single gene is his. The only things that belong to him are his own feelings, unexpected hitchhikers out of nowhere. Those are his. Hell yes. Hers, too, but only if she wants them.

Sometimes he thinks she might. Sometimes he allows himself that hope.

Not the unthinking mindless kind of hope of his own childhood. He'd had a shit load of that, none of it ever paying off. No, this thing, this new thing, was based on fact. She'd needed him. That was a fact. And then, suddenly he'd needed her. Not exactly your bright and shiny slice of knowledge. More buried, dirt streaked, ugly when you first see it. And damned tough to unearth. Something you have to dust off, and study, and polish to understand.

But still, a surprising fact, overwhelming even. And the two facts combined, her need, his hope, made you do things, instead of wait for things to happen.

But she doesn't belong to him; he can't see how she ever would. She belongs to Shawnee, who might not have even noticed that her kid is missing. Shawnee could still be stoned from last week's booty call.

Max opens the door and escorts Romey and her new bright-white cast into the reference room.

"New word," he says, pointing to the journal in front of Lenny. There are lollipops in Max's shirt pocket, and one swelling Romey's cheek. Green, from the look of her lips.

"Syndemic," Max says. "Not yet in the lexicon, but it will be."

Max sits in the yellow vinyl chair beside Lenny. He pulls a pen from the bouquet of lollipop sticks and holds it out to Romey.

"Might as well start learning to write with that left hand," he says, indicating her newly encased right arm. Max smiles at her, his eyes as innocent as Romey's. More innocent even, much less guarded.

Romey takes the pen and migrates to a small couch away from the men.

"She's a tough one. Football tough. No meds. Boom!"

Romey's head is bent to her handiwork on her cast, but she smiles at the compliment. A rare sight, that smile. Day three of his new life with Romey. One river immersion with a mad priest. One busted arm. One hard-earned smile. It's just unimaginable how many moments an adult can get wrong, or right, within any given set of minutes.

"But she might want to numb up at some point, so I'll give you something to take with you."

Lenny thinks if she hasn't numbed up by now, she never will.

"Syndemic?" he says.

Max focuses.

"Well, yes. Syndemic. First heard it at a medical conference. Nasty stuff, I'm telling you. You talk about bad marriages. Try two diseases. One disease latches on and magnifies the other. Like TB. Yeah, let's say TB, marries up with, I don't know, rubella? Things spin out of control. You might could fix one. But there's just no help for that particular combination. Deadly consequences for entire populations."

Syndemic.

The idea needles around Lenny's synapses. One bad decision, you might could fix, but combined with another, and maybe three more. Disaster. He'd been in that swirl. He could see that, yes, he could. But how about one crazy person, his mom for instance, or, more accurately, one intelligent, funny, loving person, in her own way, tying a crazy knot with another person, a son, let's say, Jude, with a different crazy tack...

"Fixing that," Lenny says. "I guess, fixing a combination like that, well, I guess there's no divorce with disease, huh?"

Max laughs, nods his head.

"Yep. Just like us Catholics. No divorce. I guess the best we can hope for, today at least, is to treat each combination, each team, as a whole different disease. It's a lot to think about. And out of my scope, that's for sure."

There's a weighted wire fisherman on the table in front of them, and Max tips him, watches the rod rock back and forth, back and forth. His eyes settle on Romey, who has her name spelled out in neat block letters along the top side of her cast. Max takes in a breath slightly shallower than it looks like he needs.

"You know," he says. "You know that I married Glenna."

Lenny picks up the journal and returns it to the shelf behind them.

"I heard," he says. "I…well, I was glad enough to hear it."

Max nods.

"She raised Ricky on her own. Mostly. You saw Ricky today."

Lenny runs his forefinger down the ridge of his stump, fiddles at the seam.

"Yep, I did. I guess that wasn't too easy for her. Out here." Lenny takes a shallow breath of his own. "He looks to be eight or nine?"

Max sits forward in his chair, elbows on knees.

"You know that doesn't add up, Lenny. Ricky's ten. Ten and seven months. I adopted him. Just as soon as we were married."

Max lifts a hand to stay Lenny from interrupting, not understanding that Lenny didn't have the words anyway.

Romey's pen is quiet along her cast, a half-drawn daisy at its tip.

"He's my son now, Lenny. And a good boy. I just want you to know, well, whatever you and Glenna try to work out between you, it'll be good with me. I just hope it'll be good with you."

The words are firm, but kind. Lenny tries to swallow, but can't manage it.

Romey abandons her chair and settles on the arm of Lenny's. Holds her pen out to him.

"You gotta sign," she says.

Lenny looks at the pen, then at Romey. Flint eyes reflecting a deeper knowledge of pain than any kid her age should feel. Can she sense that this is what they share?

Max steadies the rocking fisherman, tips him again.

"You know, Glenna's a big fan of your whole family. Your dad, he did so much for her…well…Richard…well, anyway. She and Ricky are up on your farm frequently. Helping, doing whatever. And your brother, he comes down to the house."

He looks Lenny over, observing him, waiting for him.

"My brother?" Lenny finally says. Stunned at the revelation, but relieved that it pushes him to form words over the drought in his throat. "Frank goes down to the Rader farm?"

Max hesitates.

"You've been gone a long time, Lenny. Frank's a hard worker. And well-liked throughout the county. Just shows up, helps anyone out. Anyone. Nobody works harder. So, yes, sometimes Frank. He comes. But no, no it's Jude. Jude comes around."

"Jude?"

"Yep. Jude. He visits. Sometimes just parks his car down there by the river, takes a walk up in the woods. Other times he parks himself at our kitchen table."

"Jude," Lenny says, still not quite processing.

"Look, everybody's got something missing." Max's eyes stray to Lenny's stump. "Maybe some not quite as obvious as others. But still. Your mom, given her profession, might've understood that, especially with regards to your brother, Jude."

When Lenny doesn't reply, Max stands.

"You, more so than most, know there's always a workaround. But it's not everybody who can find a workaround. Not like you did. Like you *do*."

Lenny turns away, rapidly signs Romey's cast.

Max slips another lollipop under the buckle of one of Romey's cowgirl boots. Clips her on the ear.

"I'll be ready to take that cast off in six weeks. But, Lenny, if you're not sticking around, any doctor, anywhere, can remove a cast."

Lenny slows the truck at the end of the parking lot. Pulls to a full stop.

If you're not sticking around…

Romey looks up the street, then down the street. Then at Lenny.

There's no traffic, but he doesn't want to pull the truck into the lane. He doesn't want to move them in any direction at all.

Romey puts her skinny fingers top of the gear stick between them.

"I'll shift," she says.

Lenny closes his eyes.

Anytime Shawnee opened his door, Romey trotted directly through. Headed straight for his closet when she was younger, his refrigerator when she was older. Like she'd found home.

"Which way you wanna go?" he says.

Romey seems to consider all directions, even though she can't have a firm idea of where she really is or where the roads lead. But still, she sits there, considering. Gathering her sturdy mental arsenal, solving this puzzle.

"I haven't learned to ride yet," she says. "Or shoot. Or track. And you promised."

Lenny nods, turns the truck into the lane toward the farm. Romey's hand grips the gear shift tighter, shifts the two of them into second.

CHAPTER 15

LENNY PICKS UP THE FOYER PHONE on the first ring. Like he's never left home. Same shrill consonant. Same black rotary dial. Sheer reaction, old habit.

"Yes?"

It scares him to think what else he might be doing on auto pilot. He didn't come here to drift back into old habits, old roles. He came here to confront them.

"Yes?" he says again into the phone. Only one day left until his mother's ashes float free along the mountain ridges she cherished. One day to figure things out and get the hell out. Sun shafts through the open screen door and he stretches the phone cord for a view down to the barn. The morning mist is burning off, the horses are heading up the pasture, blowing their streams of fog, heads bobbing.

Can he teach Romey to ride, shoot, and track with just one day left? Like he'd promised her? No, he could not.

The kid must've set a record by now for sustaining broken promises.

"Hello?" he tries one more time, then backs into the shadow of the foyer to replace the receiver in its cradle.

But then there's a fumbling on the other end, a familiar shuffling of crap, a rapid intake of air by someone who hasn't realized that even though he has the wealth of two hands, he actually does only have just the two hands with which to work a pay phone.

Lenny sighs.

"Raymond?"

"You gotta hand it to her, man." Raymond, sucking in deep, blowing out long and thin. Likely weed.

"Hang on, man."

He pictures Raymond, phone wedged between ear and shoulder, one hand holding the roach, the other wiping it down with one of his hippie kerchiefs before dropping it neatly into the pocket of his crisply pressed dress shirt.

Pure Raymond.

"Seriously, you gotta hand it to her."

Raymond's voice seems impossibly distant. A throwback voice. A voice he wakes to…woke to…every single morning for years. Either drugged out beside him, deep into a day-long coma, or calling urgently from the shower, hyped for Raymond's version of working at his dad's satellite bank. Counting bills, snorting, counting bills, snorting. *It's the life, man.* Lenny considers hanging up. With his mom's funeral the next day, Father Bryan would likely be by. More food would likely arrive for Freta to sort. And shouldn't Freta already be here? If he lived here, could he ever get used to Freta Hatmaker wafting in and out of the house, down the halls, in and out of their rooms?

Lenny twists the phone cord, waits for Raymond's wall of words, listens for Romey. He'd given her Max's pain killer. Is it too much to hope she'd slept soundly? Is it too much to hope she's forgotten about school? That she's settling in? Good God, does he want her settling in here on the farm?

"Raymond?"

A spoon scrapes against a bowl in the kitchen on the other side of the foyer wall. A wheelchair creaks. The refrigerator opens. Shuts.

Raymond jingles change. Cupping his fist of coins, from the sound of it, tossing them up next to his ear as if to remind Lenny, solidifying the fact that these coins only buy you so much time, man, this call is only temporary. Short lived. Just like you and me, man, just like you and me.

Never admitting that Lenny has bolted for good.

Lenny stretches the cord as far as it will untangle, leans to peer around the door into the kitchen.

His dad at the kitchen table. That face, which three days ago reminded Lenny of a wet fishing net, lifts at Lenny's entrance. His dad, shoveling Rice Krispies into his mouth before they pop their way to oblivion.

No Jude in sight. Probably already taken his car out, making his early rounds on the farm.

No Freta. No Frank.

Lenny waves the phone in greeting, steps back to the foyer, sits on the bottom step. The wood creaks. His dad's spoon hits the bowl. The jingling in his ear accelerates.

"Talk," Lenny says into the phone. "What? What is it that I have to hand to whom?"

"She don't stop, that's what."

This is not affronted Raymond, due to Lenny taking his daughter, nor cocky Raymond at having snared Lenny's full attention. More like innocent Raymond. Wonderment Raymond. The real Raymond, like the boy he'd fallen for when they both needed stuff they didn't know they needed.

"Shawnee, man. Gotta love a woman who goes *after* shit. She just goes *after* it."

Lenny snakes the phone cord back and forth across his knees.

"Raymond. What's the news here?" He instantly regrets calling Raymond by name inside the farmhouse. Keep the farm separate from the city, from his real life. Nothing else is workable.

"Shit. Shawnee. That's the news. Custody shit, man. This time. I'm pretty sure anyway. You gotta be coughing that kid up."

Footsteps upstairs. Romey crossing the hall above him to the bathroom. Still not closing the door for her tinkling.

"Shawnee's straight, man, you didn't know that. Woman's been *working* it. Normal pupils, steady hands. Kinda makes me miss her. You know what I mean?"

"Makes you…miss her."

"Yeah, well, that's what I said. Done drove out, man."

"Drove out?"

"Watch out Lens." Romey's lilt from the steps above him.

He cranes around as she edges her butt onto the banister and releases both hands. He jumps up off the bottom step and yanks the phone cord out her way just as she dismounts at the bottom, jogs around the corner and into the kitchen.

"Morning Mr. Richard," she calls.

"Romey," his dad more verbal with each passing hour.

"Hold on," Lenny says, but Raymond's off in non-stop chatter mode. Lenny places the receiver against his chest.

Romey jogs into the foyer, Pop-Tart in hand. But she turns back to the kitchen.

"You getting up today?" she says to his dad. "You getting up and out? You promised. At least try. You're gonna stand up, right?"

"Might."

Lenny thinks he hears the distant memory of his dad's chuckle.

Romey pushes through the screen and lights on the top step of the porch. The sun catches every amber highlight atop her fuzzy head.

Lenny walks the phone back deeper into the foyer shadows, up under the casing of the stairs.

"Hold on. Drove out where?"

"Your farm, man. That's where you're at, right? You answered the phone, didn't you? Where else would she be headed?"

"You told Shawnee—"

"I didn't tell her shit, man. Your stalker priest friend, he's the news. Shows up looking for you. I told you we weren't done with that holy roller. Prison don't stop a man like that. Shawnee, she shows up too. Same time. Looking for you. Talk about a freak grenade. But here's what I'm saying. Your priest-man is no match for that woman. She is intense, man. I gotta get back up in that game."

"The priest."

"Like he was all comforting and shit, you'd be back soon and so forth, not to worry. Like somehow that was going to be helpful. Okay, I did confirm that the farm was a possibility. Not like I was telling them anything. Then the stalker priest tries talking her down. Same as striking a match along your gas line. I'm telling you, it was all over in a hellish flash. All up in each other's business. Shawnee tearing up the apartment hunting for the kid's clothes, which there weren't any. The thing about you, Lenny? You got no subtlety. None whatsoever."

"You confirmed the farm was a possibility."

Why had he ever trusted a pot head with his story? For that matter, with years of his life?

Important Raymond interrupts. "I'll say this. She's just plain out straight. She's been all up in that clinic. Look, she headed for the clinic *first*, *before* she allowed herself to head out after you. I'm saying, she's got herself on a road, man, she's driving a slim little tight-ass road, which is what I can't get out of my mind, and like I've been telling you, driving it hard. She's looking for you, now. And she's looking for the kid you took. That's all I can say. Why'd you take the kid? I sure hope you can produce the kid."

Lenny starts to remind him that "the kid" they are discussing is Raymond's daughter, and that she has a name.

He thinks better of it. One parent at a time.

He walks out from under the steps. Romey's migrated down one step and has her hair pulled back in a wide, yellow band. She's tugging her go-go boots onto her feet.

How long ago had Shawnee left the city? How long would it take her to find the farm? What are the odds she stops along the way, gets high, gets lost, or turns back?

A faint and fast shadow passes the screen door behind Romey, like a hawk, swiping a few seconds of sunlight.

Freta finally?

Nope, Frank. Who must've been on the porch the entire time Lenny's been wrestling Raymond on the phone. Quiet and still. Now Frank lingers over Romey, hesitates. Then turns and cups his hands to peer through the screen at Lenny. Nods at him before easing down on the step beside her.

How to read that nod. Asking permission? Seizing control? Where do you land, Frank? Where do you land?

Lenny places the phone against his forehead, listens for Frank's murmurs out on the porch. A spoon chings across the wooden floor in the kitchen. His dad groans. Where is Jude? Maybe he'd been back in the pantry and was now sitting there in the kitchen, reading the paper, also listening to Lenny's life.

"You still there?"

"Well the question is, man, are *you* still there. Look—"

"Just hold. Can you hold a sec?"

Out on the porch, Frank and Romey simultaneously stand on the top step. As if they've made a plan. Romey reaches and taps Frank's elbow, and they head down the steps. Then down the hill. Toward the barn. Just like that.

Lenny walks the phone cord out its full length to the front screen, pulling the base off the foyer table. It dings as it hits the wooden floor.

Coins ping in his ear, one after the other.

"She says you're underestimating her," Raymond says. "She's all like—"

"Hang on," Lenny says. "Hang on."

"What?"

Lenny presses his face close to the screen door. Romey running ahead of Frank toward the barn. The horses catch her eye and she veers toward the pasture.

Romey up on the pasture gate now, Frank climbing over. The horses, flicking flies with their tails. Snorting steamy clouds.

His dad rolls to the kitchen door, looks out the front screen too, backs his wheelchair into the foyer for a better angle toward the barn.

Romey zig-zagging toward the horses, Frank closing the distance between them.

Lenny can hear Raymond working the accordion door of the phone booth. Squeak open. Squeak close.

When Raymond speaks, it's Real Raymond, though it's Real Raymond acting as if he's only concentrating on the phone booth door.

"Where is the kid, anyway?" he says.

Squeak, squeak. Squeak, squeak.

"You got that kid, right?"

CHAPTER 16

ROMEY DISAPPEARS INTO THE BARN AT the bottom of the hill behind Frank, who is leading the two horses.

Lenny takes the steps two at a time and heads after them, but the low hum of a degraded engine with what sounds like a deteriorated muffler, stays him. Could that already be Shawnee, stout, rumbling, and simmering out on the farm road?

"Hold now! Goddamn you ain't changed a wit! Running head long and full speed ahead just like always. Hold."

Buford, cutting his tractor to an idle and settling it at the edge of the yard.

Lenny glances back at the barn. "I only got a minute," he says.

Buford climbs down from his tractor, grinning.

"Well, don't let me halt progress."

Buford fumbles in his shirt pocket for his cigarettes, fishes deeper for a match. That cadence, that idle rummaging, settles Lenny. Pulls him back into their greasy rag shop days. How long has it been since someone, anyone, seemed so glad to see him?

"Just returning property to its rightful owner," Buford says, lighting up, indicating with the tip of his boot the tractor's back hitch, which is draped awkwardly in a mud-caked mess of leather and iron.

Lenny steps closer.

Buford nods. "Yep, your mama's saddle. Found it while rounding up stray yearlings along Chub Ridge. I thought you might want it back."

Lenny squats down to examine the saddle, He runs his hand over the horn where Buford hooked the iron stirrups, feels along the strap.

Buford blows smoke over Lenny's head. "Yep, torn up belt. Cinch completely gone. I'm saying, that mare was spooked. To rub a saddle clean off like that? Probably reared, dropped your mama. Then, smelling death, hell bent to shy herself of the evidence. You think?"

Then, "Sorry Lenny, I'm speaking a bit blunt."

Lenny inches his fingers along the frayed belt. Not a clean cut. Not like a sharp knife would slice. Which had been his next guess, after the cattle prod theory. Cut the belt almost through, and hope for the worst. But the leather is clawed. You couldn't rule out a desperate sawing from a dull serrated blade—a detail Jude could dream up. Rip it rough and just enough. Let the horse do the rest.

"I don't know," Lenny says.

He tugs on the saddle irons. The rigging seems sound.

"I can see your idea, though."

He lifts the saddle from the hitch with his stump, runs his good hand along the flap, then strums his fingers up and under the saddle skirt. The curly, plush wool transports him to fresh hay stalls, rough dirt trails, smoky camp fires and tents. Frayed memories, all the good stuff from childhood, so long obscured by the crap, it all rises up out of the wool. Only the finest shearling for their horses.

"Your mama sure was a good rider. Good doctor, too, if you ask me. If you ask my old man, especially. Yep. She worked some wonders around these parts, Lenny."

Buford makes his way across the lane to drop his cigarette, grind it out.

Again, Lenny is struck by the latent power of his mom. A spirit he evidently left too soon to know about. He'd been too young to take it in. Regret hits hardest when it's a surprise strike.

Buford climbs back up on his tractor, cranks it, shifts into gear.

"Just in case you were ever wondering," he calls down. "I had a few more dollars than any young buck could take off of me. Those floorboards? Just a decoy, Lenny. Just a decoy."

His laugh is partially drowned by the rasping roll of the tractor engine.

Lenny eases the saddle over the porch rail and again runs his fingers through the soft wool, lets his mind drift back to the brisk autumn evenings spent scraping commercial fleece from the underside of every one of their saddles and replacing it with the shearling, his mom carefully inspecting every inch of their work.

Pulling across the soft grain, Lenny works his fingers deeper. Across and up. Across and up. Same exact pattern as they'd laid it down. They'd padded firmly, painstaking and meticulous in their competing desires to please their mom.

Lenny massages deeper, lulled by the good times before the bad times. He winces, and it takes him a second to realize it's not from the pain of those good memories, or maybe it's partly that too, but it's from the blood percolating at the tip of his index finger when he pulls it free of the wool.

He presses his finger against his chest to stop the bleeding, then flips the saddle upside down on the top step and kneels to sort more carefully through the skirt. He pricks his finger twice more before gaining purchase on the culprit and gingerly dragging it into the open. An unclipped safety pin. Lenny holds the pin up to the light, then slowly closes it and lays it aside. Stares at the soft wool. Finally, he sorts again and pulls three more pins from the shearling, one open. He secures them, drops them back into his palm, and gently jiggles them there, like Raymond jiggling his phone coins. Which reminds Lenny of Romey.

He slips the pins into his jeans pocket, steps up to the screen door and peers into the house.

"Is Freta here yet?" he calls.

His dad, still huddled behind the screen, shakes his head.

"Lizzy's…saddle?"

Lenny doesn't have time to make this any easier. "Yes," he says. "Belt busted. Cinch gone."

He opens the screen slightly so his dad can get a better look.

"I'm…I'm sorry, Dad."

His father's forehead furrows, but since he just nods, Lenny continues.

"Jude? Is Jude here?"

His father shrugs and angles his head toward the parking area to the side of the house.

Lenny gently closes the screen door and walks to the end of the porch that overlooks the cars. His beat-up truck beside Frank's beat-up truck. The third parking space, empty. Just a dry rectangle where Jude's yellow Ford LTD should be sitting, cold and idle.

With Jude gone, Lenny feels easier about Romey. But still. The pasture is empty. So, they must still be in the barn. Or behind the barn, maybe letting the horses drink from the river. Either way, they've been out of his sight for too long.

He heads back down the porch steps, but the rumbling hum of Buford's tractor backs its way into his brain. He pauses and scans the lane down to the road, wondering what's on the old man's mind this time.

But it's not Buford's tractor.

A low slung, faded maroon Challenger chugs into view, the driver oblivious to any notion of my-side-your-side of the rutted country road. The car putts slowly past the turn-off to the farm, then halts so abruptly the back end elevates well above the white-walled tires. Lenny gauges the distance to the car, then gauges the distance to the barn, to Romey.

Safety quotient blown to hell.

Shawnee hangs her sleeveless, muscled arm out the driver's side window, strums her hand on the car door to some beat belting from the radio that Lenny can't quite yet hear. She's clearly palpating. Clearly finding her rhythm.

His dad's wheelchair creaks behind him at the screen door.

Can he trust Frank with Romey, at least long enough to get rid of Shawnee?

The Challenger jerks into reverse, backs fast across the lane's turn-off. Shawnee's sited her target. She swings in, wheels spinning, kicking up dust and gravel all the way up the lane.

Romey would come running out of the barn at the sound of her mom's Challenger.

But the barn stands quiet. Maybe Frank's teaching her to muck stalls, or brush down one of the mares. If they're wading the horses in the river, they wouldn't hear the sound of the car over the water rush.

He crosses the front yard. He simply won't look at the barn. Nor the pasture. If Shawnee is stoned, he can make quick work of her. Watch her drive away. Romey none the wiser.

But if she's straight? Like Raymond warned?

He'd rarely seen Shawnee straight. Shawnee straight puts him in a dark cove with no clear idea where to cast.

His dad sits shadowed behind the screen door. Lenny finds himself imagining, just like he'd imagined as a kid, his dad standing up and demanding to know what was going on, insisting on accountability, insisting on protection for a little kid.

The Challenger chugs into the drive, radio now blaring but abruptly cutting out when Shawnee kills the engine.

Why would his dad-as-hero notion continue to wedge its way into his brain? Even full-force, alcohol- and depression-free, his dad had never pressed anything on anyone. Except for his word map, except for Lenny's escape route.

Shawnee sticks her head out the window to accompany her stout arm.

"What ho?" she yells and wrenches the door open from the outside.

"Found your farm, Mr. SLA! Just when was it you joined the Symbionese Liberation Army? Just when did you start stealing girls?

Mr. SLA. As if this were a Patty Hearst-type kidnapping. He hopes Shawnee is joking. But when has Shawnee ever joked?

Lenny tries to convince himself that Romey would be okay with Frank. Because Frank is fine. With Jude out of the picture, Frank is fine.

Shawnee slams the door shut, tosses the keys back through the open window onto the driver's seat. Slowly she turns away from Lenny to face the expanse of neighboring farm land stretching across the other side of the lane and down to the river hidden by trees bordering the pasture.

Raymond was correct. She's straight. She has all the time in the world.

Lenny reminds himself not to look toward the barn. To think

clear. But Shawnee goes cloudy before him, her wild mass of black hair coils in a hazy arc somewhere in his line of vision. The barn pulls at him, calls to him. The barn. Check on Romey. No. Deny all primal instincts. His familiar trap, his crappy choices. His god-awful, crappy choices. Lenny tries to remember that he's good at this. He thrives inside that trap.

Shawnee comes into focus, her thin t-shirt exposing every muscle across her back, hands steady on sturdy hips. Feet apart, standing there in his dad's driveway, staring at Rosey Face and Chub Ridge. One thing about Shawnee, you never had to wait long to find out what's on her mind.

"So? My girl?" She turns from the mountains, sweeps her hand toward the pasture, the barn. "You keeping her down in the pig sty or what? Shoo-wee, sure smells like she might be in a pig sty. You gonna split my baby half-wise and roast her, or what?"

Her eyes. Straight. Direct. A woman he doesn't know.

Lenny wills a strategy to surface. Waiting her out won't work. Not with Romey so close. Retreating to a thought hole, running away, useless. He's fishing a dry shaft. The pooling behind his eyes, even more useless.

Lenny blinks.

"What have you got, Shawnee? Just what exactly have you got that Romey needs?"

His own raw-boned strike takes him aback. Straight out of Jude's playbook.

"Tell me that," his voice gone ragged. After all these years, a crystalized understanding of Jude surfacing.

Shawnee raises a clenched fist, pops it on her chest.

"I got things," she says. "I got things that Romey needs. You listen now Lenny. You just listen. I been clean. You not noticing doesn't mean I'm not clean. Certified clean, is what I got for Romey.

Help is what I got. Job is what I got. Home is what I got. All you got is stealing a child out of a bus line."

"Because you were going to…to sell her…services."

"Raymond give you that load of crap?"

"He said you had a profit scheme. But no, it was Romey. Romey told me about you and your Hippocrates stories."

Shawnee shakes her head, calling him useless without ever saying the word.

"I can teach her Greek if I want, if that helps her learn responsibility. You think your George Washington cherry tree stories are any better? I'm teaching her the ways of the street, because that street is always there, Lenny. If we lived right up your country road? Right here in the middle of nowhere land? That street would be right here. Just ask your family, just ask your neighbors. No matter our address, uptown, downtown, that street is right out front."

Shawnee shortens the distance between them, but her anger seems to have dissipated and her words drop like simple truth.

"Any profit scheme I've ever had involved me and only me, not my baby. Somebody's mixed up if they think my baby's for sale. Look, I got straight. For thirteen weeks I been nothing but straight out straight. Just look."

She turns her head one way, pauses to let her message sink in, turns her head the other way. Daring him to challenge her sobriety. Pleading with him to believe.

Lenny takes a breath. There's no rationale for casting the same bait toward the same empty fishing hole. Still, he can't pull back on the line, hatred for himself growing with every cast.

"That's nothing, that's only temporary," he chokes out, then feels himself gain momentum as the dark words, the Jude words, build. Is this the circuit inside Jude's head? Is this what Jude can't stop once it gets started, what his medications—his circuit breakers—try to interrupt?

"Temporary, Shawnee. You know it is. Nobody can make that stick. You'll go south again, it's only a matter of time. What are you going to do when straight gets boring? What is thirteen weeks, anyway? Thirteen weeks is nothing."

Spit draws inward at the corners of Shawnee's mouth, inches back out. She swipes it away with her knuckles. "You can't know that," she says. "You can't have that understanding. Answer me this: Did my Romey ever ask you to take her? Did she? Did she ever say one single thing disparaging about her mama?"

Shawnee pauses to watch him come up empty.

"You don't know me," she says. "You don't know us. You think you can just drift in on some magic carpet, take my girl? You think you're some white-ass savior? My child. My child. Raymond's too. We struggle, yeah we do, but don't be *saving* us."

She raises her arms to shove him. He raises his arm and stump to brace himself. And in that frozen moment Lenny suspects that he is no longer, maybe never completely was, hiding Romey just to protect her. He was hiding her, at least in some ways, to abate some need of his own.

A great distance opens between them, a distance, it seems to Lenny, that only a direct line of truth had put there.

Shawnee drops her arms, looks him over like he's just another hopeless cause she needs to avoid.

"Just go get my girl."

Sturdy, fierce. Just like Romey.

"I told you, Mr. No-Second-Chances. Go fetch her."

Behind him, the screen door thumps and the hinges screech. Wheels roll hollow against the porch boards. Lenny imagines his dad emerging too late from his own traps to try and turn everything back, back to…to what?

Shawnee turns toward the barn.

"Wait," Lenny says. But her face is not registering any recognition of her child emerging from the barn. Only mild puzzlement. Lenny follows her gaze to find Frank sprinting up the hill toward them.

His dad's voice, hoarse, rasping, calls from the porch.

"Lenny…where's…"

The air stirs as Shawnee pushes past Lenny, not toward the barn, but toward the porch. Lenny whips around to see the wheelchair careening down the ramp, his dad grappling with the brake.

Shawnee reaches the porch just in time to take the force of his dad tipping off the edge of the ramp full into her chest. She falls back under his weight and her head cracks back awkwardly against the walkway. The chair bounces, rolls once to land upright on its wheels in the yard.

Lenny's feet are in motion running toward Frank well before his mind can untangle the improbable image of his father and Shawnee crumpled under the ramp.

Frank, panting, seizes Lenny by the shoulders, steadying both men.

"Good god!" he whispers. "He's not…I don't think he's coming back."

"The priest? Where's Romey? What do you mean, not coming back?"

Frank shakes his head, holding onto Lenny.

"He was just giving her a ride," Frank says. "He was giving her a ride on the little Tovero. The little black-faced filly. I waited. But he never came back."

Lenny shrugs out from Frank's grasp, pins Frank's forehead with his stump, which slides on the sweat there, his good hand grips the back of his brother's head, the short hairs prickly and wet against his palm.

"You let Romey disappear with the goddamn priest?"

He shakes Frank's head.

Frank tries to escape but Lenny clamps Frank's head tighter.

"Come back from where, Frank? The woods? The Gorge Trail?"

"No," he says. "I mean yes. Up the Gorge Trail. But no, not the priest Lenny. Jude. Jude took her."

Lenny slackens his grip and Frank's eyes clear.

"Jude? How is that possible? His car…" Lenny glances toward the drive. "It's gone."

"Look, I don't know. Maybe he drove to the bridge and walked the trail back." Frank places his hand on Lenny's chest. Lenny tries to recall Frank touching him, ever, without inflicting pain.

"That's the closest intersection to the river," Frank says.

Lenny steps out of Frank's range.

"And you never stopped him," he says. "Jude took Romey into the woods on a horse and you never stopped him. Not once, Frank, not once in your entire life, did you *ever stop him*."

"How would you know what I ever did, Lenny? You left us. You gave up on us. You deserted the family. How would you know?"

Frank steps in close and shoves Lenny. Then shoves him again, lands a punch into Lenny's chest. But the force of the punch doesn't hit Lenny as hard as Frank's words.

Deserted the family.

Frank punches again, harder, and again Lenny falls back.

"I tried to stop him," Frank hisses as he lands another jab to Lenny's chest. "But you." *Punch.* "Were never." *Punch.* "Here."

Lenny ducks Frank's final punch and throws his weight forward to drive his brother to the ground. He straddles him, a knee on each side, plants his elbow and stump into Frank's shoulders, pins him into the dirt.

Frank tries to roll, but can't get purchase. He gives up, squints up into Lenny's face.

"You're wasting time, Lenny," he breathes out. "You could cut Jude off. At the bridge. But if he gets to his car before you? You may…you may never find Romey."

Lenny holds Frank down a second longer, then releases and stands up over him.

"If you're messing with me, Frank? I swear—"

"Stop blaming me for your troubles, Lenny."

CHAPTER 17

THE VISION HITS LENNY AS HE sprints up the slope: Shawnee's sturdy arm arching the Challenger's keys back through her open car window. He veers toward the maroon blur at the edge of the yard.

A blur, because it's difficult to pull his eyes from the mystifying sight of Shawnee staggering under his dad's weight, slow waltzing him back in the direction of his wheelchair, her hair wet with sweat and glistening from black to silver and back to black in the sun.

Lenny reaches the drive as Shawnee drops his dad into the wheelchair. She turns toward Lenny, her new target. A ball-hawking middle linebacker.

Lenny swings the Challenger door open, grabs the keys, slides in. The familiar jolt of one-armed logistics hits him. Never fails. Overwhelming fear.

Gear shift situated on the steering wheel, unfortunate, and to the right, also unfortunate. Calculations and permutations run through his brain, his old friends, guiding him to a correct solution. There's always a solution.

He glances through the windshield at Shawnee making her own calculations. Maybe just now realizing that Romey is truly missing. Behind her, his dad appears dazed, stricken, trying to gather himself. Frank stands on the hill below. Lenny hesitates a second, taking in his brother's pent up anger.

But you... were never... here.

Lenny reaches across the steering wheel to crank the key, wonders if it's possible to have misread Frank all these years. He'd only been fourteen when he left. What else had he missed?

The Challenger coughs into action and Lenny steadies his good hand along the steering wheel.

"Hey!" Shawnee yells, evidently the full light of his intention piercing through. "Hey!"

Lenny smashes the clutch clear to the floor, releases the steering wheel and reaches to shift into what he hopes is reverse. The gears grind but he's guessed correctly.

He whips the Challenger around, releases again to shift into first. Holds the wheel steady with his knee, swings toward the lane, all the while keeping an eye on Shawnee who has taken off across the yard to cut him off at the turn.

She's beating him. Her legs pulling across the high brown grass, arms cranking. She jumps the ditch into the lane and he swerves hard to miss her, then swerves back toward her to keep the Challenger out of the ditch.

She jumps away and he spins out onto the lane. The smudged rearview mirror reveals Shawnee running full force down the lane as if there's still a chance she can catch him.

She's yelling, but he focuses behind her, on Frank, who is emerging from the farm house.

Lenny cranes around to look out his side window.

Frank, with a rifle under his arm.

Lenny floors the gas pedal, ducks low, braces for gunfire.

But the only thing he hears is the huff of the engine and the grind of the tires as he wrestles the Challenger out onto the farm road. The backend fishtails twice before he steadies it down the center of the long straight stretch ahead.

Lenny does not want to measure Romey's safety quotient. There's no guarantee Jude is even headed for the bridge. The main fork of Gorge Trail runs along the ridge toward Rosey Face then drops steep toward Gorge Bridge. But there are other forks. He does not want to imagine Jude riding the little Tovero now, with Romey perched…where? Behind him? In front?

He can't think about it.

Lenny runs the Challenger out the long straight stretch as fast as he dares. By road, it's a long way to the bridge. Much shorter by horse trail. And Jude has a head start. Can Lenny make up enough time? Even by boat, it's shorter. That had been his first hurdle, all those years ago, paddling away from the farm. To race his boat beyond the bridge and down into the open water, before being caught.

He'd thought about pausing only once, just north of Gorge Bridge at the clearing just below the Rader farm, wondering if he should dock there, run up from the clearing to find Glenna one last time.

But he hadn't paused at that clearing, had he?

He'd paddled on under the bridge, leaving her behind. Leaving all of them behind. He'd had to do that, right? He'd had to leave. *Go or hold.* His dad had known he could not hold, not any longer. So he'd laid out his escape route. How hard had that been for his dad?

Jesus. He'd paddled straight through, not looking back, unsure whether someone was chasing him. His shoulders ached until that moment of release, that moment his boat slid under the bridge and caught the sweet relief and the terrible hurt of big river freedom.

It was such a surprise, the current picking up beneath him on the far side of that bridge.

The Challenger's tires squeal on the asphalt as the road curves sharp to the right, then roll smooth and quiet for a few seconds, then squeal on the next curve, as Lenny winds his way up toward the lower saddle of the ridge.

Is that what Jude is doing now? Banking on catching that same luck at the bridge, banking on riding out clear and free to wherever he hid the car? Wondering whether anyone is chasing him?

The Challenger reaches the saddle, hits another long straight away. Same straight stretch where his brothers and their friends took bets drag racing. Lenny braces the wheel with his stump, reaches across and shifts into fifth. The Challenger shutters but he needs to make up time. In a minute, he will reach the forest and start the final climb, curling to the ridge top. One of Jude's buddies, Jimmy somebody, had tried to make up time, racing here, and crashed at the far end of the straightaway. Died at the scene. Jude had them all back out racing the next night. *Gotta honor Jimmy, boys.* Lenny guns the Challenger. That had been the summer of Glenna Rader, so he'd mostly stayed away from it. Lenny lifts his foot from the accelerator, but hesitates, gliding at high speed. His foot hovers over the brake. Had either of his brothers ever hit this speed?

He should never have brought Romey back.

What would Jude's story be? He'd taken her for a ride, all innocent and easy, but then? What? Another experiment? An accident?

A deer darts from the side of the road and curves back sharply across the ditch and Lenny finally hits the brake, spinning the Challenger's tail, rocking it violently as he fights with his good hand to gain control. His left foot misses the clutch and he pops to a jolting halt perpendicular to the road, dead center across both lanes.

Lenny sits for a moment facing the deer, which has also spun around and squared itself off to the car.

A doe, head up, alert.

"Where the hell am I going?" Lenny says.

Jude could've turned the Tovero north toward Chub Ridge instead of south toward Rosey Face.

What if he'd parked his car the other direction, down the east valley?

What if he'd already tied off the filly to a tree, was cruising out on the highway at top speed?

Jude could've pulled up anywhere.

What's his brother's plan? And how long has he been planning it? Or did it just kind of come up, knowing that if he waited long enough, Lenny would get distracted. Off guard.

Which is precisely what had happened. *That's when you make your move, boys. Got to wait for just the right moment. The wind's got to be with you.*

Then you release the wheels of the go-cart. Then the go-cart rolls off the roof.

And Frank? Still the accomplice? Frank going along with Jude's plotting? Frank leading Romey down to the pasture, to the horses, to Jude? *Tell Lenny I've taken the trail to Gorge Bridge, Frank.* Frank always did as he was told. Jude would be practical, steady, unyielding, carrying out his plan. He was headed upstream, not downstream. Jude has plenty of money and plenty of time to do whatever he wants. And, according to Frank, no adult Lenny knows is going to call out Jude. Jude the supplier.

The doe drops her head, then lifts it once more to catch scent before pivoting back into the forest.

Lenny reaches across the steering wheel, cranks the ignition, shifts the gear. He spins the wheel with his stump, swings the Challenger around at a brisk but safer clip. Every instinct tells him it's useless to look for Romey at Gorge Bridge. Jude would know that's the first place he'd look. But then, the bridge is also Lenny's only clear hope of finding her.

He drives into long opposing curves to the ridge top then pauses above at the crest, just above the bridge crossing the ravine between Rosey Face and Chub Ridge.

Rosey flush with brilliant sugar maples in the fall. Chub, her stocky twin.

Lenny eases the Challenger down the elbow and onto the bridge, edges over to the rusted guard rail, cuts the engine and gets out to peer over the rail to the river below. That distance down through the gorge never fails to hollow out his chest. Black magic, where the river rolls gently from the north, picks up speed to the south. Scary black magic, just to make yourself look.

But in looking, he can see the futility, the naivete of the notion that he can stop Jude.

He would need to hack and thrash his way down the ravine, then wade out and swim through the deep water there. Hike from the clearing at Glenna's farm up to the trail. Then, soaking wet, somehow stop Jude. Stop the filly. Without scaring it, without spooking the filly into rearing and dumping Romey. Or, if they've already reached the Rader's farm, chase down the filly on foot before Jude reaches his car.

A deluded notion, that Jude would not have a bigger, better, more sophisticated plan than Lenny ever dreamed up as a teenager escaping the farm.

He's going to have to turn himself in, because who else would report Romey missing? Shawnee, yes, Shawnee would be pissed off enough to risk a close encounter with the law. But that's the same as turning himself in. Her finger would point directly at him. He's going to have to admit to kidnapping, and take a chance that the Sheriff's department will want to find Romey. Hope that Sherriff Fletcher is not one of Jude's paying customers.

Lenny watches the slow deep water on the north side of the bridge. Hardly a ripple. He walks to the other side and watches the white rapids on the south side.

Could be days, could be weeks, but eventually they would find Romey. Where? In what condition? And find Jude. And whatever Jude's up to. Lenny thinks maybe if he helps bring Romey back safe, well, maybe his own violations could be forgiven. Not by the law, of course. But by Romey.

And what then?

She would go to the state. Sure she would, at least until Shawnee can prove she's clean. Likely he would never see her fuzzy head again, never feel her skinny fingers pick across the seam of his stump.

Lenny wipes sweat from his brow, picks up a rock from under the guard rail, heaves it arching toward the south side of the bridge. As it arcs into the dizzying nothingness below, it occurs to him that in the care of the state is better than wherever the hell she is right now.

Were these the same thought tracks his own dad traveled over a decade ago? His father, weighing his own heart against a kid's survival. Is that why he never pursued Lenny? Just let him go?

You could love somebody more than was good for them. Or, you could love them just the right amount.

Had his dad loved him just the right amount?

Lenny walks back across the bridge to the Challenger, cranks the engine once more, is pulling into a three-point turn when a glint on the ridge catches his eye. He eases the brake and searches across the ravine, scanning until he locates the silver flash among the trees, along the opposite ridge, well above Glenna's farm.

Then nothing, then silver, then nothing.

Lenny waits, the Challenger idling under him. Silver, nothing. Again. Again. The unmistakable rhythm of it. That stilted gate. A horse. Shortening its zig-zag to account for the downhill slope. And a glint of a stirrup along its flank, veiled in deep woods.

Well hell. Jude, it's got to be. Picking his way down the ridge. Jude headed south, after all. Jude accepting the simplest plan available, just as Lenny had a decade ago. Heading for the bridge.

Meaning that Frank had told the truth. Or what he knew of the truth.

Lenny gauges the distance between the Tovero and the bridge, then himself and the bridge. The safety quotient. He wouldn't put odds either way. But with Romey in sight, there's only one way to bet.

Lenny reverses the Challenger, pulls back to the guard rail, jumps out and heads full tilt down the embankment.

CHAPTER 18

WHAT IF YOU CAN'T STOP HIM?

Then you lose her.

What if you lose her?

Lenny hits the woods, clear and cool down through the hemlocks, the tiny cones rolling beneath his skidding feet. His sweat instantly chills. The miracle of the mountains, no matter the temperature, it's always cool in the shade. Lenny quickly locates well-worn deer and mule routes switch-backing down the mountain, but to save time opts for the clean gully washes where water, left to itself, takes a direct path to its destination. He slides on his butt in the deeper cuts, rises, slides, rises again and again down the mountainside, until, sooner than expected, he's at the base of the embankment thrashing through deep brush that whips and gouges at his face. To avoid a rhododendron thicket, he travels an upstream detour before swinging back toward the rush of the river.

Soon, cold water sucks at his shoes and he's sweating but shivering in the shallows.

He swipes his stump across his eyes to clear the damp debris, then searches the ridge up the opposite shore. He waits, and sure enough, catches a clear view of the horse as it enters a clearing, carefully picking its way around a switchback. The glint of a deer rifle along its side winks in the midday sun. The horse pauses, looking for the best footing, then swivels toward the river, sunlight catching it full in its face. A face which is not black, but white.

Lenny wills his lungs to steady so he can focus on the opposite bank. Maybe the sun is just reflecting oddly? Creating the illusion of a white face, and it's really the black masked filly carrying Jude and Romey?

But no, this is his mom's big, white-faced mare. And sitting up high in the saddle above the winking rifle, with his face also turned toward the sun, is Frank.

Probably spotting Lenny. Little Lenny, still stupidly hopeful, always ready to believe.

His parents as his protectors. Raymond as his home base. The priest as his savior.

Had any of that ever panned out?

And now Frank. Luring him in. Frank, robotically following whatever path Jude set before him, Frank reeling Lenny in over the past thirty-six hours with his false objectivity, his fake confidences. Had that been the plan? Let Jude take Romey, for whatever crazy experiments. Arrange a shooting accident for their kid brother. Let their father drown in his booze.

But why? What's the point? What was ever the point?

And just why is he standing here knee-deep in a goddamn river, looking for something that's not even his, that will never be his?

The air that was whipping through his lungs slows, as the white-faced mare emerges from the trees, putting Lenny well within range of Frank's rifle.

Why does he continue to care? He's just so tired of caring.

Lenny raises his face to the sky and tries to heave his voice clearly over the rush of the river to Frank.

"Go ahead!" he shouts, attempting to ram his words into Chub Ridge, echo them back off Rosey Face.

He waves his good arm at Frank, then lifts his stump to the sky.

"Go ahead Frank! Take a shot! Easy picking!"

But even he can't make out his words against the current rushing toward the bridge.

Sweat or river water or both drip into his eyes and he can no longer see the relentless flash of the deer rifle nor the bright white face of the mare. Lenny grabs the bottom of his t-shirt and swipes it across his eyes, leaving his stump in the air though, maintaining the target.

"What are you waiting on?" He chokes the words out into a throttled cry.

The mare pushes across the outcropping in full trot directly toward the river bank. A horse is hard to manage at that steep of an angle. But Frank doesn't waver and the horse doesn't attempt to shy. Instead, its head draws in concert with Frank's tug on the reins and they turn upstream, away from the bridge. Moving fast.

Toward what?

Lenny scans the opposite shoreline to the clearing of Glenna's farm.

Then he's running through the shallows, his shoes soggy and weighted, paralleling Frank's path across the river.

His brain can't think up anything and his eyes can't see anything except upstream, upstream, north, north. Frank is headed north, to the bend in the river. And in that bend standing in full view is the black masked filly.

Relief at finding the filly hits Lenny in the chest just before dread of its empty saddle hits him in the gut.

The filly's reins loop low and tie off on a young sugar maple. Her head is down, her soft, black muzzle almost touching the ground. Abandoned. Exhausted. No Jude. No Romey.

What are they doing? What is his plan?

The stupid hopeful part of his brain envisions Romey breaking free and running back across the ridge, back toward the farm. He would like to start worrying about whether she would know which trails to follow, whether she would get lost. The other side of his brain, the one that understands crappy choices, begs him to think clearer. Begs him to remember that the best-case scenario, Romey running for the farm, is a fail. Begs him to remember that his brothers lured him here with a purpose.

He has to move faster, he has to cross the river, because that's the most likely path to Romey.

Lenny kicks off his shoes, hits smooth sand through the shallows, and dives into deeper water, deeper than expected, outside of his memory deep. Flailing against the chill and the unexpected weight of his pants and shirt, he's under, then back up, choking, searching for the horses, searching for Jude, for Romey. But a sudden relentless sun flashing across the water's surface blinds him. Has he forgotten how to swim? He treads with his stump, his legs churn through a cool deep shaft beneath the surface. Finally, he manages to pull his hand through the heavy current to his face, his thumb and fingers to his eyes to clear his sight.

Where are they? Have they spotted him?

No Jude. No Romey.

No Frank, no rifle.

But up past the river bank, in the clearing, sits Old Man Rader's flat boat. Or Glenna's, now. Moored on its side, bottom facing south, slick with mud like it was recently pulled from the river muck. It appears to waver a little in the sun.

Lenny lowers his head under water, feels with his feet for the bottom, momentarily locates a jutting rock and pushes off, propelling himself up and forward, his soaked, mutinous clothing dragging him back down, again and again, as he draws closer and closer to shore.

Just as his knees scud into the knobby bottom of the opposite shallows, the first shot rings out.

Lenny ducks his head low, crawls parallel to the shore, toward Romey, toward Romey, river pebbles digging into his good arm and the seam of his stump, his feet floating behind. He angles further into the shallows and lies there, belly down. The river rocks up into his mouth, cold and gritty down his throat.

Could they see him? Surely they could pick him off. What are they waiting on?

He startles at the next shot's reverberating pop and whizzing trajectory. Frank must have a perfectly clear bead on him.

So, if Lenny's still breathing, what's Frank aiming for?

Unsteady from his pull through the river, Lenny eases through the shallows trying to give his eyes time to adjust, trying to get a feel for where his brothers are and the most direct line to Romey.

The black masked filly whinnies, a lilting bell against the river current's rush. Then an answering whinny, from the other side of the clearing. Lenny eases his shoulders out of the water for a better view. Sure enough, up near the trail Frank's mare fidgets, her front feet nervous and skittered, her white face high and tugging against her reins. Like the filly, tied off to a sapling. No rider. No deer rifle at her side.

Up in the clearing, the Rader's flatboat shimmies again in the wide expanse between the two horses. A breathing boat; a boat with a pulse. If he strains, maybe he could even hear empty fiberglass yelps as the light waves ping off the shell and ricochet back to the ridge. But the boat steadies too quickly, too firmly, to be the result of some random array of distorted light.

Lenny sheds sheets of water and silt as he rises up out of the water.

There is no other place Romey could be.

He splays the river as he high knees across the sharp rocks. His bare feet pound firm ground in full charge toward the boat that breathes.

Lenny doesn't pause when the boat births a long, protruding arm, black and vacuous. Jude's .22. Yes, Jude would be there too, along with Romey. She has to be there. Yet not making a sound. Romey's silence.

The malignant arm ignores him, ignores his shitty choices, his dilemmas, and instead swings toward Frank's mare on the hill. In mid-stride Lenny scans her direction, and what he sees immediately stops his momentum. Frank emerges from the woods beneath the trail, fully absorbed in his own bull charge. Leading with his rifle.

Not toward Lenny, but toward the breathing boat. Toward Jude. Toward Romey.

Lenny redirects for Frank.

"No!" he yells, close enough, finally, for Frank to hear him above the rush of the river, but getting no acknowledgement from his brother.

"No!" he yells again, pausing as his voice kicks off Rosey Face and back at him. *No, no, no.* "Frank, Romey—"

"You don't think I can stop him, Lenny?" Frank yells. "Well, I'm stopping him."

Without breaking stride, Frank hoists his rifle to his shoulder and fires. The fiberglass hull of the boat screams and shatters. The horses behind each brother half-rear; their saplings nod and sway.

Jude rises from behind the boat, his rifle pointed skyward. Jude's expression, delivered direct from childhood. Pissed that Frank shattered the boat's hull, pissed that Frank is not listening to reason.

How many times do I have to tell you, boys?

"Stopping me from what?" he yells. "I've only ever taught you what needs to be taught."

Frank reams out another shot and Jude's .22 drifts away from him. Jude follows it with his eyes as if the gun and his arm are just a couple of unexplained curiosities.

Lenny recognizes at once a man with the use of only one arm.

"Why?" Jude cries out, still looking puzzled at the absolute disobedience of his appendage. "You? Stop me?"

Jude laughs, and it's hard to tell whether he's laughing at Frank, or at his rifle still wildly swinging. Jude tries to lift his functioning arm to steady his useless arm, manages to grasp his rifle but he catches it wrong and it fires into the dirt at his feet.

Lousy choices. Lenny needs to stop at least one of them, either Jude firing randomly or Frank regaining forward motion and firing toward the boat.

Lenny sprints on up the slope and into the clearing. "Stop shooting! Just stop!"

Both brothers finally yield their eyes to him, but only for an instant. Neither changes course.

"Should've done this years ago," Frank calls out as he fires off another shot, hitting Jude in the other shoulder, finally spinning Jude's rifle out of his hand. It falls barrel first over the hull into the mud.

Jude lurches back, overcompensates forward, staggers to find balance.

"Look at my arm," he calls out, knocking the skiff sideways and lurching toward Frank. "You can't even shoot straight."

Lenny has only a moment to register what's behind the boat—which is nothing, no go-go boots, no fuzzy halo, no Romey—before he plows into his brothers.

They fall apart, but lunge back toward each other. Lenny grabs Jude by his collar, yanks his face up close to his own.

"Where is she, Jude? Where the hell is she?"

Jude's face contorts in pain, but his legs still thrust his weight forward, his eyes still glare bewilderment over Lenny's shoulder at Frank.

Lenny releases Jude and spins around into Frank's rifle barrel.

With his good hand, Lenny seizes the barrel and twists it as he swings his stump upward into the rifle which rams the butt into Frank's chin.

Frank's head rocks back and Lenny pries the rifle from his brother's arms, whirls the other direction, swinging it by the barrel to pound the stock into Jude's nose.

"What the hell did you do with Romey?" Lenny yells.

But he can't hear himself.

On impact, the gun fires and Jude falls like a bird shot out of the air.

Lenny glances down, expecting to see the black ooze of blood seep from Jude's shirt. But the heat in his hand is the barrel, not the stock. Which means the barrel is not pointing toward Jude. But toward Frank.

Lenny swings around.

Frank is lying on his back, steady drops of sweat drizzling from his hairline in perfect tandem with the dark red trickle from the bud on his right temple.

The beads mix, sweat diluting blood, sliding down Frank's ear lobe to drip into the muck below.

CHAPTER 19

LENNY RELEASES THE RIFLE AND IT falls to the ground between his brothers. A deep, cold shivering overtakes him, a chilling mix of shock and sweat and river water. He sucks in air, kneels beside Frank, feels for a pulse from his brother's still perspiring neck.

But Frank has disappeared, gone elsewhere. Drained, diminished. No longer his brother.

Lenny's knees grate into the dirt and he glances over at Jude, who appears to be in a coma sleep.

Lenny scans Frank's torso, searching in vain for any posture in death.

His brother's chest, his shoulders. The star lineman, known around the county, if you could believe Max, which he guesses he does, as a man of heads-down hard work, a man who turns neighborly favors.

Where is that linebacker?

Sweat drips from Lenny's temple to Franks' temple, rolls into his brother's hairline. What is recognizable in that face?

Lenny reaches his hand toward Frank's chest, but withdraws.

Had Frank been protecting Romey?

Maybe so. But maybe, also, protecting his little brother. Finally. Or had he just been angry?

Lenny would never know, because Lenny had never known this man. Instead, he'd made his own blind assumptions. *Blind faith, motherfuckers. Blind faith.*

Frank finally took his own action. And now plenty of folks would spin their own stories. And those stories would turn against him, against Lenny, against the brother who had run, who had deserted his family, who had returned to tear them apart.

Lenny reaches out again and this time he presses his hand to Frank's chest.

"There's no safe zone, man, there's no hiding," he says to the chilling body beside him. "Hell, Jude must've told us that a million times."

Lenny rocks back on his butt. Suddenly and utterly exhausted, he eases down to lie flat between his brothers. Listens to the river rolling. Listens to Jude moaning. The sky is blue and cloudless. He'll need to do something about Jude. Tough to stomach, the idea of helping Jude, just to spell it out clear. But it dawns on him that Jude is a witness. He is the only person who could convince anyone that what happened here was an accident.

He rises to his knees, edges over to Jude.

Blood seeps into his brother's shirt at the upper right shoulder, and along the left bicep.

So, Frank missed wide at point blank range. Twice. Obviously not trying to kill their brother. Just so tired of Jude, so tired. That's what they'd had in common.

A guinea egg of red and purple blooms across the bridge of Jude's nose. From Lenny's swing of the rifle butt. Unlike Frank, aiming for nothing but dead center.

Jude cries out in pain and his eyes open wide and deranged. "Safe," he murmurs. "Safe."

Safe.

Romey. How could Lenny have forgotten Romey.

Lenny leans in close to Jude's ear. "Where is she, Jude? What did you do with Romey?"

Jude sucks in air.

"Safe," he breathes out again.

"Shit you say. Where, Jude. Where is she?"

Jude sucks in deeper. "Not the girl. You. Father said."

Lenny lowers his face to within inches of Jude's face.

"What the hell's Dad got to do with Romey, Jude?"

Jude exhales into Lenny's face, his breath metallic and bloody. Every few words, he appears to float away, then float back.

"He wanted you. Gone. Little Lenny. Father knew best. He knew. Me and Mother…already too much…for him."

"Jesus, Jude." Both brothers now, confirming his dad's word map.

Lenny had been right to take his dad's escape route. And he'd been wrong.

He shakes his thoughts back to Romey.

"If you've got last words, Jude, I need them to be about Romey."

Jude lifts his head to look over at Frank's body.

"I won't die." Jude smiles then contorts in pain. His eyes and lips remain tight, and Lenny wonders if he is holding something in, like a scream. Maybe they are both holding in screams.

To help hold his in, Lenny reaches down and presses on Jude's left bicep, directly over the wet wound.

His brother's face swallows itself whole. Sweat breaks out under the red-blue bulge on his forehead.

"God, Lenny," he bleats out. "Up on the trail. Where else? Left her…at the spring, the hideout." His chin drops, his eyes close.

"You left her…"

Lenny blows into his brother's face to keep him awake. Jude's eyes flutter.

Lenny blows harder. "Alone?" he says. "Jude. Was anyone else up there? Did you see anyone else?"

Jude turns his head away and vomits into the dirt. He spits, tries to lift an arm to wipe his mouth which causes him to writhe in pain.

"She knows…the hideout." Deep breath. "She knows…the spring…that old man…he's with her." Deep breath. "She's not… stupid."

Jude stops to catch more air and his eyes drill sightless into the sky as he finishes off his thoughts.

"I hid…your kidnapped kid…once her mom showed up."

Lenny stands, removes his jacket, rips it down the middle and wraps Jude's shoulder and arm the best he can. He lingers over Jude a moment, trying to drum up some feeling—rage? pity? relief?—about the tears now streaming down Jude's face and angling off his neck. Was he crying for himself? For Frank?

If history held, Lenny would never ask and Jude would never tell him. Lenny wishes he knew whether he cared.

"Look, Jude," he finally says. "I'm going to the spring. But first, I'll take the horse up to Glenna's and get help."

Jude turns his face away from Lenny.

"I don't care what you do," he breathes out. "I just wish you hadn't shot my brother."

#

As Lenny heads for the mare, Glenna emerges from the trees, carefully choosing her way down the access drive. A long cotton shift drops loosely over her baby belly, and her shoulders are wrapped in a pale-yellow blanket. Her sleek black hair reflects sun from the clearing. She loses then regains her balance before she spots Lenny.

"I heard shots." Her voice scrapes against itself. "Lenny, did I hear shots?"

The yellow blanket floats free as she takes in the two brothers lying on their backs like felled trees, heads pointing in opposite directions on either side of Lenny. Panic churns in her eyes.

"Glenna," Lenny says. He starts to head toward her, but stops himself. "Glenna…listen to me."

"Lenny…what?…why?"

"Glenna…I need you to go…I need you to go and get help. I need you to call Max, call Sheriff Fletcher."

He waits until she stoops to pick up her blanket, then he turns and runs for the mare tethered at the base of Rosey Face.

CHAPTER 20

LENNY LETS THE HORSE TAKE HER lead through the thick, fall foliage. She tries to match Lenny's urgency, stumbles, then recovers her footing up the steep incline. She knows her way, and it's a good thing because all he can see is the mix of sweat and blood dripping from Frank's temple.

He tries concentrating on the mare's rhythm. It's been a long time since he's ridden a horse. His own legs seem too long, his torso too thick, and his head too far from her mane. His thighs ache within minutes, his bare feet sting in the stirrups, but he's glad for the distraction. Glad not to have to think. Not to have to visualize what he's left behind by the river, nor what likely lies ahead of him at the spring. Let his brain freeze right here in its tangled unholy mess of a moment. Just hang onto the rhythm of this horse. Let each brother lie in the goddamn muck.

Lenny buries his face into the mare's mane, but can't keep his thoughts from flying. Jude removing Romey from Shawnee's reach? Frank protecting Romey from Jude? His father…painting his word map then letting his youngest son bring it to life? How does it all calculate? Does it even calculate?

He can't keep it all clear of his heart.

So. Concentrate on the horse. Hang on, let the mare do her work.

As she rounds off the first knoll he urges her into a canter through a small flat before letting her settle for the final push up to where the mountains join in their long, grassy connecting notch. The same copse where he'd rescued Glenna from his brothers. Although he's pretty sure Glenna would've figured a way out without him. Now the grass is stiff and brown, crackling under the mare's hooves. As she slows to a trot, Lenny slides from the saddle and hits the ground running for the old hideout at the edge of the grove.

Of course, the brush that once hid the shack appears freshly cleared. The bastard. The goddamn lizard-eyed bastard. Lenny accelerates as he reaches the shack and crashes shoulder first directly through the decrepit door, which splinters and slides in pieces across the cabin floor.

One room, just as he remembers, smelling of fresh cedar and musk, but now also, oddly, of flint. Neatly swept. Empty bowls, bowls from the farmhouse kitchen. Bowls not for kittens. Goddamn bastard. No wonder she'd been gone so long. She must've kicked her short legs into high gear up Gorge Trail to the hideout. Feeding kittens. How naïve could he be?

Lenny peers into the bowls. Washed clean.

He heads back for the shattered doorway, but an odd outcropping at the far side of the room begs him back, nags his memory. Nags, because it was never a piece of his memory. Because it wasn't ever there. The cabin sits flush against the face of the mountainside, with just enough space for the mountain laurel growing outside to appear painted onto the lone window at the back. But now, the smattering of light from the window catches a newly constructed makeshift shelf. Lenny steps closer, peers into the dimness. Not a shelf. An altar. A goddamn altar. Bastard has wrenched up splintered floorboards from under the window and lashed them together with old twines from a once stronger rope. Small votive candles line the altar rail, their glass cylinders reflecting what sun could reach them. Candles recently extinguished, hence the flint odor.

Lenny takes one more step toward the altar, peers underneath. Tucked against the wall is Romey's backpack. Her shoes neatly tucked under the straps. Shit…the bastard. Lenny looks around for anything that could serve as a weapon. He picks up one of the clean bowls, raises it to smash on the altar, but its crystal shine stays him.

A shiny clean bowl. In a shack with no running water.

So. They've found the spring. He thinks back to Romey's insistence that she hadn't been "practicing" in the river. She hadn't been lying.

She had been practicing in the spring.

She'd tried to tell him that. And if he'd asked just one question…

Lenny reaches with his good arm and yanks the cross bar of the altar from its moorings. Candles scatter across the floor. He hefts the altar board, gauging his ability to swing it. One of the two rusty nails still protruding from the end pierce the skin at his wrist. He flips the board end over end, nails up.

Lenny leaves the mare to graze in the clearing, locates the narrow, rocky trail leading to the spring. He runs up the incline, jumping from stone to stone, the altar board wedged up under his good arm, his stump out wide for ballast. He hopes to God, hopes to all of the priest's gods, that the priest is still just "practicing". The old man had called up *forever* waters for Romey's baptism. How far would the priest go to repay *all debts* on Lenny's ledger? Frank's oozing temple flashes through his mind. Having shot one brother today, and not caring much about what happens to the other, he probably has no grounds on which to hope. Still, he needs to hope and he needs a hope he can sustain. A hope that will keep Romey safe. He tries out hoping that Jude was delirious and that Romey is, after all, alone. Alone and wading knee deep, only knee deep, floating sticks across the sinkhole to the base of the cliff. Maybe she's learned to scale the rock face, shimmy up to the outcropping. She'll be tossing rocks from above, splashing them into the spring below. He could re-hang a rope to the big oak up there, teach her to swing from the clifftop out over the spring to the opposite bank. Like his father had taught him and his brothers when they were too young to know they weren't happy. When their father likely knew, but was still trying.

The moisture from the spring greets him as he draws close to the top of the rise. Just over the edge, the moss, the ferns, the sod, the hemlocks, the cool, the damp, the rock face, he can smell it all. He will soon be bathed in the opaque sauna from the sinkhole. He could call it paradise, if it wasn't for the incantations striking his ears, rote melody, floating over the incline, so much a peaceful blending with the chirping of the birds and the rustle of the breeze that he at first had not recognized its oddity. Chanting, chanting. A familiar southern-slanted Latin.

Exi ab ea, immunde spiritus, et da locum Spiritui Sancto Paraclito.

Now that his brain parses it, the melody boils in Lenny's ears, and his neurons translate the words rising deep from his memory.

Go forth from her, unclean spirit, and give place to the Holy Spirit…

Lenny pushes his way through the brush, pauses to catch his breath above the spring, and to seek out Romey. What he finds instead is the old man up to his thighs in the foamy water, his croaky, sing-song Latin-jabber rising in the mist, his back to Lenny, shirtless, his bony vertebrae in a sacred bow to the water.

His hands dip low in the spring, like he's preparing to wash his face.

Exi ab ea, immunde spiritus, et da locum Spiritui Sancto Paraclito.

Lenny scans the surrounding bank, searches beneath the rocky outcrops and along the edging of dried autumn brush. He needs to picture Romey clear of this unholy ritual. He checks the side of the cliff face clear up to the small outcropping above, and finds that someone has indeed hung new rope, looped it high and secure to the oak tree there, just as they had done as kids. If the rope were not looped, but instead hanging low, he could strangle the old coot with it. But he will make do with the old man's altar.

"Where the hell is she!" Lenny shouts. "Where's…"

He can't bring himself to call her name without knowing she's safe.

"Where is she?"

The priest's spine solidifies at Lenny's intrusion.

Still bent toward the water, the old man rotates on his skinny axis, and Romey's skinny body floats into view, face down.

Her cutoffs bubble and water eddies along her white t-shirt, laps against her cast as her spindly arms drift wide atop the steamy surface. Wisps from the back of her kinky halo protrude between the priest's submerged fingers.

Lenny never feels his feet fly down the embankment to the sink hole, but he's there when the priest slowly releases his hands, raises his arms wide as if to praise the surrounding woods, to praise the sky, to praise all that is anything to anyone, giving Lenny a wide expanse of open target.

Lenny swings and the rusted nails find their home in the old man's forehead and chin as if Lenny had planted them there with a sledge hammer.

The priest fulcrums backward, arms still spread like a cross now felled atop the water, and Romey pitches up, sputtering, spitting, cast windmilling, legs churning to stand in the cold pool.

"Did I do it right?" she calls out.

She coughs, rubbing her eyes.

"Did I come out slow and holy, like you said, Mr. Damien? Was that it?"

The priest floats atop the water, his altar nailed to his face.

Romey spots Lenny standing there, his lungs heaving in the thick air.

"Lens?"

She looks from Lenny to the priest. Back again.

Then her small hands begin treading air toward the old man.

Seeing her alive, seeing her vibrant and thinking, hearing her say actual words, sends urges through Lenny he doesn't believe he's capable of controlling. Snatching her up and running with her, for one. Running from the farm, from Shawnee, from his dead brother and the brother who's alive. From his father. Running again, running from his past. Their past.

They could make it. No one would really care, right? Who would care?

Romey stares down at the priest. Her face becomes a dripping rock.

"Lenny...did you?...what did you do?"

Her eyes wide. Such deep, deep pools of slate within which he cannot fathom the networks and connections and disconnections forming, letting go, reforming.

Lenny glances at the old man, then faces Romey.

"I thought you were...I thought he had..."

But she's not hearing. She's bulldozing in slow motion against the heavy water. She lifts her good arm and with more force than he imagined she could drum up, shoves him hard in the gut.

"What?" she yells, as he falls back. "What are you so *afraid* of?"

Tucking her cast tight to her chest, she rams him with her shoulder, and this time he goes down on his butt in the cold water. She pulls a bare foot from the water and jabs it into his chest.

"You know what you are?" she whispers. "You are just one loaded barrel full of loathsome fear!"

Lenny wants to respond, to tell her that she's got him all wrong. But when he opens his mouth, he realizes that she's got him all right. She's summed him up perfectly.

Romey has her hands on the old geezer now, cradling his head under her rapidly disintegrating cast and leveling the board with her good arm to lessen the torque against the water's surface. Two strings of blood flow and dissipate into the spring, one from his forehead, one from his chin.

Lenny sighs.

The nails are too short to kill him, he wants to say to her, though with the board nailed across the old man's face and the rest of him under water, it's a difficult thing to read.

He wants to tell her, *The geezer's faking, enjoying his theatrics. Hell, no one dies, not immediately, from being nailed to a goddamn cross.*

He wants to tell her, but he just sits there in the cold pool of water.

Romey places her face down close to the board, her nose almost under the water, and peers in.

"He's breathing!" she says.

She places her bony fingers along the board's underside, next to the old man's nose.

"The nails," she says. "I think I can..."

"Romey, don't!"

Lenny struggles to his knees in the spring, but he's too late.

In one swift motion, she pops her palm up and the board snaps free of the priest.

Romey shoves the altar away. It floats across the spring, dark amber-tinged nails to the sky, pivots off the rocks at the base of the cliff and swivels its way back.

The old man's eyes open and his head bobs atop the water under Romey's support.

"What the hell," Lenny says to him.

The priests runs his lizard tongue over his wet lips. Blood from his forehead drips into one eye and he blinks it away. He chokes a little on his own spit.

"I forgive you, son," he croaks out.

Lenny slams his hand across the surface of the pool, sending a sheet of water over both Romey and the priest.

"What the hell. You held her there, you held her head under the goddamn water. I thought—"

"Not hurtin' her," the priest says. "Convertin' her."

Romey scoops water with her free hand and dabs at the old man's face.

The geezer, still floating in her support, considers Lenny.

"There's a difference, motherfucker," he finally says.

Lenny leans back, bracing himself on his good arm. Raymond was right, he'd never be rid of the priest.

"Converting her to what?" Lenny says.

The priest pushes up to sit in the water beside Romey.

"To whatever helps, son. To whatever helps. Thought ye would a know'd that much by now."

Whether Lenny goes to prison, or runs, finally, for the great Atlantic Ocean, whether he takes Romey, or leaves Romey, the priest...the priest will always be with him.

Lenny looks skyward, lets the sweat pool in his eyes. Then quickly lifts his stump and runs it across his face to clear his vision.

There, above them on the cliff, lies Ricky, belly down along the outcropping, peering over the ledge.

Lenny closes his eyes for a long moment, struggles to get them back open. The boy is still there. Black shiny hair, intense eyes, taking in everything below.

Lenny calls up to Ricky, "Can you ride?"

The boy understands immediately, like the two of them have been running these hills, wading these creeks, swimming these rivers, farming this land together for years.

Ricky unloops the rope from the great oak, gathers upward on the twines for purchase, and swings clear across the opening to the rise on the other side of the sink hole. He drops neatly off near the path leading downslope to where the mare will still be grazing in the copse.

Romey would not allow Lenny to help her guide the priest to shore, or help ease him onto a boulder to rest, or help wash his wounds. So instead, Lenny stands knee deep in the water and listens to the mare's hooves hit the dirt along the Rosey Face trail.

Listens to his son going for help.

CHAPTER 21

"I SEEN YOU FOUND THAT SADDLE."

Freta Hatmaker lifts her long skirt, climbs up on the fence rail. Straddles it too close to where Lenny leans, peers down at him through her veil of graying hair.

Lenny edges away, trying to keep his eyes on Romey and Ricky down at the far end of the pasture, near the river. Ricky saddling the filly, having promised to teach Romey to ride.

Shawnee paces off to the side, one of Romey's No. 2 pencils speared in her hair. Likely still fearing her womb creatures, still worrying over Romey's impending bloom. Still staring down each second of the next minute, each fraction of the next second. Stubbornly sober, it appears, though she wasn't allowing him close enough to find out. Shawnee, keenly observing Ricky, though, like he might be a great source of handy knowledge.

He might.

Again, Raymond is correct. Shawnee sober is something to behold. And Romey needs something to behold. Lenny wonders if he'll ever get any closer to Romey than he is right now. Right now, with a length of a pasture and a rightful mother and God knows what else lodged between them.

"Yes," he says to Freta. "You know I did, and you know what I found in that saddle's wool."

He digs into his jeans pocket and feels for the safety pins, all closed now. Hands them to Freta.

She snatches the pins from his palm and quickly clips them onto the waist of her skirt.

"I know'd what you found, I know'd what you found. You done told my man, you did."

"Yes," says Lenny. "I did."

"I would not a hurt your momma. I would not. Pin in a saddle woulda scare't her, that's all."

"I know," Lenny says.

"Like I scare't you. Weren't you scare't?"

Lenny studies her face, much less a mask now, studying him back.

"Yes," he says. "Yes."

Sometimes I was scared of my mom, he wants to say.

Sometimes, feeling the scars along her wrists, I was scared.

Freta's head bobs twice. "You being here's not fair. Not when my boys ain't."

Lenny turns to look for Buford, and finds him watching his wife from the top of the slope, up by the farmhouse. Buford's hands deep in the pockets of his coveralls. His baseball cap tipped back, bill pointing toward the sky.

Buford had waited through their mother's funeral, then through Frank's service two days later, before making good on his promise to commit Freta.

Lenny wonders if she'll go easy.

Hell, he wonders if he, himself, will go easy.

He'd run into Sheriff Fletcher in the church parking lot immediately following Frank's funeral. The Sheriff waving his cigarette at him.

Lenny let himself be pulled aside. Watched the Sheriff blow smoke toward the blacktop.

"Murder, kidnapping, assault. Quite the prodigal return, son."

Lenny loosened his tie, removed his coat.

"The assault…" Lenny said, but the Sheriff cut him off.

"Assault won't stick. Your funny little freaky friend, you sure he's a priest? He's not all that much disposed to talk."

The Sheriff shrugged as if to question the universe, took a deep drag on his cigarette.

"From what I can study up on in the archives, you two have quite the history. But let's leave that be. Let's talk murder. Your one living brother, Mr. Jude, is correct when he says you ran from the scene."

Jude.

The fence post shimmies from Freta's fidgeting, probably noticing Buford now descending the hill toward them.

Jude, still recovering in the hospital from surgery, steadfastly refusing to attend either funeral regardless of their dad's offer to delay the services.

Still repeating to anyone who would listen, "Lenny shot my brother. I would never have shot my brother."

"You know why I ran," Lenny said to the Sheriff.

"Uh huh, I do," the Sheriff said. "Glenna backs that up. Murder wouldn't stick anyway. Your prints are all over that barrel. Frank's prints are all over the stock. Just like you said. So, your story's ringing a bit truer than Mr. Jude's."

Lenny suspects that Jude will have an easier time recovering from being shot than from Frank finally leveling a rifle and pinging him, twice. Plus, by god, intentionally didn't shoot to kill. For Jude, that fact was going to take him on a circuitous path to healing.

Again, Lenny fights against the image that he guesses will never leave him: blood mingling with sweat. Dripping, dripping.

The Sheriff held his cigarette out to Lenny.

"You might have to start smoking in prison. Cause from what I can see, out of the three felonies, the kidnapping just might ride."

The Sheriff looking Lenny over, assessing, making his judgements.

"Unless you can give me something else to go on?"

Max and Glenna, his dad, they'd all tried in their different ways to persuade Lenny to tell his story. Tell Romey's story. But none of them knew Romey's story. They could only guess. None of them knew Shawnee, or Raymond, or why Lenny took Romey from them, or how things like that could swing around on you in such a flash. They had no idea where their misperceptions, their assumptions, could land Romey. They had no idea how Romey's story stood right now, right this minute.

Nobody did, certainly not Lenny. Nobody could parse the delicate crosshairs of a child's life.

"Nothing, huh?" the Sheriff said. "Well, that mama's pretty upset, aiming to file. I reckon we'll just see what that little girl has to say."

What would Romey have to say? Lenny's pretty sure she will simply stay to her nature and tell the truth. And the truth? Would that get him off, or put him behind bars?

"I'll be around in a day or so to sort this out. You not going anywhere, correct?"

Sheriff out of uniform, in his Sunday best, grinding his cigarette into the church parking lot with his shiny penny loafer.

Freta tugs at her skirt and lifts her foot over the fence to balance so she can face the pasture. Her back to Lenny. Her back to Buford, now within earshot.

"You know what became of my boys," she says.

"I know," Lenny says.

"Swine flu," she says. "Your momma says, your momma says she got the same sickness what I have. Like looking into a mirror, she says. Only different. She can manage. She says. But I don't manage."

Buford veers for the gate as Freta hops down into the pasture and turns to face Lenny.

"Your momma says to paint. She says to breathe. In and out. In and out. She says to climb the mountain. She says to dig the dirt. But still. She never handled her boys. No better than I handled mine. If she is so smart, she ought to have better handled her boys."

Ricky, finally up on the filly, stretches a hand down to Romey, who is trying her best to hold her re-casted arm out of the way while she mounts. Shawnee attempts to edge close enough to give Romey a boost, but the filly prances and Shawnee shies away.

Romey holds her foot steady to give her mama a chance to help out, motions a couple of times for Shawnee to try again, but finally Romey gives up, angles her foot, wedges it into the stirrup, and clambers her own way up behind Ricky.

Lenny tries to settle his mind by envisioning a day when Romey might forgive him for taking her without asking her permission.

For standing in the way of her baptism.

For assaulting the priest.

That day doesn't come to mind.

"I'm not coming back," Freta says. "Not ever. I just loved your momma."

"I know," Lenny says. "I know."

#

What if there's no fish?

Then we catch crawdads...

What if there's no crawdads?

Lenny kneels in the wet sand along the river, downstream from the farm, where he'd spotted a bottle among the reeds, a bottle similar to the one into which Romey had tucked her message and implored Ricky to toss to the river currents.

God, his dad had been so patient with Lenny's *what ifs.*

What if you didn't find that hole, Dad? You said yourself there were plenty of pilots who didn't.

The two of them, Lenny just a kid, just learning to fish with one arm. His father thinking, casting, eyeing his lure arcing through the air, jerking his rod, popping his jig within inches of a nearby stick up. Landing the bait precisely where he'd aimed.

Sometimes you just gotta take your chances and drop through the soup, Buddo.

Lenny reaches into the bank's high reeds, plucks out the swamped pop bottle. Sure enough, the cattail plug is still in place. He methodically rubs the mud from the shaft and lifts the bottle to the early morning sunlight. Jiggles it. The note inside jiggles too.

Somewhere behind him, back in the trees, a horse whinnies.

Lenny wedges the bottle, now possibly his only sure tie to Romey, into his back pocket.

Romey, still mute around him, still staring him down. Shawnee too.

Sheriff Fletcher, evidently a man who believes in providing as wide a latitude for as long as possible, has sent word that he would be around today to "tend to business." Which means Lenny will be arrested. He wonders what he'll see in the Sheriff's eyes. Accusation? Concern? Sympathy?

Lenny makes his way up from the river and finds the white-faced mare. The horse must've pulled loose from her hold and followed him downstream. She bobs her head in relief. He rubs her muzzle, then blows on it, long and slow, calming her.

He could ride her bareback into the deep hills. Ride until someone stops him. Or doesn't stop him. Who's to say whether anyone would try to catch him? Who's to say whether anyone would follow? Hell, who's to say his dad hadn't sent Glenna, or little Ricky, to set the mare free, knowing she would follow him? Providing his son yet another escape route. Knowing all along that a clear path might not even exist. But still, laying the possibilities out. Hoping, hoping.

He could ride directly up and over Rosey Face, head west through the valleys.

But Romey. But Ricky.

What if he leaves them?

Then they'll make their own way.

What if he stays?

Same goddamn deal. One way or another, same goddamn deal.

Lenny slides his good hand over the mare's flank.

Her soft, pale nostrils quiver in anticipation. She raises a hoof, and Lenny reaches down to cradle it.

Such a tiny shock absorber for such a massive animal. At most, six inches in width. Growing from the coronary band down to the toe. Quietly replacing itself every single year. A complex tissue, powerful, resilient, fragile.

Lenny grabs a fistful of the mare's coarse mane. The key, with one arm, is to throw your stump over her neck and pull her into your chest for leverage. Swing up.

He tugs on her mane. Go or hold, go or hold.

She bobs her head, blows gentle, *come on, come on.*

Lenny leans into the warmth of her shoulder, then quickly he releases her mane and swings his stump, wild, wild, once, twice, in front of her eye. Cocks his head back and yells *Hayah! Hayah!*

She rears away from him, startled at his betrayal, startled at her own confusion.

She rears again, hesitates, backs herself to a halt a just few yards away, head down.

Lenny charges at her again, yelling, *Hayah! Hayah!*, circling her, flashing his stump, coming at her from her blind side before she relents and shies and rears one last time.

The mare bolts, her lone, back hoof—no bigger than Lenny's one good hand—supporting all eight hundred pounds, while the other three hooves dance useless in the air.

Just like that, she hits her three-beat canter for the switch-backed trail that will take her home.

ACKNOWLEDGMENTS

You guys! This journey could not have happened without you. Gail Ansel & Simi Monheit—there are no words. Roy Dufrain, Megan McDonald, Shanda Bahles, thanks for sticking with me year by year, scene by scene. And to all our small writer's group and all the students and instructors from Stanford's OWC community, I'm so grateful. Special thanks to Sarah Stone for teaching me how to stay on track and to Josh Mohr for teaching me how to jump off track: your passion and daring underpins every word. To Diane Goettel of Black Lawrence Press, thanks for loving Lenny, Romey, and Father Damien and for providing such a nurturing, professional publishing experience. (And thanks for being such a close reader.) To BLP editor Angela Leroux-Lindsey, wow! I owe you! To Anna, Ty, Rick, Lindsay, and Joe, thank you, thank you, thank you for never needing to read my novel to know that writing it meant the world to me. And to Charlie, Jackson, Ellie, Henry, Zoe, and Ben, your wild hearts beat on every page. To all my extended families, your unconditional support and love is unmatched and I'm trying hard to return it ten-fold.

And, of course, thanks to my mom for making the mountains of Western North Carolina a main character in my own heart's story.

DANIELS grew up in the mountains of Western North Carolina, attended Brevard College and graduated from the University of North Carolina, Chapel Hill with a master's degree in education. She is a 2016 graduate of the Stanford University Novel Writing Program. When Daniels isn't writing, she can be found in her garden, hiking, or shooting hoops with her grandchildren in her backyard in Oak Ridge, Tennessee.

www.ingramcontent.com/pod-product-compliance
Lightning Source LLC
Chambersburg PA
CBHW030606310726
48979CB00003B/591

9781625571380